accidentally
PERFECT

accidentally PERFECT

MARISSA CLARKE

This book is a work of fiction. Names, characters, places, and incidents are the product of the author's imagination or are used fictitiously. Any resemblance to actual events, locales, or persons, living or dead, is coincidental.

Copyright © 2022 by Marissa Clarke. All rights reserved, including the right to reproduce, distribute, or transmit in any form or by any means. For information regarding subsidiary rights, please contact the Publisher.

Entangled Publishing, LLC
10940 S Parker Road
Suite 327
Parker, CO 80134
Visit our website at www.entangledpublishing.com.

Amara is an imprint of Entangled Publishing, LLC.

Edited by Heather Howland
Cover design by Elizabeth Turner Stokes
Cover art by Maridav/Shutterstock,
Anna-Mari West/Shutterstock, and
Diana Taliun/Shutterstock,
Interior design by Toni Kerr

Print ISBN 978-1-64937-189-8
ebook ISBN 978-1-64937-190-4

Manufactured in the United States of America

First Edition March 2022

AMARA

ALSO BY MARISSA CLARKE

ANDERSON BROTHERS SERIES

Sleeping With the Boss
Neighbors With Benefits
Chance of a Lifetime

ANIMAL ATTRACTION SERIES

Dear Jane
Three Day Fiancée

*For Sally Johnson, friend, cheerleader,
and maker of darned fine vodka tonics*

CHAPTER ONE

There were good days. There were bad days. And then there was *this* day.

Lillian Mahoney gritted her teeth as the TV camera moved in closer to the food-prep table. She'd known they'd be filming this segment of *Good Day Manhattan* outside, but she'd been assured it would be a closed set.

The set was totally *not* closed.

Since Lillian had created the Living Sharpe brand almost five years ago, she'd forbidden its namesake, lifestyle guru Niles Sharpe, to participate in interviews or make public appearances, and yet here he was, in front of a live audience, with the potential to ruin everything she'd worked so hard to create.

Behind Niles and the show's host, Sylvia Baynard, a crowd of onlookers had gathered and were all but shoving each other out of the way to get their faces and hand-drawn posters in the shot.

Niles, of course, was loving all of the attention. All the face-to-face fawning from the crowd pushing up against the metal barriers around the tiny stage was like food for a starving man—a starving man who was supposed to be making fondue, not making eyes at every woman in the audience.

She shot a glance at her sister and co-producer, Erin, who looked as horrified as Lillian felt. There was little hope this would end well. She crossed her arms over her ribs protectively. For years she'd protected the Sharpe image as if it were a fragile egg. Now, like Humpty Dumpty, it could come crashing down never to be put together again.

"Salted caramel fondue is one of my favorites during apple-picking season," Niles said, giving a pretty woman in a tight *I heart NY* T-shirt leaning over the barricade a wink before grinning at the camera.

Lillian groaned in her head. He hadn't even known what fondue was until yesterday when they'd practiced this recipe in her kitchen—the kitchen they passed off as *his* in all their episodes of *Living Sharpe*.

Left to right, she chanted in her head, unballing her fists long enough to cross her fingers. *Left to right like we practiced, Niles.* A live performance was a terrible idea, but people were starting to get suspicious because the famous Niles Sharpe always declined public appearances and live TV shows. Maybe this would throw them off the scent. *Good Day Manhattan* was a great gig in that it was local and hit the right market without the risks of a national program if Niles screwed up.

"First, we'll need to heat our water and sugar over medium heat." Niles added the correct ingredients in the correct order to the pot and Lillian sighed with relief. They always had to do multiple takes when filming *Living Sharpe* episodes.

"How long do you heat it?" the host, Sylvia, asked.

"Um…" He stirred vigorously—too vigorously—and squinted his eyes like he always did when trying to remember something. "It depends on the pot and the heat source. Just until it reaches a rich, golden color." He shot Lillian a glance, clearly wanting a pat on the head for actually remembering something fundamental. She gave him a nod, and he beamed. "Yeah. Just be sure not to burn it."

"So, you've become a real household name, Mr. Sharpe," Sylvia said as an obvious time killer during this boring stage of making the recipe. "What got you into the life-style business?"

"Call me Niles, please, Sylvia," he said in his velvety voice while flashing his movie-star smile.

She blushed, like most women did when he turned that devastating smile on them. His looks were a big part of the success formula—well, that and all the research, testing, marketing, and hard work from Lillian, Erin, and the entire Sharpe team. "Okay then, *Niles*, what got you into this business?"

"My grandmother's chocolate chip cookies," he said with a nod. "Best cookies ever. I wanted to be like her for as long as I could remember. I want to make her proud. Hopefully I have." He waved at the camera. "Hi, Grammy!"

A couple of feminine sighs came from the audience crowded around the tiny stage. Lillian fought the urge to roll her eyes. The real reason he'd become a household name was anything but sigh-worthy. She'd found him in a bar and made him the viral sensation that launched the company. She wasn't even sure he *had* a grandmother. Still, this story worked to their advantage, so they kept it in the repertoire.

"Ah, see how we have a nice, even layer of bubbles across the top?" Niles said. The cameraman maneuvered up and over to get a shot inside the boiling pot. "Should be soon now." He shot Lillian a look as if seeking confirmation. God, she hoped it would be soon. Her heart couldn't take more of this stress. She swallowed hard, hoping her smile looked casual and genuine.

"So, let's talk about what you dip in salted caramel fondue," Sylvia said. "I see you have a plate of apples and some strawberries." She picked up a tiny disc. "Are these—"

"My famous waffle wafers," Niles interrupted. "The recipe is on our website and is featured on episode… Ummm…" Again, he began whipping the contents of the pot like he'd experienced a power surge, when really, he'd experienced a brain blackout. He shot a startled glance at Lillian, who held up two fingers and then four. "Yeah. Episode Twenty-Four." He grinned and slowed his manic beating of the caramelizing sugar before he began flinging it into the audience like a malfunctioning KitchenAid mixer.

"Okay. See the deep golden color? Now we add three tablespoons of butter, and once that melts, the heavy whipping cream."

Left to right, Lillian coached in her head.

He added the ingredients in the correct order and continued stirring.

Lillian allowed herself to relax a little at this point. Rehearsal and drill had paid off. She should have selected a less burn-sensitive dish, but time constraints and the expectation of something practical yet unusual from Niles Sharpe made this the perfect recipe. Besides, fondue was one of her favorites.

"Ooo. That looks wonderful," Sylvia said. "I can't wait to taste it."

Niles gave a woman in a yellow dress in the audience a smile, and Lillian fought the urge to clear her throat. *Pay attention, Don Juan.* If only his attention span was as impressive as his libido.

"Now, the last ingredient is some salt."

As if the entire world had been set to a slow-motion setting, Lillian watched in horror as he grabbed the bowl farthest right—the one full of flaked sea salt he was supposed to use only a pinch of sprinkled over the top as an attractive garnish, rather than the measured teaspoon of salt in the left bowl, which was supposed to be added to the pot—and, never breaking eye contact with his well-endowed front-row groupie, dumped the entire thing into the caramel mixture.

Crap, crap, crap. The world may have been moving in slow motion, but Lillian's thoughts zipped and pinged in hyperdrive. She'd known something like this would happen. She should never have agreed to this. Every possible scenario played out simultaneously in her head— none of them good. In fact, all of them terrible.

A woman in the *Good Day Manhattan* crew held up a notecard with "15" on it written in red Sharpie. Good. Maybe they'd cut away before the tasting, because that stuff was going to be flat-out awful with an ocean's worth of salt in it.

"We are so honored that you came on today, Mr. Sharpe—I mean, Niles—and I can't wait to try your salted caramel fondue!" Sylvia said. Niles picked an apple slice, and they both dipped and lifted their bites in salute to each other.

Surely it had been fifteen seconds. *Please cut away,*

Lillian begged in her head as Sylvia lifted the waffle wafer to her mouth and took a delicate bite. The woman was a better actress than expected, because other than a slight furrowing of her forehead, she didn't give anything away. Niles, on the other hand, grabbed a napkin and spat his bite of apple out with a muffled curse as the camera cut away.

"Well, that was more like caramelized salt than salted caramel," Sylvia said with a laugh.

Lillian was relieved she had a sense of humor, unlike furious Niles, who was stomping her way. Thank God the camera was off. "What the hell was that?" he said, glaring at Lillian.

No, no, no. Not time for one of his characteristic temper tantrums. Way too public.

"How did that happen?" he said between his perfectly straight, gritted teeth.

"You know exactly how it happened," Lillian replied in a tone so low it wasn't even a whisper. Nobody in the crowd around them could have heard her, which was imperative in order to not do any more damage.

"Five years!" Niles practically shouted. "We've been together five years, and you do *this* to me?"

Aaannnd this was why they never did live appearances or interviews. Niles's ego and his abilities were way out of sync. So, evidently, was his temper. This was not the time for one of his childish tantrums.

"Please keep your voice down," Lillian said so that only he could hear.

"You sabotaged me. You mixed up the ingredients on purpose," he said so that everyone within a ten-mile radius could hear.

"Watch the segment, Niles, and then I expect an apology," Lillian whispered. "A really, really good one. Not like the last one. You should probably present said apology with baked goods, preferably low on salt, and maybe flowers."

He threw his arms up and shouted. "We're through."

If only. Sadly, he was the face of Living Sharpe, and she and Erin were the brains. They were stuck with one another.

He stomped over to Erin. "That's the last straw. Either she goes or I go."

It wasn't until then that Lillian dared a glance around. Phones. Everywhere. This entire drama had been filmed by dozens of onlookers, many still focused on her. *Oh, freaking perfect.* Her drama king had found a stage.

"Go to the greenroom with Suzanne, and I'll meet you there, Niles," Erin said, nodding toward a Sharpe crew member at the ready.

Face red, he pointed an accusatory finger at Lillian. The sound of phone camera clicks came from behind them. "You can't just send me away. She sabotaged me."

"Oh, for Christ's sake, Niles," Lillian said under her breath.

He folded his arms across his chest like a petulant child. "Her or me," he stated as if Erin were the only one with a say in the matter. Lillian still pulled the biggest salary because she created the business, but Erin was in charge of marketing and, more importantly, keeping Niles happy and productive, so perhaps it was natural he'd make his appeal to her.

"Go inside with Suzanne, and I'll be there shortly," Erin said, pointing an authoritative finger toward the doors into the building flanked by barriers lined with rapt fans and the ever-present phones recording this entire thing.

"And you'll take care of *her*?" He tipped his head in Lillian's direction as if she were a problematic stranger rather than the person who dragged his drunk butt out of a college bar and made him who he was. Inside her chest, sadness and anger warred in a painful tug-of-war. Anger was winning big-time.

"I'll take care of it," Erin assured. "Meet me inside."

With a dramatic *harrumph* and an applause-worthy swagger, Niles strode away, stopping a couple of times to sign autographs. Once he'd entered the building with Suzanne on his heels, Lillian and Erin both huffed out breaths.

Erin had left her job at a big advertising firm almost four years ago to join the Living Sharpe team at Lillian's request... Well, it was far more than a request. Lillian had begged, groveled, and even threatened to kidnap her big sister. They'd just sold the *Living Sharpe* TV series and launched the kitchenware line, and Niles had become uncontrollable with his inflated ego filling every room to the point of bursting. Erin had adopted the role of big sister to Niles and helped keep him even and on task, something Lillian had struggled with from day one.

"It was just an accident," Erin said, in that annoying big-sister way.

"There is no such thing as an accident in this business.

There are careless mistakes and intentional negligence." Lillian's cheeks heated as her anger bloomed up her neck and over her face. "I'm going with the latter in this case."

Erin tilted her head and gave Lillian that hush-now-you're-overreacting look she'd perfected twenty years ago. "It'll blow over," she said, gesturing to two folding chairs that had been abandoned by the *Good Day Manhattan* crew members who were busy striking the set to clear the area.

Lillian scanned the dwindling crowd. A couple of people still had their phones out, clearly hoping Niles would come back out or that something else exciting would happen. "I'm going to head home."

Erin gave a thumbs-up to one of her crew members who was loading up the Living Sharpe equipment and the morbid remains of the fondue fiasco, then placed a hand on Lillian's shoulder. "When was the last time you took a day off?"

"I don't take days off."

"Exactly. You work every day, all day, and you have for years."

That was true, but look at the payoff. They'd grown so big so fast it was mind-boggling, and Lillian was proud of that. She'd grown this business from the ground up, single-handedly for the first year before she convinced her sister to help.

Right now, that sister was looking at her with an irritatingly worried expression. "What do you do for fun?" she asked.

Great. Now Erin was slipping into her big-sister role

with Lillian as well as Niles. "I *work* for fun."

"Oh, yeah, that's a blast, Lils. Do you"—she lifted a brow—"date?"

"I'm dedicated to my work. You know that. I don't have time or interest in"—Lillian mimicked Erin's suggestive brow lift—"dating."

That wasn't exactly true. She went out, but not recently because they'd been winding up that season's episodes. Besides, dating services were terrible. The guy was never anything like his profile. She closed her eyes. Just like Niles Sharpe, the entire facade was a lie, but with Niles, that was all on her.

"You two have worked closely for over five years," Erin continued. "He lives in your house, even."

"He does *not* live in my house. He lives in the guest house out of necessity." If he were out in the wild, he'd blow his image for certain.

Erin held her hands up in surrender. "Okay. Whatever. You guys are still up in each other's business twenty-four seven. Maybe you and Niles need a break from each other."

God, if only. "Don't you think I'd love that? It's like having a high school–aged little brother to look after, and I'm sick of it. Sick of *him*."

"Clearly, he feels the same way. Admit it, Lils, you're pretty intense."

Lillian's face flushed hot. Her own sister was taking up for Niles Freaking Sharpe?

Erin patted Lillian's shoulder. "I'm not saying he's justified or his behavior is okay, but you and I both know his reality is not the same as, well, *reality*, right?"

She could say that again. Niles lived in an alternate world that rarely intersected with hers or anyone else's for that matter. But, in fairness, his face and voice had been instrumental in their success. Perhaps the primary reason for it.

"Look," her sister said, "Season Three is in the can, and we don't start back up until October. This would be a good time for you to take some time off."

Lillian snorted. Like she could just do nothing.

Erin put her hands on her hips. "Okay. I'll put it this way: You need to disappear for a while. If we lose Niles, we've lost the business."

Pressure built behind Lillian's eyes, and she imagined herself like one of those cartoon characters that had steam come out their ears when they got mad. "If we lose *me*, we've lost the business," she shot back like a petulant child.

Erin rolled her eyes. "Are *you* going to quit?"

"Of course not," she said, feeling remorse for the outburst. Calculated and calm was her style. Clearly Niles was rubbing off on her.

"Well, he's not as practical or forward-thinking as you are. He just might be silly enough to quit if he really thinks you screwed up the appearance somehow. I can work with him to see what happened here, but he needs to calm down first. I think he's pretty serious about quitting. A couple of crew members said he's approached them in the last few weeks about leaving with him."

Niles wouldn't walk. No way. Lillian slumped into one of the folding chairs. *Would he?* In truth, he'd mentioned it several times recently. He'd even threatened striking out on his own last night at rehearsal when he'd burned the sugar for the second time. She'd written it off as a hissy fit and nothing more.

Nah. No way he'd leave. He'd last five minutes trying to pull off the Niles Sharpe persona without her. The guy couldn't even boil water. She took a deep breath. Still, what if Erin was right and he was that far out of touch? It would leave them high and dry for sure. Without the face, the brand would fail. The company she'd worked so hard to build would fold instantly.

She crossed her arms over her chest and watched the woman in the yellow dress who'd winked at Niles. She was waiting patiently by the door for him to come out.

Something inside Lillian's chest tightened. She'd worked so hard to make the Living Sharpe enterprise a success, and Niles just showed up…barely, and he had people waiting for him. She had…nobody waiting for her.

With a sigh, she closed her eyes. She had work. And a big house. And a cool car. And no free time to enjoy anything. Maybe her sister was right and she did need some downtime.

Erin must have sensed her capitulation. "You don't need to worry about a thing. I'll stay at your house and take care of everything. I even have a place you can go. Before I joined you guys, I thought I wanted to move to part-time or even remote, so I bought an ocean cottage at a foreclosure auction." She got a dreamy look on her face. "I've always wanted to live on the water."

This surprised Lillian. She'd not known this about her sister. She thought back and couldn't remember a time when they'd talked about the future outside of Living Sharpe in the last five years.

Erin sighed. "Waves lapping the shore. Seabirds calling. Peace and quiet." She paused for a moment, staring at nothing before shaking her head as if to clear it. "The cottage is in Maine. I've never seen the place, but the pictures are nice. I've had a company keeping up with maintenance since I bought it, so it should be ready to go."

Lillian's chest tightened, and she consciously stilled her hands in her lap. "So, you're sending me away?"

She gave that indulgent big-sister smile that made Lillian feel seven again. "I can't very well send *him* away, can I?"

"Let's put him in a hotel or something."

"You two need time apart, and I don't trust him to behave like Niles Sharpe should if he goes somewhere out of our reach, if you know what I mean."

Oh, yeah. She knew what Erin meant. It would be a constant frat party. He still acted like that carefree twenty-one-year-old she'd met at that bar near campus. "We can make each other rich," she'd told him all those years ago. "We can retire at forty." And she hadn't been wrong. Living Sharpe, LLC was a wonder. They'd grown from two people with a YouTube channel to a team of twenty with a worldwide fanbase for their TV show, online platforms, magazine, and even a bakeware line sold at fancy kitchen stores. Keeping Niles happy was important.

"What will I do for that amount of time? I can't stay idle; you know that." Even as a child, she'd been go, go, go nonstop, only slowing down to eat and sleep.

"Well, we still have the second half of next season to map out. That can be done by video conference. You're always looking for new recipes and home tips. Maybe there will be something new or different there."

Okay, well, that at least appealed. Lillian stood so the *Good Day Manhattan* crew member could take her chair. She watched the crew strike the remainder of the set, efficiently packing up and moving on to something new. *Something new…*

Yeah. Erin could be right—time away from Niles and a change of venue would benefit them both. Like she said, the second half of the next season hadn't been set yet. A segment on fresh seafood and another on coastal living could be good. And maybe Erin's cottage was in one of those charming towns that attracted artists and she'd feature some of their works. In her mind, she imagined cool stores full of pottery, jewelry, and paintings from the hands of talented local artists. They could do a clothing segment chock-full of L.L.Bean coastal outdoor vibes. She pictured the images she'd seen of the rocky Maine coastline with lighthouses and sailboats. Tourists hustling in and out of pubs and art galleries. Lobster rolls and local artisan beers.

A change of location could do her creative side a favor. Refill the well, as the saying went.

"Okay. I'll take you up on the cottage," Lillian said. "But I'm going to warn you. You'll be begging me to come back. He's going to get on your last nerve by the end of the week."

"He's *always* on my last nerve," Erin said.

Lillian had never been to Maine, but she'd seen lots of pictures. And Kennebunkport was there, right? There would be lots of things to do to distract and inspire her. Yeah. She could imagine taking some time off in Maine. How bad could it be?

CHAPTER TWO

"Come on, Bessie," Lillian coaxed her new BMW convertible, eyeing the flashing orange light on her gas gauge. She was running on fumes now. "You can do it." She stroked the dash, then gave it a couple of pats for good measure. "Just a little farther."

She'd passed the roadside sign, "Blink, Maine, population 204," about a mile back. Surely there would be a gas station—though, the past two had been closed, completely in keeping with the rest of her awful day. From the corner of her eye, she gave the map on the screen in her dash a glare. It had shown the last station as open, though the thing even had boards on the windows.

She switched music tracks to something more mellow than her "get happy" playlist she'd had on a continuous loop for the past few hours. Usually, upbeat songs lifted her mood, but tonight they'd only highlighted the obvious: this day had sucked. With a sigh, she consciously relaxed her shoulders. The worst was over.

She switched the music off. Maybe Erin had been right. Downtime would do her good. She'd been running full steam ahead since the Living Sharpe enterprise began to take off what felt like a billion years ago. She and Niles just needed a cooling-off period, then the team could get to work on next season's programming. Secluding herself would afford time to research new topics and refill her creative well without distraction.

Maybe the town of Blink would be a good reset.

That is, if she ever got there.

There was nothing on this winding coastal backroad. No signs of life at all. A little bit of dread and a huge chunk of regret churned in her stomach. If she ran out of gas out here, it would probably take hours and hours for AAA Roadside Assistance to get to her. She shuddered as she imagined being stranded.

Wait. Were there bears in Maine? She gave her soft convertible top a wary glance.

She turned her music back on and hummed along in a failed attempt to push bears out of her brain. The terrain was hilly and twisty and the road dark. She should have planned better and waited until morning to take off on a ten-hour solo road trip. But oh, no. Full steam ahead, she'd hit her house at a run, made a bunch of calls, tied off some loose ends, hired a new social media manager, and packed. The packing was pretty minimal. She planned to hit all the local stores for ideas for the upcoming season. The more she'd thought about it, the more she'd liked the idea of taking a working vacation. Too bad she hadn't thought ahead enough to consider that small-town gas stations were not open twenty-four hours. She'd always been a spectacular planner. Not so much this time.

Again, she marveled at the absolute blackness around her. Huge trees lined the road on either side, whipping by in the outer margins of her headlights. The bears were probably just outside that light, lurking in the woods for an unlucky passerby to run out of gas. Yep. Definitely should have waited until this morning to leave. She'd be much more comfortable if she had a view of the coastline to distract her.

When she came out of a particularly sharp turn, her heart leaped. Lights! Yes! At least if she ran out of gas here, she wouldn't be in the middle of nowhere. She thought again about the Blink sign... Population 204. 204? How did a place this tiny even rank a population sign? She'd spent her whole life working in a city of over eight million people. She couldn't even imagine living in a place like this. No theatre, no nightlife, no restaurants. Again, she soothed herself with images of quaint harborside art galleries and coffee shops. It was only temporary. A reset.

She heaved a sigh and tapped her fingers on her steering wheel, focusing on the warm lights coming from the windows at the front of the small building up on her right. The only lights she'd seen for miles on her journey to the middle of nowhere. Well, at least she'd be where there was electricity in the middle of nowhere.

She squinted to read the hand-painted sign in her headlights. STARFISH DINER. Thank God above. She'd kill for a cup of coffee—and a tank of gas, of course.

"We did it, Bess. Just a few more—"

And just when she was certain her day couldn't get any worse, her car motor sputtered. Grumbling every swear word she knew, she pulled off to the side of the road as the car fizzled out right along with her last remaining shred of composure.

She shifted the dead car into park and rested her forehead on the top of the steering wheel. After blinking back tears she refused to allow—she never cried, never—

she took a deep breath and reached for her purse. She snorted. Why bother? Her wallet had been lifted at the McDonald's several towns and many hours back. This time, a tear broke through, and she wiped it away with her sleeve, then checked her makeup in her rearview. All good.

"Look for the bright side," her mom had always said. "When things are bad, make a list of the good things." Well, her makeup was still okay. She had run out of gas near civilization, at least. Her stolen wallet could be easily sorted out with her bank. She had a twenty-dollar bill in her console for emergencies just like this. And hey! At least it wasn't raining.

With a deep inhale, she opened her car door and struck out for the diner. The side of the road was rocky and uneven. She should have at least changed her Ferragamo pumps before leaving New York to something more practical. No. She loved these shoes. They were one of her pairs of power shoes, and they made her feel feminine and invincible. She adjusted the purse strap on her shoulder and lifted her chin, then glanced into the woods off the side of the road. Yeah. No way she could outrun a bear in these shoes, but she could impress it with her sense of style, right? She picked up her pace and pulled out her phone and called Erin. No answer. Of course there was no answer. It wasn't even daylight yet.

Crack. Aaaaand, there went her heel on her favorite shoes. She leaned down to check the damage with her fingers. Yep, broken off and hanging on by a strip of leather. She'd be making an entry on this date in her planner officially ranking this as the worst day ever.

As she hobbled awkwardly toward the building, a car approached from behind, making her want to bolt into the woods and take her chances with the bears that may or may not live in Maine. Googling the answer to that bear issue would be task number three after contacting Erin and updating her day planner.

"Need a lift?" a man's voice called out as a dirty pickup truck pulled up beside her. It had huge tires with knobby treads, and a logo that said Wright Boat Works in a circle around a sailboat was on the door.

Oh, sure. She was going to hop into a truck with a strange man in the middle of freaking nowhere. While it was still dark out. "No thanks." She'd found it safer to not make eye contact growing up in the city, so she stared straight ahead at the sign with the bright blue starfish on it.

"You sure?"

Of course she was sure. *Never ever get in the car with a stranger*, her mother and her own common sense had drilled into her. Eyes ahead, she tried to limp along with dignity and purpose, her broken heel making a scraping sound with every step sucking the dignity part right down the drain. "Yes, I'll walk. Thank you."

"Is that what you're doing?"

At the hint of humor in his voice, she glanced through the open window at a handsome man in his mid-thirties. Only he didn't have any humor in his expression at all. In fact, he wore a frown. She returned her attention to the sign that was now only a few yards ahead and lifted her chin. Maybe if she ignored him, he'd go away and find another victim for his mass-murder spree or whatever he had going on in the middle of nowhere at the crack of dawn. Normal people should be asleep. Yeah, like her. Again, it struck her how being impulsive never paid off. She should have waited until this morning to head out.

"Suit yourself," he said before slowly pulling away and, darn it, right into the diner parking lot. She glared down at her aching feet and broken shoe. Maybe he was just a decent guy offering to help her out. Regardless, it looked like she'd have to face him after snubbing him.

Shaking her head, she pulled out her phone again as she struck out across the oyster-shell-and-gravel parking lot of the diner. There were several vehicles in the parking lot close to the door, including scowling guy's truck. Why would anyone be up at this time of day? Five in the morning was early, even for her.

Hey, Er. Call me when you're up, she texted, then shoved the phone in her purse.

Boom! Lillian jerked upright at the loud clap of thunder and hurried as best she could with one missing heel toward the diner...right as it started to rain.

"Perfect," she said from between clenched teeth as she yanked the door open. The cheery chiming of little brass bells broke through the hiss of rain and frustrated pounding of blood in her ears as the door closed behind her. For a moment, she shut her eyes and pulled herself together. When she finally met Karma, she had a word or two for her. After a deep inhale through her nose—an inhale filled with the scent of freshly brewed coffee—she opened her eyes.

Things could only get better from here, right?

"Well, hi there," a woman with a round face and graying temples said from behind the long counter facing the door. "Welcome to the Starfish Diner."

Shooting a self-conscious glance around, Lillian noticed there were only a few other people in the diner, and all of them were staring at her, including the scowling guy from the truck—yep, still scowling. She looked down at herself and almost groaned. She was still in her clothes from the *Good Day Manhattan* shoot—her charcoal suit skirt with a white silk blouse. A completely soaked white silk blouse. She might have more than words for Karma when she met her and maybe a creative suggestion where to put her broken favorite shoe.

"Why dontcha have a seat in the booth over there, hon, and I'll be right over."

"Thanks." Lillian could hardly hear her own voice over the pulse in her ears and could physically feel the other patrons' stares like pin prickles as she awkwardly wobble-hopped her way to the booth, broken heel hanging on for dear life. With a grateful sigh, she sank into the booth in the corner behind three older men, her back to them. Ordinarily, she would never have chosen the seat that only gave her a view of the wall, but the idea of facing these people after her wet T-shirt contest grand entrance? Nope.

"How about a cup of coffee?" the woman said, coming to stand beside her booth. "You look like you could use some warming up." The woman laid a towel on the booth bench next to her, and Lillian shot her a grateful smile as she wrapped it around her shoulders. Behind her, the bells on the door jingled.

"I'm Sally." She placed a menu on the scratched yellow Formica table.

On cue, Lillian's stomach growled. "Do you take Apple Pay?" she asked hopefully. Most places in Manhattan did, but this certainly wasn't the city.

"Nope. Sorry," Sally said. "We take cash and card."

She needed to save money so she could put as much gas as possible in her car in case the local gas station—please, God, let there be one—didn't take Apple Pay, either. "I'll just have some coffee, thanks."

When she glanced over her shoulder at Sally's retreat, her breath caught. The man from the truck sitting at a stool at the end of the counter closest to her wasn't even pretending not to stare. Her eyes locked with his, and she almost laughed when she realized she was playing a weird game of *Don't Blink* in Blink, Maine. What a day.

As if he'd suddenly found her a waste of time or effort, he swiveled on his stool and turned his back to her. A very fine, broad-shouldered back, she noticed against her will.

Whatever. She came across all kinds back home; Grumpy Guy was nothing special. Again, her stomach growled, probably loud enough for the next town over to hear it. Sally placed a cup of coffee in front of her along with a couple of plastic containers of creamer. "Sugar's on the table, hon," Sally said. "You sure you don't want some breakfast?"

"Positive. Thanks."

The woman gave her a doubtful stare, then a quick nod.

Lillian picked up her coffee mug. "Is there a gas station nearby?"

Sally wiped her hands on her apron. "Nearest one is

ten miles or so south of here. The station closest closed down a while ago. Not enough business."

It was the boarded-up one she'd passed on her way here. Great.

"Damned shame," one of the old men in the booth behind her grumbled. "Emmett had to go live with his kids in Boston when the station closed down."

The door jingled again. This time, Lillian did turn to look.

"Hi, Gus!" Sally called out to a man with gray hair wearing a dark blue shirt with a business logo patch and jeans. He was dressed just like Grumpy Guy at the counter. Lillian's gaze flitted to his back, and as if he could feel her looking, he glanced over his shoulder at her, met her eyes, then shook his head and turned back around, as if she were offensive somehow. Since he could feel her look, she hoped he could feel her screw-you glare focused on the area between his wide shoulders.

"How's Alice?" Sally asked as the man named Gus slid onto the stool beside the guy with the attitude.

"Great," he replied with a smile. "Said she'd be by to drop off some eggs later today."

"Be with you two right away," Sally said, collecting Lillian's menu and hustling away. "Usual?"

"Yep," both of the men said in unison.

How would it feel, Lillian wondered, to live in a place so small, people not only knew your name but your spouse's name and what you wanted for breakfast? She traced her finger over the handle of her mug absently. The barista in Lillian's usual Starbucks knew her order and first name, but this was something else entirely. One more strike against Blink.

"Anybody know whose car that is up on the road?" Gus asked from the counter. Grumpy Guy, who he'd been sitting next to, elbowed him in the ribs and gestured with his head to the corner where Lillian sat. Gus turned to face her. "Did you break down?" he asked, looking directly at Lillian.

"I ran out of gas," she said. "I'm about to call roadside assistance."

He smiled and stood. "Aw, no need for all that. I've got some cans in the back of my truck. I'll get you all fixed up before my eggs are ready."

Grumpy Guy shot him a look that would have boiled those eggs.

"Oh," Lillian said, turning sideways in the booth to face him as he approached. "That's not necessary. I…" Her voice trailed off when the man held out a callused hand.

"Gimme your keys, and I'll get you taken care of."

"That's really not—"

"Oh, for Christ's sake," Grumpy Guy grumbled. "Stop with the act and give him your keys."

Stunned, she dug her fob out of her purse and dropped it in Gus's still-outstretched hand.

"Who pissed in your Wheaties this morning, Wright?" one of the old guys in the booth behind her asked in a raspy voice after the door closed behind Gus with a jingle of bells.

Grumpy Guy—Wright?—didn't answer or acknowledge the question. Sally grinned as she placed coffee in front of him and patted his hand, like a mother would do.

"You hush, now, Roger. Mind your own business," Sally admonished.

"Been meaning to ask *you* the same question, Roger," the other man in the booth behind Lillian said.

"Life pissed in my Wheaties, and you know it, Seamus," the man with the raspy voice named Roger grumbled. "Can't seem to get things started up since…you know."

"Well, maybe it would help if you changed clothes. You look like you've been wearing the same clothes since Mabel's funeral."

"That was a year ago."

"Yeah. I stand by my statement," Seamus said.

"I wash. This shirt is clean."

Lillian wanted to turn around to see the man so badly it hurt. Instead, she pulled out her compact and pretended there was something in her eye while she snuck a peek at the guy they'd called Roger. He was easily in his eighties with a bald head and thick glasses. The other guy had been right. He looked like he'd slept in his clothes. The collar of his plaid shirt was folded under on one side and stuck up on the other, and deep wrinkles turned the plaid pattern into zig-zags.

A weird prickly wave traveled up her arms to her neck, and she lowered the mirror. She knew exactly what had caused the sensation. Sure enough, Grumpy Guy was giving her the same boiling stare he'd given Gus when he'd offered to help her.

He arched an accusing eyebrow, and she arched hers in return. With a huff, he turned back around. She fought back a smile at her little victory.

The bells on the door jingled, and Gus came back in

with Lillian's suit jacket and a big grin. "Nice car," he said, placing the key fob on the table. "Parked it in the lot and brought you this, since it looks like the rain got ya."

"Thanks." She pulled the twenty out of her purse. "My wallet was stolen on the way here, and this is all I have on me. I need enough to cover coffee, but the rest is yours."

Gus shook his head and walked over to the counter, making a shooing motion with his hand. "Glad to do it. People should always help each other out. It's what we're put here for." He glanced at her as he slid onto his stool and winked. "Just pay it forward."

"Thank you so much. I'm... I..."

"Your car has New York plates," Gus said. "Where-abouts in New York?"

Grumpy Guy turned to look at her, and for some irritating reason, that made her skin heat. She slipped on her suit jacket to cover her sheer, wet blouse, and then switched sides of the booth so that she had her back to the wall. The move wasn't graceful thanks to her broken shoe, but at least she didn't have to twist her head around like an owl to talk to Gus.

"Manhattan, mainly," she answered finally, reaching across for her cup of coffee. She had her apartment there, but she also owned a house in Long Island where they filmed most of the *Living Sharpe* episodes, passing it off as Niles's place. It was more of an estate, really, complete with chef's kitchen, vegetable and flower gardens, pool, two guest houses, stables (which she'd converted into offices for her team), and a duck pond.

Grump rolled his eyes and turned back around. Actually *rolled his eyes.*

"Well, welcome to Blink," Gus said with a smile.

"Thank you." She loosened her death grip on her coffee mug.

"I went to New York City once," the man with his back to her in the next booth said. She could see them now. The man in the rumpled shirt, named Roger, faced her. Across from him with his back to her was the man who'd just spoken—Seamus. He had wavy gray hair with hints of red on the sides. "I liked it," he said. "Couldn't imagine living there, though. No offense," he added with a smile to her over his shoulder.

Lillian could totally relate. She couldn't imagine living *here*. "No offense taken," she said. "It's not for everyone." She could feel Grumpy's eyes on her again but refused to look his way.

"So, where ya headed?" Sally asked as she set two huge plates of eggs and sausage in front of Gus and Grump.

Sheesh, it was like an interrogation room, not a diner, and the steaming plates of food only added to her torture. "I'm…" Well, it's not like they weren't going to find out. They obviously knew everything about everyone anyway. "I'm staying in Blink for a while as a little mini vacation." There. That was perfectly truthful without any specifics.

Sally clapped her hands. "That's wonderful!" Then her smile faded a bit. "You know we don't have a hotel here, right?"

Lillian didn't know that, but it didn't surprise her. "I'm staying at a friend's place."

"What friend?" Roger asked.

Holy smokes. So much for no specifics. "You probably don't know her." Now every eye was on her as they waited for…what?

"Oh, we know everyone around here, hon," Sally said with a reassuring smile.

"She's never been here. It's my sister. Her name is Erin Mahoney." Nobody moved at her sister's perfectly generic name, expecting more. "She bought a cottage on Overlook Road a few years ago."

"Emmett's place," Seamus said. "Bank took it. Sold at foreclosure auction to some out-of-stater."

Again, all eyes landed on her. Well, crap. Emmett was the gas station owner who had to move in with his kids. No doubt the sale wasn't celebrated around here. "I'm really looking forward to staying here for a while." She cleared her throat. "Erin says she's hoping to come spend some time here soon, too," she lied. Evidently, that was the right thing to say, because everyone seemed to relax a bit.

"So, this Erin doesn't plan to sell it to a developer?" Roger asked in his raspy voice.

"No," Lillian answered. "She said she plans to retire here."

"Well, then, double welcome to Blink," Gus said around a mouthful of hash browns.

Whew. Hopefully that was the end of the interrogation.

"How long are you staying?" Grump asked.

"Not sure. Does it matter?" She knew it was confrontational, but he was rubbing her the wrong way.

He shrugged and turned back around. He picked up his fork and stabbed a piece of sausage. "Not really."

The sun was finally rising over the trees, and Lillian took another sip of coffee, marveling at the gorgeous colors ranging from light lemon yellow to vivid tangerine highlighting the clouds. At least she'd have sunrises to look forward to as she was bored to death in this place.

"You ever find the keys to Mabel's car?" Seamus asked Roger.

"No. I can't find anything." He let out a deep sigh. "Mabel did all that kind of thing. She kept everything in order."

"Including you!" Seamus said.

Roger gave a choked laugh. "Yeah, especially me."

Lillian pulled out her phone to text Erin and let her know she'd arrived safely in Blink.

"I wish I could do what she did, but I can't. Hell, I can't even figure out where things are when I go to the grocery store."

For a while, the only sounds around her were the scrapes of silverware on plates.

"Sometimes I think I'm ready, you know?" Roger said.

"Ready for what?" Seamus asked.

"You know," Roger answered.

Lillian's heart squeezed in her chest. The poor guy.

"Now, don't go talking like that," Seamus said. "You're too far ahead in poker. I need a chance to earn my money back."

Both men laughed.

Gus's words from earlier played through her head. *People should always help each other out. It's what we're put here for.* Her heart rate increased as pieces clicked into place. She was stuck here. Idleness made her anxious. For five years, she'd worked eighty-plus-hour weeks. No way could she just stare at sunrises and do nothing during this banishment. She'd given money to her local women's shelter and several other charities, but since starting Living Sharpe, LLC, she hadn't volunteered in person. She'd been too focused on building her business. "Pay it forward," Gus had said. Who better to help this man get his house in order than the mastermind behind lifestyle and homemaking guru Niles Sharpe? She could use her expertise to actually benefit someone else. Someone who really needed it.

Don't be impulsive, she reprimanded herself. *Nothing good comes from not having a well-thought-out plan. Think this through.* But something in her rebelled. This felt right. It wasn't impulsive—it was opportunistic philanthropy.

"I can help you," she blurted. "It's my job in New York. I organize, plan, and cook." When neither of them reacted or even moved, she felt the niggling of doubt drizzle down her spine but ploughed on anyway, moving to the other side of her booth and getting on her knees to face them over the back of it. "I can help you make sense of what you need in stock and provide you with a list of tasks and a schedule to keep your household running smoothly. I'd need to come do an inventory of your pantry and cleaning supplies first, of course."

Roger rubbed his chin as if he couldn't figure out what to make of her. His friend looked equally perplexed. She was confused, too, honestly, but it felt good to break out of her calculated routine.

"Let me help you," she said. "We can try it for one day, and if it's not beneficial, we part ways."

Finally, the old man spoke. "How much?"

"How much what?" she replied.

"How much you gonna charge me to organize and inventory and do all that stuff?"

She shook her head. "Nothing. I'll do it for free. Like Gus helped me, I'll help you."

. . .

Caleb had to give the stranger this: she was a helluva good actress.

Even though his dad had clearly bought into her act and was all but strutting like a rooster at the mention of his name, Caleb knew better. Nothing was free. Especially coming from a city woman wearing slick clothes, driving a BMW convertible, and propositioning the richest man in Maine's Downeast region. The fact she honed right in on Roger proved without a doubt that she was after something. Something with lots of zeros in front of the decimal point, no doubt.

His dad had swiveled on his stool to watch the conversation with an adoring look on his face, like he was watching a Disney princess movie rather than a bank heist flick.

"That's mighty kind of you," Roger said. "But I'm not sure."

"His wife died," Seamus said.

"Yes, I know," the woman answered.

Caleb rolled his eyes and took another bite of eggs. Of course she knew. She probably knew everything about Roger McGuffy, including his Social Security number, date of birth, and amount in his bank accounts. Why else would she turn up here out of the blue and offer to help him for no pay?

She was pretty, though; he'd give her that. Tall and curvy with shoulder-length brown hair that was escaping a clip on the back of her head as it dried in curls. He sliced off another piece of sausage. Yeah, he knew all about dark surprises hidden in pretty packages like this one. She was up to something.

"Free, huh?" Roger said, rubbing a hand over his week-old whiskers.

"Yes. Let me help you."

Man, she was good. Voice and expression 100 percent sincere.

"Okay," McGuffy said with a nod. "How 'bout sevenish tomorrow morning?"

Still facing backward in the booth, she gave a little bounce on her knees. And again, Caleb couldn't help but notice her ample curves as they bounced and jiggled right along with her.

"Great! What's your address?" she asked, grabbing her phone from the table behind her.

Like she didn't know. Caleb shook his head and bit off a hunk of toast.

The men in the booth laughed.

"You'll find me," Roger said, standing and throwing some bills on the table. Seamus stood and added a few more bills to the stack.

"I'm Lillian," she said holding out her hand. "Lillian Mahoney."

"Roger McGuffy. See you tomorrow, Lillian." He shook her hand and followed Seamus to the door.

The bells made racket when the door shut behind Roger and Seamus. The woman named Lillian Mahoney didn't even wait until the bells stopped smacking the glass door before she snatched up her phone and texted someone—probably her accomplice.

Caleb took a sip of coffee and watched as her fingers flew over her screen, smile on her pretty face. Good thing Emmett's cottage was right across the harbor from his place. No way was he going to let her take advantage of Roger—or anyone else in Blink, for that matter. He planned to keep an eye on her.

And with irritation, he realized he was looking forward to this mission way too much.

CHAPTER THREE

Lillian glanced at the map app on her phone. The house should be on the left once she crested this hill. A lump formed in her throat as the image she'd originally had of a quaint, white cottage with green shutters morphed into something out of a horror movie in her mind. Nothing about Blink was as she'd imagined it, so why would this be any different? The thing was probably falling down with holes in the roof and bats and rats and things that skittered and slithered into holes in the baseboards. She shuddered.

"Take a break. You need to get away," Lillian muttered in her best imitation of her sister. "It'll be fun." Yeah. As fun as a migraine. Woo-hoo. As she crested the hill, the theme song from *Jaws* played in her head as her dread grew over the condition of the cottage. *Duh dun…duh dun…duhdunduhdunduhdun…*

She braked, staring at the building in surprise, and checked the address on her phone again. Yep. This was the place. To her relief, the outside looked okay—cute, even. It was small, with naturally faded gray cedar shingle siding and teal accents on the windows and doorframe. Not at all what she'd been expecting. Maybe her luck was turning. The only other house she could see was about a city block down the road. It was big, like maybe it had been a hotel or something at one time, and it was in rough shape.

She turned off the road in front of the little cottage with a relieved sigh. She wanted out of this car, out of these damp clothes, and out of her pitiful broken shoes. What she really wanted was a long, hot bubble bath, but that might be a dream too far. There was no garage on the property. In fact, there wasn't even a driveway, just a shell-and-gravel area in front of the house where, in her opinion, there should be a flowerbed full of perennials with a side kitchen garden for herbs and spices. Right now, though, it was her personal parking spot.

She grabbed her purse from the passenger seat, pulled out the key Erin had given her, and ran her thumb over the shiny, lacquered keychain. She'd been so angry when she left, she'd shoved it in her purse without a glance. It was bright, cheerful yellow in the shape of a lemon and said, "when life gives you lemons, add vodka." She chuckled and got out of the car. If it weren't obscenely early, she'd totally take that advice—that is, if she could find a place that sold booze in Nowhereville.

Key in hand, she wobbled up the steps to the porch on her broken heel. There were two wooden rocking chairs on the porch placed on either side of a round iron table that had seen better days. The chairs and table should be painted in cheery colors that coordinated with the bright teal of the house trim, Lillian decided, turning the lock.

"Coastal colors to make your porch pop," Lillian said, imagining the headline of a *Living Sharpe Magazine* article. Yeah. This getaway could turn out okay.

The smell of the house hit her right away when she opened the door. "Tricks for removing musty odors from your weekend home," she said in a newscaster voice.

Entering the living room, she turned a full circle. The cottage was bright but suffered horribly from the effects of a bad 1970s makeover. "Harvest Gold and Avocado Green: The new stainless?" Nah, not even the Living Sharpe team could sell this combo.

Crossing to the back of the room, she smiled at the row of windows, which appeared original to the house—the real kind with wood muntins between wavy panes of glass. The kind you'd pay a fortune to buy salvaged or have replicated in the city. Only one of the three windows didn't open. "Salvaging your antique windows," she said in her headline voice. Nah. She'd leave that to the old house renovation people. Her company's specialty was tips for making the home beautiful and efficient. Niles Sharpe fans wanted innovative, unique ideas with a touch of practical.

After opening the rest of the windows that functioned in the house, she stepped out on the porch and gasped at the view. The cottage was near the top of a hill overlooking the harbor below, and beyond it was a rocky shore with blue water that called her as much as that bubble bath she'd imagined earlier. The sunrise she'd admired from the diner would be killer from up here. She sucked in a deep breath of clean, cool air. Holy cow. This place was postcard gorgeous. Pulling her attention from the shore, she focused on the harbor below—well, it was sort of a harbor, she supposed. Most of the structures ringing it looked unused. On the far side from her, there was a big wooden building with boat slips in front of it. Most of them were empty except for a half-dozen or so fishing boats with wire traps all over their decks—lobster boats, maybe? There were two sailboats—one of them was huge. There was also a small, dark brown wooden boat with a motor on the back, and a houseboat that was not in a slip but instead tied up to some pilings directly across the harbor from her cottage. A golden retriever mix ran happily along the wooden walkway between the boats and the building, half-heartedly barking at seagulls sitting on top of the pilings. A small dog followed along, yipping enthusiastically enough to bounce with each bark. This must have been the usual routine, because the birds didn't seem impressed or bothered.

She squinted as two trucks pulled into the lot next to the wooden building. Gus and Grump got out of them and disappeared inside. That had to be Wright Boat Works she'd seen in the logo on their shirts and on Grumpy Guy's truck. He must be a boat mechanic or something. That suited. He didn't strike her as someone who would have a people-centered job. Maybe not even a people-adjacent job.

With a sigh, she leaned her elbows on the porch railing and rested her chin on her hands. She wondered where the touted 204 residents lived because other than the boat business, one other building on the harbor with tables and umbrellas out front, and the two-story house next door to this one, the area around the water was either undeveloped or the buildings looked vacant, which struck her as odd.

The harbor appeared to be a natural cove, rather than man-made, and it was beautiful, with rocky slopes angling down to blue water. Other harbor towns she'd seen were jam-packed with businesses, which made this place strange. It was just her luck to find the only coastal town that had absolutely nothing going on. It had a diner and a boat-repair business. Great.

With a sigh, she strolled back into the house and wandered into the kitchen. Small. Way too small. She turned a circle. It could easily be opened up to the living area, which would give it a more open feel and could allow for expansion. But that stove. It was gorgeous. Not as old as the house, of course, but probably from the thirties or forties. She could remove the obvious more recent additions—well, recent as in the last five decades—like the damaged, peeling Formica and first-gen Amana Radarange microwave, and install modern/retro features that would complement the stove.

Wait. Stop. Full stop.

No repairs. No remodel. No improvements. No nothing. She was going to stay a week or so and get out of here. That would give her enough time to help Roger, do some next-season planning, and allow Erin plenty of time to calm Niles down and get him back on track.

She scanned the living room through the kitchen door. The sofa was hideous, as was the rest of the furniture. "First-world problems," she muttered under her breath. Erin could sort all of this out when the time was right. Lillian didn't have to make everything here show-ready like she did in her own home. Nothing would be filmed here. She only had to survive the boredom. She glanced at the brown and umber floral sofa. Survive the boredom and looking at that sofa every day.

Her phone rang, and she grabbed it out of her purse where she'd dropped it on a little table right inside the door. "Ellen Lu - Social Media Director" flashed on her screen. Oh, good. The media director she'd hired before she left New York was already on the job, and early, too. She smiled. She'd really liked Ellen at the interview. She was young but had the online experience and maturity to pull off the perfect mix of professional and fun across the Sharpe social media platforms.

"Hi, Ellen!" Lillian said, wandering through the open door to the porch to check out that amazing view again.

"I quit," came through her phone in a rush.

Lillian shook her head to clear it. She surely had misheard. "I'm sorry. I didn't catch what you said, Ellen."

After an exasperated sigh, Ellen said, "I quit. There's no way I can handle this."

Wait. She'd been hired because she'd handled social media for a national sporting goods outfitter in addition to running her own fashion channel that had a huge following. Living Sharpe should be a great fit for her—a unified look with a unified message, as they'd discussed.

"It only requires one post and responses to online comments and inquiries across our seven primary platforms. That's only seven posts and related responses a day. Less than you did for your previous employer." She was about to launch into a placating speech about tips for settling into a new job culture when Ellen made a frustrated sound that might have been a growl.

"Have you been online today, Ms. Mahoney?"

"No."

"I suggest you check it out. I appreciate the opportunity, but I'm out."

And with that, the call ended.

Numb, Lillian slumped against the front doorframe and stared at the blank phone screen. What on earth was going on? Erin called in just then, but Lillian muted the ring and instead opened Twitter.

Mistake. Wow, was that a mistake. She should have gone with a kinder, gentler platform first. The mentions and messages to Living Sharpe went on and on. All of them pretty much the same. After a few seconds of scrolling, Lillian wanted to join Ellen and say, "I quit," and from the angry, accusatory messages, she was pretty sure their fan base would applaud.

Her phone rang again, and this time she took her sister's call.

"Don't go on social media today," her sister ordered.

"Too late." She flipped over to Facebook and scrolled through the hostile comments under yesterday's post advertising Niles's appearance on *Good Day Manhattan*.

"Ellen quit," Erin said.

"I know." On and on the comments went. Some of them threatening. Niles's fans were super angry at her.

"We should have anticipated this," Erin said.

Lillian didn't answer. She'd seen the phones at the filming but had never imagined Niles's fans would misconstrue his words like this. They thought she'd sabotaged him. Worse, they thought she and Niles were…ugh. The mere thought of Niles as her lover was nauseating.

"They think you and Niles are—"

"Don't say it," Lillian said with a groan. The image would be too much.

"And that you—"

"I know." Lillian cut her off as she flopped down on the

hideous sofa. All around her, a cloud of dust puffed from the cushions, launching her into a coughing fit.

"Don't worry, we'll handle it…somehow," Erin soothed.

Still coughing, Lillian pushed to her feet and glared at the sofa on her way to the kitchen.

"You okay?" her sister's voice came from the phone.

"No. But I will be. Can I call you back?"

"Sure."

"If you don't hear from me in five minutes, call the cops and tell them that the sofa is the prime murder suspect." When her sister didn't respond, she added, "It was a joke, Erin. I'll call you right back."

She pulled a glass out of the cabinet to get some water, but nothing came out of the tap. Broken. Everything. The water, the Living Sharpe social media platform, Niles, her lungs, her favorite shoe. *Ugh.*

She dug a mint out of her purse and popped it in her mouth, staring out the window at the little harbor below. Eventually her coughing settled down, as did her racing heart. The social media feeding frenzy on her would settle down, too. Heck, it might even bring in new followers. So what if people think she and Niles are a couple and she intentionally screwed him over? Big deal. It wasn't nearly as bad as if someone had found out Niles was a complete fraud.

Below, Grumpy Guy sauntered out of the big wooden building and made his way to the huge sailboat. As if he had spidey senses or something and could feel her staring, he paused and looked up straight at her cottage. Surely he couldn't see her through the window at this distance, but it felt like he could not only see her but see straight into her. She took a step back.

Her heart, which had finally slowed, kicked back into high speed. *Wow, the guy's hot*, she thought as he climbed the ramp into the huge sailboat.

Hot? In addition to everything else in her life, clearly, her brain was broken, too—or at least her hormones were.

With a groan, she trudged down the front porch steps toward her car to retrieve her bags. Her car, Bessie, made a happy chirp when she hit the unlock button on her key fob, right as a pickup truck pulled into the little shell drive in front of the cottage with "Handyman Hank" in black letters on the sides.

A woman got out of the truck with a big grin on her face. "You must be Lillian Mahoney," she said, practically bouncing around the front of the truck. Her denim overalls were covered in paint. All different colors, like she'd been in a paintball fight and lost in a big way. Even her ballcap and work boots were splattered with paint. "Welcome to Blink." She extended her hand as she rounded the front of the car. "I'm Cassidy James. I've been keeping an eye on the house since your sister bought it. She called me yesterday and asked me to get the place ready for you."

It figured Erin was on top of things. It's one of the reasons they worked so well together. Lillian shook the woman's hand, which, thankfully, was not paint splattered. Cassidy appeared to be a bit younger than she was, maybe in her mid-twenties. Lillian leaned in and pushed a button on the dash, and the trunk of her car popped open. "Thanks."

"I'm here to turn on the water and gas." Cassidy

shrugged. "Well, they're already connected by the power and water company, but I shut them off at the house as a precaution, since nobody was here. Other than that, I think everything is in working order." She was talking superfast, and Lillian had to concentrate to keep up. Little or no sleep wasn't helping, either. "There's no heat, I'm afraid," the too-energetic woman continued, "but the fireplaces appear to be in working order—not that you'll need them for a little while. The plumbing is all good now, too. I replaced some of the exposed pipes at the back of the house that didn't fare well in that last winter freeze. Replaced it with PEX, so that shouldn't happen this year." She gestured to the open trunk. "You want some help?"

"Uh, sure." Lillian was a little overwhelmed, wrapping her head around this unusual woman who spoke too fast. "Do you live in Blink?"

Cassidy nodded as she grabbed the handle of Lillian's bag. "On the other side of the harbor, but you can't see the house from here because it's up in the woods." She craned her neck to look through the back window of the car. "This all you have? I guess you're not staying long."

She certainly hoped not. Lillian grabbed the remaining bag from the trunk and followed Cassidy up the stairs to the porch and inside the house. "I travel light." Actually, she'd planned to buy what she needed here, but it looked like that wasn't going to pan out, considering there were no stores whatsoever.

"There's no bed in the master, so I guess you'll stay in here," Cassidy said as she disappeared into a room at the front left corner of the house. Lillian followed her into the tiny room with a mattress on a box spring on the floor. "Didn't look like anyone had ever slept on that mattress," she said. "And the bedding is new. Erin had it shipped, and I put it on when I was here to fix the pipes."

Thank God for small favors and clean sheets. "Is there a post office in Blink?" Lillian asked.

"Not officially, but you can go to Amanda's place at the harbor, and she'll do UPS and FedEx. She also has a mailbox, but USPS only picks up a few times a week."

Good. She could use the company account and not her precious remaining cash. She'd also hit Amazon up for an essentials delivery.

"Her business is just this side of the big boat works building. See?" She followed Cassidy to the window to check out what she was pointing at. With a squeal, the woman waved so vigorously toward the harbor, it looked like she was trying to fly. Grumpy Guy was waving back.

"So, what's his story?"

"Caleb Wright? He's the best. If you need anything at all, he'll be there for you."

Lillian fought back a snort. It was unlikely she'd be asking him for a thing. For some reason, he'd taken an immediate dislike to her. She opened her mouth to ask for more information but decided against it. Who cared anyway, right? Not her.

"I'll turn on the water and gas now. I should have started here before going to help Mr. Finch first," Cassidy said with a grimace as she flipped the light switch and the room remained dark. "Your sister said you wouldn't be here until tonight. Figured I had at least until five today." She looked at her watch, which was also paint splattered.

"Wow. It's not even eight in the morning yet. You must have driven through the night."

"I did."

She grinned. "So, are you running from or to?"

Exhaustion was seeping through Lillian's muscles, even with all the caffeine she'd chugged at the diner. "Pardon?"

"The only time people who aren't long-haul truckers drive through the night is if they're running away from something or are super excited to get somewhere." She shrugged. "Never mind. I've overstepped. I tend to do that. Sorry. It's obvious, anyway. Nobody's ever excited to come to Blink." She flipped the light switch again. "I hope it's burned out and not an electrical issue. No biggie either way. I'll fix it."

Keeping up with Cassidy's line of conversation was like following a tennis match. No, faster. A ping-pong match. "Uh, okay."

"So, I'll turn on the water and gas. Then I'll come back after you get settled in and fix anything else that needs attention. Just give me a call to let me know what's broken and when you want me to drop by." She dug a business card out of the top chest pocket of her overalls and handed it to Lillian.

And just like that, the chatty, energetic woman strode out of the room and out of the house. Lillian moved to the window and watched her as she grabbed a wrench from her truck, then leaned over to pull the cover off something at ground level near the road, wrench in hand.

Lillian jumped as a loud hiss and bang came from the

kitchen. She rushed into the kitchen, then heaved a sigh when she realized she'd left the faucet on when she'd tried to fill a glass earlier. After a few seconds, the sputtering stopped, and slightly brown water flowed in a steady stream from the faucet.

Her sigh was melodramatic, even to her own ears, as she imagined it was her problems washing down the drain as the water went from murky brown to crystal clear. Lillian shook her head. Obviously, she needed sleep if she was pathetic enough to create home-improvement metaphors for her life.

Cassidy bounded into the kitchen. "Oh, you already opened the tap. Thanks. The crud in the pipes should purge right away, and you're good to go. Gonna go turn on the gas for your water heater and stove. Be right back."

Lillian looked down at the business card in her hand. *Miss Fix-It* was centered in block letters with Cassidy's name and number below. The background was colorful paint splatters. She liked the layout and the card. Honestly, just from the few minutes she'd spent with Cassidy, she liked her, too. Weird. She was usually a little slower to warm up to people.

She looked at the colorful, artistic card again on her way back to the bedroom. They were forever doing home repair tip segments on *Living Sharpe*. Maybe she could get Cassidy to give her some ideas. She took her planner out of her shoulder bag on the corner of the bed and slid the card into the front pocket, then added several items to her endless to-do list.

- *Call bank re: stolen cards*
- *Call DPS re: license theft*
- *Research bear population in Maine*
- *Find post office and mail shoes to cobbler*
- *Find grocery store, hopefully in this county or region*
- *Bake something as a thank-you for Gus*
- *Talk to Cassidy about home tips for the show*

Cassidy stomped into the house and called out, "Gonna check the pilot lights and get out of your hair. I'm sure you're wiped out after a drive like that."

"Thanks," Lillian said, closing her planner. Cassidy was right. She *was* wiped out. Emotionally and physically. Funny how it never occurred to her that she was overdoing it back home. It's like the energy and vibrance of the city supercharged her and kept her going. She glanced at the horrible seventies sofa and cracked Formica countertops. Just like the town, time seemed to have frozen this cottage in place.

"You are so gone, sofa," she threatened, wagging a finger. "You're out of here even faster than I'm going to be."

A weird prickly wave of being watched tickled up the back of her neck, and she turned to find Cassidy smiling at her from the open front door. "I'm happy to take that off your hands," she said.

Lillian swallowed and waved in what she hoped was a casual gesture. Man, she needed sleep if she was conversing with a sofa. "That'd be great."

"This place is up and running. Give the water a while to heat. The oven and stove lit right up when I tried them out. I'll be back for the sofa tomorrow if you're serious about getting rid of it."

"Oh, believe me, I am. It's offensive on every level imaginable."

Cassidy tilted her head and studied her for a moment, then glanced at the sofa before saying, "I'll see you tomorrow, then. Around five okay?"

"Sounds good." Lillian's phone rang as she watched her bound down the front steps. "Thanks, Cassidy," she called as she answered her phone.

"Oh, my God, Lils. You said you would call back. I was honestly about to report a missing-persons case and tell them to check a sofa's alibi and bring it in for questioning."

Lillian laughed. "Sorry. The person who you hired to look after the place was here turning on the gas and water."

"Oh, yeah. They were supposed to get the house ready for you, but I guess you beat them to it, since you sped out of here in a huff."

"I do *not* huff."

"You most certainly do."

She leaned against the doorframe. "No, I don't. Niles huffs."

"Yeah, well, he's better at it; I'll concede that. He's having a field day with the online disaster right now."

Lillian opened Instagram and was not surprised to see the same kind of nasty comments and threats she'd found on the other two platforms she'd checked earlier, and her stomach churned. She pushed away from the door and paced a slow circle around the small living room. "About that. Maybe Living Sharpe should issue a formal statement."

After a pause, Erin sighed. "While I was waiting for you to call back, I talked with our attorney and the publicity and marketing team leaders. The consensus is that we should do nothing at all and just let it blow over."

Lillian stopped her pacing and gasped at a particularly awful comment. She closed the app. "Not sure this is going to blow over. My God. They think I'm Niles's lover." She made a choked sound and shuddered.

"We've been advised to not reply to any comment and have been encouraged to stay completely off social media except for our scheduled promotional posts. Also, they suggested you stay out of the limelight until the dust settles."

"Limelight? When have I ever sought attention like that?"

"Good point. I know you don't want to ever be on the lens side of a camera, but if you've looked at the platforms, you know that there is probably a bounty on your head from the Sharpies."

"Sharpies?"

"An avid group of Niles's groupies."

"This is ridiculous."

"I totally agree."

Lillian lowered herself gingerly onto the sofa in order to avoid a dust cloud and covered her face with her free hand. She'd created a monster, and now she was the one being hunted with pitchforks.

"How's Blink?" her sister asked in a voice infused with way too much cheer.

"Great attempt to change the subject," Lillian said. "Blink sucks. I guess the good thing is that I can guarantee

you it's Sharpie-free around here. I'm not even sure
there's wifi." She'd been surprised she had a cell signal,
honestly.

"Good. Lay low and try not to advertise who you are.
You really can't come back here right now. Some of these
threats are pretty...threatening. Lawyer's looking into
reporting some of them to law enforcement."

Lillian groaned and rolled her eyes. She sat very still
so as not to press her luck with the sofa, which was
behaving itself at the moment. "I'll say it again. This is
ridiculous. Fix it, Erin. No way can I stay here for long."

"I'll do what I can, Lils," Erin soothed.

She could imagine her sister's indulgent smile and
held her breath as she carefully stood, relieved to not be
followed up by a cloud of dust like Pigpen from *Peanuts*.
"Call me if you need me."

"I always do."

Lillian smiled. Erin was right. She always called if it
was important. Living Sharpe could not be in better
hands—outside of her own, of course. And with that, she
said goodbye and strolled to the bedroom, not even
bothering to pull back the quilt, and fell into a much-
needed nap, where instead of her usual dreams about
work and coaching Niles through another TV segment,
she dreamed about blue water crashing against a rocky
shoreline and a highly irritating grumpy hot guy who
needed no coaching at all.

CHAPTER FOUR

Caleb found it difficult to focus on his work, which, admittedly, was pretty low-level today. He refolded his sandpaper and went back over the same area, running his hand over the smooth wood to feel for any imperfection.

For the last few hours, he'd kept an eye on the cottage across the harbor through the large starboard window of the *Elizabeth's Wish*. Lillian Mahoney's fancy little car was still parked in front. The frivolous convertible was as out of place in Blink as its owner was. Cass had dropped by Emmett's cottage earlier but hadn't stayed long, to his relief. He wanted to know what this woman's game was before she tricked someone in addition to Roger into letting her "help" them, or whatever nonsense she was peddling. Squinting, he could tell the front door was open, but he couldn't see her—not that it mattered. She couldn't get into much trouble in that little house by herself.

He frowned down at the sandpaper in his hand, frustrated at how little he'd accomplished so far today. The owner wanted the walnut railing refinished on the stairs and a cracked newel post on one side replicated. Smaller than his usual job, but his dad was already doing some motor work on the *Elizabeth's Wish*, and the exterior of this forty-five-foot sailboat was going to need a total rework in a year or two, so he'd accepted, hoping to cultivate a return client or maybe pick up some new ones by word of mouth, which was how he operated. Caleb had never taken out an ad for his business. His work spoke for itself, and people who did what he did were rare these days.

"Hey! I finished putting in the fuel filter. How's it going in here?"

Caleb smiled at his dad, who was peeking in through the door. His dad knew better than to walk inside with his work boots on. "Great. I need to fabricate the replacement newel post before I stain it. Thought I had a suitable piece in the barn, but it was fir, not walnut. I'll need to drive to Machias in the next day or two if you need anything from town."

His dad nodded. "I'll let you know. Hey, uh, Beth's helping Mom make a pie. Says she's spending the night with us."

Caleb clenched his jaw and returned his attention back to the stair railing.

"Wanna join us for dinner?" his dad asked.

"No." He glanced through the window at the little car in front of the cottage. "Thanks for the invite, though." Not only did he need to keep an eye on Lillian Mahoney, he didn't want a rehash of his and Beth's argument from last night. She was still asleep when he left this morning—more like when he snuck out like the coward he was. Dinner would be a lot nicer for everyone if he stayed put.

His dad leaned into the cabin from the doorway, obviously to see what Caleb was looking at through the window. Lillian Mahoney, now dressed in pants, was getting into her car.

"Hell on wheels," Caleb muttered under his breath.

"She's pretty, huh?" his dad asked with a huge grin.

"Yeah." She was pretty, all right. Pretty and dangerous. She backed out of the driveway and headed south on the road ringing the harbor. Maybe she'd decided to leave. That would be good. Right? Of course it would. He lost sight of the car behind the pines on the west end of the harbor.

"Nice car," his dad observed as it reappeared between patches of pines.

"It is."

"And she seems to be a nice girl, helping Roger and all," his dad said pointedly.

He spun on his dad. "See, that's the thing. I don't think she's nice at all. I think she's up to no good. Why would anyone offer to just help someone like that?"

For a moment, his dad looked surprised; then, something else crossed his face. Something that made Caleb wince. Pity. That same pitying look he saw so often fifteen years ago. "Maybe, son, you can think back to a time when you thought the best of people and looked for the good in them, rather than the bad."

Direct hit. Caleb swallowed hard but said nothing. He placed the battered, folded sandpaper on the work tray he'd set on a table next to the bannister and watched as the red convertible pulled up outside Amanda Miller's shop several doors down. "I've grown up since then, Dad."

"You've gotten older, anyway," his dad grumbled.

Caleb stepped onto the deck with his dad and removed his shoe covers, pitching them in the trash can just outside the door. He whistled, and Scout and Willy trotted toward the ramp from where they were sleeping in the sun on the dock. "I'll see you in a bit," he said to his dad, intending to walk to Amanda's shop to head off whatever malfeasance Lillian Mahoney had in mind.

Amanda's place was part convenience store, part hardware store, part pharmacy, part post office, and part gossip mill. On Friday and Saturday nights, she sometimes put out plastic lawn chairs and threw impromptu porch parties in front of her place—BYOB affairs, which were a huge hit, since there was no bar in Blink. Amanda had taken over her family's business, Miller Mercantile, five or so years ago, but there wasn't any real demand anymore thanks to the shrinking town population and Amazon. Amanda dabbled in a little of this, a little of that, and she knew everything about everyone, including him, and that wouldn't do at all.

Eyes narrowed, Caleb watched the woman get out of her car.

"She's innocent until proven guilty, son."

He met his dad's eyes. "No. She's *presumed* innocent—that doesn't mean she's innocent. Big difference. And I don't presume anything anymore. I want proof."

That gut-wrenching look of pity crossed his dad's face again, and Caleb wanted to roar. Instead, he said, "This has nothing to do with Ashley." *Dammit.* He'd promised himself he wasn't going to say her name out loud to either of his parents again. He shoved his hands in his pockets and forced himself to maintain eye contact with his dad.

"You keep telling yourself that, son, and you just might start believing it, but I never will. I know better. I know who you are, and it's not who I'm hearing right now."

Caleb shrugged, brushed past his dad, and headed

down the ramp.

"You're the man up all night playing dolls with a sick two-year-old," his dad called after him. "You're the man who rebuilds houses for neighbors who can't do it themselves and fixes down-on-their-luck lobstermen's boats for free on the down-low."

Caleb shot his father a look over his shoulder as he reached the bottom of the ramp.

"Oh, yeah. I know all about that," his dad said, arms folded over his chest.

Evidently, nobody around here could keep a secret. Caleb patted both dogs on their heads, and they fell into step beside him.

"Oh," his dad shouted after him, "you're also the man who takes in dogs nobody else wants. I know exactly who you are."

Caleb gave his dad a dismissive wave over his shoulder, hoping it came across as unaffected and relaxed—the total opposite of how he felt. His dad was right about one thing for sure. He'd changed. And it made him sad. He wished he could throw off his suspicion and doubt. See the good before the bad…especially in himself. But he was broken, and he knew it. Maybe someday his dad would accept that fact and stop trying to stuff him into a mold that didn't fit anymore.

Ahead of him on the wooden walkway that circled the developed part of the harbor, Lillian Mahoney was picking her way over the rough, uneven boards toward the door of Amanda's shop. She wasn't in her snazzy little skirt anymore, but the pants she wore seemed just as impractical, and the shoes… He looked down at the spiky heels of the tall shoes and fought the urge to shake his head. It was a wooden walkway connected to a pier at a harbor, not a fashion runway. Hopefully, the con she was running was as underdeveloped as her common sense.

As she neared the door, she glanced up from her treacherous path and noticed him. She came to a complete stop, and her eyes narrowed. Oh, yeah. She knew he was onto her.

After drawing a deep breath, she clutched the straps of the huge bag over her shoulder, lifted her chin, and took two more steps. The problem was that her left shoe only took one more step, the heel remaining wedged between planks.

Caleb coughed to cover a laugh at the mortified look on her face. His dad's words ran through his head. *I know who you are.* Helping her, not laughing at her, is who he was, suspicious or not, and a wave of shame washed through him at how callous he'd become. Scout and Willy bounded over to her with kisses and wags. Instead of being pissed-off as he'd expected, she laughed and leaned down to rub the dogs.

Okay, well, that was…different.

She kicked off the remaining shoe and yanked the stuck one's heel from between the planks, giving both dogs scratches on the chin with her free hand.

"Yours?" she asked, gesturing to the dogs as she picked up the shoe she'd kicked off.

His mouth went dry. She really was pretty. Her hair was thick, shining like mahogany in the sunlight, and the pants showed off her long legs. He cleared his throat. "Yeah."

"Huh," she said airily. "That surprises me."

He frowned. That made no sense at all. "Why would them being my dogs surprise you?"

Barefooted, she made her way to the door of Amanda's shop and stopped on the rubber doormat. "Well, they say a dog reflects their owner's personality." She placed her shoes on the mat and gracefully stepped into them, balancing herself with a slender hand on the doorframe. "Clearly, they are nothing like you."

Caleb glanced at the two dogs falling all over themselves, wagging and working for her attention. He didn't know whether to be offended or impressed by her assessment. "That's because they are fairly recent rescues," he said with a lift of an eyebrow.

"Oh, that explains it." She leaned down to rub them on the shoulders. "I'm sure they'll turn surly, judgmental, and unfriendly before too long." With a final pat for each adoring dog, she disappeared into the shop.

Well, shit. He deserved that, he supposed. He'd made it crystal clear from the start he was onto her ploy, so why did it bother him?

He snapped his fingers to call the dogs, and they slowly came to him, looking longingly over their shoulders at the shop door. "It doesn't bother me one bit," he told the dogs. So what if she thought he was surly, judgmental, and unfriendly? Maybe it would keep her looking behind her while she tried to screw over Roger McGuffy or anyone else.

She's innocent until proven guilty, his dad's voice whispered in his head.

Maybe his dad was right, and she simply wanted to

help Roger?

He shook his head. No. It was way too coincidental that she, super fancy city woman, ended up in the tiny nothing of a town and bumped right into the richest man around. She'd said she was on a short vacation. Who would choose to vacation in Blink? He glanced around the boarded-up storefronts on the harbor. It was like a ghost town from a bad horror movie. Nobody vacationed here. Nobody did anything here—except for plan for the day they could leave.

Still, his dogs liked her, which was pretty strong evidence she wasn't an outright villain. He turned to walk back to work, but his feet didn't want to move. If this was a con, it was a really long one. He'd looked up the tax records for Emmett's house, and her story checked out. It had been purchased by an Erin J. Mahoney several years ago through an online bank auction. He assumed Erin was the sister she'd mentioned. Two years is a long time to wait, and Roger's wife died over a year ago. Why buy that far ahead, and why wait another year after he's widowed to approach him, since he'd be more emotional and probably an easier mark closer to his wife's death?

He took a couple of steps away and stopped. Maybe Mahoney wasn't really her name, and she was only going by it in order to link herself to the house as cover. Maybe—

Stop. This whole line of logic was ridiculous. He should just ask her.

The dogs' tails went into hyper speed when he turned and strode toward the shop after her. He looked down at them. "You guys really need to tone it down and learn to play it cool." Deep down, though, he knew that if he were a dog, the thought of being rubbed on by Lillian Mahoney—or whatever her real name was—would have him wagging and panting, too.

Which was a completely unhelpful thought.

He opened the door as she paused at the counter, looking both ways in the empty store.

"Hello?" she called hesitantly.

"I'll be right out," Amanda's voice called from the back. She was probably in the office.

Lillian turned and gave Caleb a resentful glare, and he resisted the urge to take a step back. "Shopping?" she asked.

"No."

She glanced past him to the door, where the dogs waited, all but crying to get inside.

"At least you're honest," she said.

"Good thing one of us is," he replied. "How are you planning to shop without your wallet?" There was no way she'd made it to the bank. Other than her trip to Amanda's, her car hadn't left.

Lillian's forehead furrowed, and she took a deep breath, no doubt to unleash on him, but was cut off before she could even finish her windup.

"Hi!" Amanda said, strolling through the door behind the counter. She looked Lillian up and down and grinned. "New to town. Welcome to Blink!"

They were about the same age, but the contrast between the two women was striking. Amanda's gaudy brightness clashed with Lillian's muted elegance.

"Hello." She took Amanda's hand and shook it. "I'm

Lillian Mahoney."

"Amanda Miller. You on the hunt for something specific?"

From the corner of her eye, Lillian watched him lean against the end of a shelf of canned goods and fold his arms across his chest. Good. He wanted her aware of him.

"Oh, hey, Caleb!" Amanda said. "Be with you in a sec."

"Take your time," he said, staring straight at Lillian. "Tell Amanda what you're on the hunt for. I'd love to know."

A confused look crossed Amanda's face, and Lillian's eyes narrowed before she turned her back to him. "Thanks for asking," she said to Amanda. "I have something I need help with. Cassidy told me I can mail something out from here?"

The other woman smiled. "You bet."

Lillian pulled a box out of her bag, sneaking a peek at him before setting it on the counter. "I have a corporate FedEx account. Can we send it through that?"

"We can, but I'll need your info."

Lillian punched some stuff on her phone and turned it toward Amanda, whose face lit. "Wow. You work for—"

"Not for. With," Lillian said, cutting her off. "Do you need the account number?" Again, she glanced over her shoulder at him, clearly uneasy as she shifted her weight foot to foot on her spindly heels and tapped her fingers on the counter.

"Yeah." Amanda took her amazed gaze from Lillian's face to the phone, then entered something on her computer. "Got it. Now, I need the address where it's going."

"Usually a label is autogenerated and I print it, but I didn't have a printer, sorry."

"We're in Blink. We do lots of stuff the old-fashioned way. Address?"

Lillian scrolled the screen on her phone and set it on the counter. Amanda squinted and entered information on her computer. "Cool. We're all set." Behind her, the label printer whirred to life. "What else do you need?"

"That's it for now." She looked longingly at the candy bar rack next to her elbow. "Well, except for this." She pulled a Snickers bar from the stack and placed it on the counter.

"Maybe you should buy some boots," Caleb said, giving her ridiculous high-heeled shoes a pointed stare. "You wouldn't want to end up with a broken neck." That last little bit sounded more like a threat than concern.

"Get lost, Caleb Wright," Amanda scolded. "Come back later."

"Wait, what?"

"Out." Amanda pointed at the door. "Like my momma says, go back and get up on the right side of the bed, or stay in your room."

Worse than being ordered out was the smug look on Lillian's face. She was now allied. Woman-bonded. Paired up with the biggest gossip in the Downeast region, and he'd been kicked out. Perfect.

Amanda was a force beyond him, so with a shrug, he pushed off the rack where he was leaning and casually sauntered to the door, where his dogs were anything but casual as they scratched and whined to come in. His leisurely stroll and untroubled opening of the door were all for nothing as Willy and Scout shot past him, skidding across the wood floor to get to Lillian, who made a knife-twisting show of kindness to them as they wiggled and wagged and kissed her.

Traitors.

It took three whistles to get the dogs at heel and out the door. He'd never seen them go for someone like they did Lillian. Maybe it was because they never met anyone new other than clients. Maybe she had a steak in her bag or something. Or maybe that weird pull he felt toward her had nailed them, too.

Instead of heading back to the *Elizabeth's Wish*, he went to the Wright Boat Works barn and climbed up to the loft office. This room used to fill him with joy, with its cross-sections of famous yachts and mechanical drawings of different kinds of vessels he'd pinned to the walls from the time he'd been able to climb the stairs. Boats. It's like they'd floated through his blood since birth. They were his first love and all he'd cared about until he'd met…

With a sigh, he stared out the window overlooking the harbor and Amanda's place. Lillian was in there now, no doubt getting an earful about him and everyone in Blink. Ammunition for whatever scheme she was running.

He smoothed his fingers over the brass and chrome of the vintage compass on the desk as he watched. He should have warned Amanda.

What if he was wrong, though? God knew he'd been wrong before. So many times.

"Caleb?" his dad called from down in the shop.

"Yeah. I'm up here."

"Oh, good. Can you help me install a lower unit I just

rebuilt? Too heavy for this old man."

"That's what the hydraulic lift is for," Caleb called out good-naturedly.

"That's what my son is for!"

Motion caught his eye through the window, and he watched Lillian exit Amanda's place. The grin that tugged at his lips felt odd and foreign. Even more so when he chuckled as she tromped toward her car in… Were those children's rain boots?

Instead of driving off, she dumped several grocery bags and her huge purse in the car and closed the door. How'd she score groceries with no way to pay for them? He should have stayed in the store.

Phone in hand, she walked to the end of the wooden walkway and climbed the trail to the top of the rocky hill overlooking the harbor. Her hair whipped around in the coastal wind, and she caught it up in her hands. She stared down over the harbor, then, to his surprise, she looked right at the window where he was standing.

Busted.

He froze, not sure if she could see him through the glass at that distance.

Yep. She saw him all right, if her hand gesture was any indication. That defiant action combined with whatever those were on her feet dragged an unexpected laugh out of him. And it felt…good. God, he hoped he was wrong about her, because he really missed laughing.

"Caleb Wright!" his dad called from downstairs. "Get your butt down here and help me."

With one last glance at Lillian, he turned away from the window.

CHAPTER FIVE

Amanda was awesome. Lillian had felt a bond right away. She loved her short, curly hair that framed her face perfectly—a look that Lillian could never pull off, just like she could never rock Amanda's colorful bohemian vest and bright red shirt. Once Caleb had left, it was like the air lightened and she could breathe. When Lillian had explained her problem with her stolen wallet, Amanda had extended her a line of credit, probably because she was a huge fan of the show, which she wanted to talk about ad nauseum. Thankfully, she hadn't blurted out the name on the FedEx account in front of the town grump.

She didn't want to think about what Caleb's reaction would have been to *that*.

Lillian reached the top of the little hill and turned around to enjoy the view of the harbor. Like a magnet, her eye was drawn to Wright Boat Works, and motion in a window high in the building caught her attention. The jerk was still watching her. What'd he think she was planning to do? Rob the tiny mercantile store? Ugh.

"Yeah, hi!" she said, flipping him the bird. Even from this distance, she saw him laugh. Stunned, she lowered her arm and watched. The grumpiest guy she'd ever met could laugh. *At her*, but still it was good to know he had a mode outside of grouchy.

Shaking her head, she struck back out on the path. It felt good to climb and move. She felt like she'd been cooped up forever. When she'd asked for the prettiest place in walking distance, Amanda had sent her here. Something impossible in her heels. She looked down at the ridiculous boots and groaned. Thank God none of the team were here to see her like this. She'd never hear the end of it.

She stepped over a large, jagged rock in the path the size of a baseball and brushed her hair off her forehead. Amanda was a good resource. She knew the closest store—not close, for the record; the best hikes; the nearest bank—again, not close; and had the dirt on everyone in Blink. She'd seemed pretty pissed at Caleb but would only say that he was one of the nicest guys ever and was simply having a bad day.

She'd resisted the urge to push Amanda for more information. The last thing she wanted was for the guy to find out she was interested in him, even if it was only to find out why he was so awful.

Cresting another rise in the trail, Lillian gasped. The beauty made her chest ache, and the crashing of the waves below caused an adrenaline dump similar to how she felt right before Niles went live yesterday. God, was it only yesterday? Time seemed to stand still here.

She pulled out her phone and texted a photo to Erin.

As she shuffled her way awkwardly down the path toward the water, she was grateful for the boots and a good sense of balance. At the bottom, there was a smooth area in the shape of a crescent moon that appeared to be made of small rocks and was partially protected from the waves on one side. She could definitely make it down there if she focused on where she put her feet.

Speaking of feet, she'd really put hers in her mouth today—like every time she talked to Caleb, but something about him irritated her. It made no sense that both Cassidy and Amanda said he was the nicest guy ever. Was it her, or was it simply his demeanor and they were used to it?

Stepping off the path and onto a large boulder, she tilted her head back and took in the ocean wind and spray. Heaven. Why was this place not booming with tourists, artists, and bird-watchers like every other town on the coast? She'd researched after her nap, and none of it made sense.

She startled when a silhouette of a person rose over a cluster of rocks to the left of the little rocky beach. A woman…no, a girl. She looked to be high-school age and appeared to be furiously texting on her phone. Not having kids or being around them much, Lillian was bad with guessing ages. The girl climbed down onto the beach, and the sun hit her face, which was clearly red from crying. Lowering her phone, she covered her face and slumped down onto the rocky beach.

One of Lillian's and Erin's mottos was "Women take care of each other," which was why they had a predominantly female business with very low turnover. In fact, the only pain-in-the-butt employee was Niles. Seeing this young woman so upset made Lillian's entire body ache with empathy.

Picking her way carefully, Lillian approached the girl, making a wide arc so that she was in her field of vision and didn't surprise her.

"Hey," Lillian said in a soft voice. Obviously too soft to

be heard over the sound of the water and wind. "You okay?" she said a little louder, and the girl jerked her head in her direction.

"Oh." She pushed to her feet and wiped her eyes on her sleeve. "Yeah. I'm good."

Now that Lillian was closer, it was clear the girl was a young high schooler. Not wanting her to bolt, Lillian sat down on a flat rock several feet away. "I'm new here," she said, picking a benign topic.

The girl gave a huff that sounded like a choked laugh. "Yeah. If I don't know you, your parents, pets, and favorite flavor of cookie, I assume you're not from here." She sat back down, and Lillian sighed with relief.

"I'm here on vacation."

This time the girl did laugh. "Why?"

She gestured to the water. "Because it's beautiful."

"So is every other town on the coast that isn't Blink."

Lillian chuckled, and the girl gave her a shy smile. She had long, straight brown hair parted in the middle and bright blue eyes the color of the ocean. She had on a T-shirt with what was probably a video game logo—it was familiar to Lillian, but she wasn't a gamer; no time for that at all. The girl's cargo pants were rolled up above a pair of super-sturdy looking boots with thick tread on them. Lillian shook her pants legs to cover her own boots, but the girl didn't seem to notice and was staring out over the water, nose still red and face blotchy.

"You wanna talk about it?" Lillian asked.

"You don't even know me," the girl said.

"Sometimes a new perspective is helpful."

The girl slid her a look and shook her head. "Nothing

will help unless you can get me a new family and out of this stupid town."

Lillian's throat tightened as she remembered the turmoil of high school. At least she'd had the distractions of New York City only short subway rides away. This girl was stuck in the middle of nowhere.

For a while they said nothing, watching seagulls dive a few yards out from shore. One tucked its wings in, plunging its head underwater and coming up with something in its beak. Immediately, the flock swooped in, trying to steal its catch.

"My dad is the worst. He's the biggest jerk ever," the girl blurted out, not taking her eyes from the birds.

Lillian said nothing, chest aching at the girl's obvious pain.

"He treats me like a baby. I'm sixteen years old." She threw her arms up in frustration. "He thinks I'm too stupid to take care of myself."

"Parents sometimes overprotect because they are afraid."

"Oh, yeah. He's afraid all right. Afraid I'm gonna end up like him. I'm not like him."

Lillian nodded. "Okay. That makes sense. What happened to upset you this much?"

"Other than him being an overprotective, old-fashioned old man?"

She smiled at the girl. "Yes. Other than that."

The girl ran a hand through her hair, and her fingers got stuck at the ends of the long, straight strands. She jerked them free with a huff and tied her hair in a knot at the nape of her neck. "He won't let me go camping with Brandon."

"Tell me about Brandon."

The girl's entire face changed, becoming softer and wistful. "He's a senior. We go to the same high school, but he's not from Blink. He lives in the next town over, which makes it impossible to spend time together, since I don't have a car because Dad thinks I'm a baby." She sniffed. "I've hardly even seen him since school let out for summer."

"Does Brandon have a car?"

"Yeah, but he says it's too far to come see me all the time."

It struck Lillian that it couldn't be that far if they went to the same high school, but she decided to keep that to herself for now. "Tell me about the camping trip."

"It's me and Brandon and another couple from his grade. Julie and Ben. I don't know them, but Brandon says they're awesome. We'd be camping on his uncle's property in the mountains."

"Far away?"

She shrugged. "Half an hour or so. Dad acts like it's days away and says I'm too young to go camping with a guy."

Lillian held up her palms. "Don't hate me here, but I think lots of parents would feel the same way. Maybe there's a compromise that could make both of you happy?"

She dug her boot heel in the rocks. "Compromise? *My* dad? No way." She snorted.

Lillian remembered feeling exactly like this at sixteen. "How about you ask him if you can go hang out at the campsite until a reasonable hour, and Brandon will drive you home, then he can go back and camp with his friends. Maybe you could even meet up with them again in the morning."

She rolled her eyes. "That is so embarrassing. He's a *senior*."

The fact she was uncomfortable asking her boyfriend to take her home so they could be together didn't line up for Lillian, but again, she remembered being sixteen, so she let it go.

"What does your mom say?"

Her only answer was another snort, so clearly that was a dead end. Lillian felt for the girl, but she totally understood the dad. At sixteen, lots could go wrong, especially with a guy who didn't seem invested enough to drive from his nearby town to see her regularly. Or maybe the dad was really that bad and Brandon didn't want to have an altercation.

"Do you have any other family members or friends who would pick you up if your dad agreed to let you go if you came home early?"

"My grandparents make my dad look lenient. No way."

"Uber or Lyft?"

"Ha. We're in Blink, Maine."

She said the town's name as if it were a curse word. The flock of gulls had moved farther out and were only little specks now.

"Dad's so…" The girl stomped her foot over the hole she dug with her heel. "He's so worried we're gonna have sex. Like that can only happen if we're together overnight. Maybe old people like him think that only happens after dark."

Lillian fought back a smile, as she was probably old enough to be this girl's mom if she had gotten an early start. "Why don't you run the compromise by him? You get to spend time with Brandon, but you'll be home early. Sometimes people surprise you if you give them a chance. Give your dad a chance."

"It'll never happen," she said with a resigned sigh. At least she wasn't crying anymore. "He's as predictable as a clock. Everything around here is. Nothing changes. It never will."

That's the vibe Lillian got from Blink, too. It had to be hard for this girl. Heck, it had to be even harder for her parents and grandparents, raising a teen in Nowhereville. "So, what's the worst thing that can happen? If you don't run it by him, you won't be able to go. You are in the same place as if he'd said no. And what if he says yes?"

The girl shrugged and placed her hands on her knees. Lillian noticed that the tips of her fingers were slightly stained purple.

"Are you an artist?"

The girl's eyes widened, and she met Lillian's eyes for the first time.

"I was noticing the stains on your fingertips," she said, gesturing to them with her chin.

She stared down. "Oh, no, that's from helping Hemom make a blueberry pie. She's practicing for a contest at church."

"Hemom?"

She blushed. "It's silly. My dad's parents are Hemom and Hedad, and my mom's are Shemom and Shedad. I evidently chose those names when I was little. My mom's dad wasn't a fan of being called Shedad, but Hemom said it made her sound like a superhero, so it stuck."

Lillian found it adorable. She turned her face toward the wind coming off the water and raked her hair off her forehead.

The girl's phone dinged, and she pulled it out of her pocket. "I've gotta go. Next round of pies needs to go in so we can taste test at dinner."

As she stood, it dawned on Lillian that she hadn't even introduced herself. "I'm glad we met. My name is Lillian."

The girl smiled for the first time. "I'm Bethany."

Lillian snapped the cover off her phone and pulled out a business card she kept there for times just like this when she didn't have her purse or planner. "Here." She handed it to Bethany. "My cell is on there. I'd love to hear how this turns out if you're comfortable enough to text me. No pressure, though."

Bethany looked down at the card, and her eyes grew huge. "Oh, my God. You work for Niles Sharpe?"

"With, not for," she said.

"I love him. My grandmothers and I watch that show every week. Is he as cool in person as he is on the show?"

Her obvious excitement was not contagious, and Lillian fought back a groan. No. Not cool at all. He was a royal pain in the butt. "You bet."

"Wait until I tell everybody I met someone who knows Niles Sharpe!"

Oh, crap. She held both hands up. "I need to ask a favor of you. I'd really appreciate it if you kept that between us. I'm here for vacation, you know, and don't want any attention at all." She doubted her presence in

Blink would be an issue for people here. Doubtful the scandal had made it this far, but still, Erin had told her to keep it to the chest.

Bethany looked crestfallen. "Can I at least tell Hemom?"

What harm could telling one grandmother do? "Sure, but tell her it's secret."

She grinned. "Thanks for sitting with me. I can't believe I accidentally ran into someone who actually knows Niles Sharpe."

"I'm glad we met, too."

The girl who climbed the rocky path away from the beach wasn't anything like the one Lillian had met. She smiled and snapped the cover back on her phone. If nothing else meaningful happened while she was here, at least she'd helped her out.

Lillian sat back down on the flat rock and turned her face to the wind. She imagined herself at Bethany's age with New York City at her fingertips. It had been so different for her as a teen than for this lonely girl in this tiny town that didn't have a movie theater or even a proper store.

She glanced down at her bright yellow boots with goofy lobsters all over them and frowned. A proper store would be a good thing right about now, but she'd have to settle for online shopping until she could get to a city that had a branch location of her bank to get replacement cards and some cash.

She picked up a smooth pebble and rubbed it between her palms. What she really wanted was to return home. Hopefully Niles would come to his senses, what few he had, and she could leave by the end of the week. A week should be long enough for Erin to turn him around.

She threw the pebble toward the waterline, but it fell short. At least she would have afternoons full of online conferences and her morning organization project at Roger's house to distract her.

She climbed the path to the top of the ridge overlooking the harbor. Her eyes immediately sought out the second-story window of Wright Boat Works, and Lillian found herself irritatingly disappointed to find no one there.

Evidently, Niles wasn't the only person who needed to come to their senses.

With one more glance at the empty window, she headed down the rocky path toward the cottage and what she hoped would be an epic online shopping spree.

CHAPTER SIX

Caleb wasn't surprised when Lillian Mahoney left her house promptly at ten 'til. She struck him as someone who would be punctual. Nor was he surprised that she was way overdressed. Business pants and high heels like yesterday at Amanda's, only today, she wore a pale peach blouse instead of white. Clearly, she didn't plan to do any real housekeeping for Old Man McGuffy in that outfit.

She looked nervously to her left, up into the woods behind Emmett's cottage as if she was scared a Sasquatch was going to nab her as she scurried up the path. When she hit the paved area leading to the house, she dashed for the porch, still looking toward the woods. Her heels clicked on the wooden steps, and at the top, she grabbed the support post, catching her breath.

"You're a little jumpy," he observed from a comfortable chair at the far end of the porch.

She screeched and rounded on him, hand rising to her throat. After a moment, her eyes narrowed and she let out a big breath, still clutching the post.

"Guilty conscience?" he asked with a smirk.

"No," she ground out through gritted teeth. "A well-developed fight-or-flight instinct when people sneak up on me."

He leaned back in the chair. "Sneak? I was here first. What do you plan to fight or run from?"

She released her death grip on the post and clutched the handles of her leather shoulder bag instead. "Why are you here?"

"I have some business with Roger." He brandished the paper bag in his lap. "A delivery."

With a huff, she strode to the door and lifted her hand to knock.

"He doesn't live here."

She rounded on him. "Amanda says he owns the huge white Victorian house up the road from me. That would be this house." She banged on the door as if she were imagining it was his face, which made him smile.

"He used to live here when Mabel was alive, but he moved into the guest house behind this one after that. It was probably too much for him to be where they had lived for so many years."

It was as if the loss of anger deflated her the way air leaves a balloon with a small leak—as if she really gave a crap about Roger—but it didn't last long. She straightened her spine and took a deep breath through her nose. "If you're here because you have business with him, why aren't you at the guest house, then?"

He gestured east, over the harbor. "For the view."

She followed his gesture, gazing at the gold and crimson hues painting the tops of the water and cliffs like a canvas and gasped. "Wow."

He agreed. He'd lived in Blink his whole life, and the sunrises never failed to awe him. The only thing he didn't like about living on the water was being down too low to see the best sunrises.

After a moment, she cleared her throat and started

down the steps. "Thanks for pointing out where Mr. McGuffy lives. Have a good day."

He smiled as she navigated the stairs in those heels. He'd have to admit she was really good at it. Most women he'd watched in heels walked like a newborn deer, all wobbly, taking mincing steps. This woman clearly had practice and probably some hellacious calf muscles. He couldn't wait to find out what her background was and why she was here.

"Thanks. I think it's going to be a great day," he said, following her.

Again, she glanced up into the woods behind the houses and picked up her pace, trotting up the path and onto the stoop of Roger's guest house.

He studied the trees. Was her accomplice up there or something? "What's spooked you?"

She brushed the front of her blouse, like she could brush her tension away. "Nothing." She let out a huff of breath when he only lifted an eyebrow. "Okay, fine." She looked up to the sky as if for strength. "Bears. I'm watching for bears."

He couldn't help himself. He laughed. Hell, he'd laughed more since she'd come to town than he had in ages. "Bears? Seriously?"

Her eyebrows drew together. "Yes. I looked it up on the internet, and there are bears in Maine, and most of them are in this region."

He shook his head, trying not to laugh again. "Poison ivy and ticks are the most treacherous things for you around here. Well, other than your shoes."

She looked skyward again. "It's not funny."

Maybe she was serious. He climbed up another step to the stoop, putting him one below her and about even in height. "I've lived here my whole life, and I've never seen a bear in Blink. You're a lot more likely to be hurt by a moose."

Her brow was still furrowed in worry. And for some reason, he wanted to placate her. In a calm voice, he said, "I've seen bears a couple of times up in the mountains, but they mind their own business."

"Sort of like you should," she snapped.

Good. She was back to her prickly self. "Why are you here?" he asked.

"To help Mr. McGuffy."

Now it was his turn to look skyward. "No. Why are you in Blink?"

She shifted her bag to her other shoulder. "For vacation, like I said."

"Do you usually play maid to widowers on your vacations?"

"Of course not. I'm just helping a poor old guy who clearly needs help."

Poor. Right. He wasn't buying it.

She placed her fists at her waist and took a deep breath. "You've been rude to me since I got here. Is it because I turned down a ride when you offered? Because hopping in a car with a stranger is a bad idea on a billion levels."

"That's not it." He crossed his arms over his chest. "I want to know why you are really here. Why would someone like you come to Blink?"

Her lips drew into a tight line, and for a moment, he

thought she might come clean. She studied his face for a long time, then said, "My life is none of your business."

Dammit. And she'd seemed so close. "It's my business when it's in my town. You either have an agenda or you are on the run."

"I don't *run*. Well, except for bears."

"That means you have an agenda."

"Yes—to get away from *you*."

He stepped in front of the door before she could knock. He looked her up and down, from her silky designer blouse to her fancy shoes. "You're clearly successful. What kind of work do you do?"

"The successful kind," she shot back before giving him the same up-and-down perusal he'd just given her. When she reached his work boots, she wrinkled her nose. "What kind of work do *you* do?"

He looked down at himself, from the wood stain and varnish blotches on his shirt and jeans to his boots covered in dust from walking up here. "The dirty kind."

She reached around him to knock on the door, but he beat her to it, giving three loud raps. Roger opened the door almost immediately. Caleb held out the paper bag he'd been gripping, and Roger took it, rolled it open, stared inside, then grinned. "I love test week."

Roger stepped back from the doorway and gestured Lillian inside. "Good to see you, Ms. Mahoney."

"Bye-bye," she said to Caleb with a dismissive wave. She shot him a smug look over her shoulder as she entered Roger's house. If only he'd thought ahead to have his phone out to take a picture. The look on her face when she realized he was sticking around was priceless.

"So where are we going to start, Ms. Mahoney?" Caleb asked with a grin as he followed her in. "I'm your assistant for the day."

CHAPTER SEVEN

Lillian's teeth were clenched so tight, it felt like her molars might crack. She'd give Caleb Wright this—he had some nerve. First, he followed her to Amanda's store, then he ambushed her on the porch, and now he interjected himself into her job for Mr. McGuffy. What was his deal?

She took a deep breath and tried to relax her face. She'd been half kidding when she joked that he thought she was planning to rob Amanda, but maybe that hadn't been too far off track. He clearly thought she was up to something awful, but what? She admired the fact he was doing this out of some bizarre sense of loyalty to his neighbors, but it was seriously misplaced.

No. She wasn't going to think about it anymore. She was here for a reason. Time to do what she did best: create order. She set her bag on the nearest chair and faced Mr. McGuffy. He was wearing a different shirt today than yesterday at the diner, but it was equally wrinkled, as were his khaki pants.

Past his shoulder, she could see dishes piled up in the kitchen sink. In the room to her right, which had a large, flat-screen TV, a huge pile of clothes took up one recliner while the other was surrounded with magazines and newspapers. No wonder the guy was at wit's end.

Lillian slipped her planner out of her bag and turned to a clean page. "Most homemaking experts say to start at the front door when tackling a house, but I like to start at the most important room in the house."

"The TV room?" Roger said.

Caleb grinned at him, then gave her a sly look. "No, no. The most important room in the house is the bedroom— am I right, Ms. Mahoney?"

She wanted to wring his blasted neck. He had loaded the way he'd said "bedroom" with so much innuendo, she had to force herself to not blush. Instead, she looked him right in the eye and said, "Well, I guess the room we consider the most important depends on our priorities. I consider the kitchen the most important room in the house, so we'll start there."

She stomped into the kitchen and began making notes in her book. Before she had the second item in her schedule for the kitchen entered, Caleb sauntered over to her. "Clearly, you underestimate the importance of a good night's sleep if you value the kitchen over the bedroom."

"Clearly, you underestimate the value of a home-cooked meal if you don't rank the kitchen first."

Again, he looked her up and down with those piercing blue eyes of his. Then he lifted one of his eyebrows with cocky cynicism. "You can cook?"

How dare he? "I can do a lot of things."

"Of that, I have no doubt." His voice was low and rumbly and full of… Lillian had the urge to fan herself.

Stop. She shook herself mentally. He had some warped idea she was here to do something nefarious. He was trying to ruffle her. Not a chance. She had five years of working with Niles, which gave her nerves of steel and a heavy dose of patience few people had.

"Since you profess to be here to help and seem focused on Mr. McGuffy's bedroom"—she ripped a blank sheet of paper out of her planner—"why don't you go in there and make a list of changes you think would make it a more effective, enjoyable space?" She shoved the paper in his hand and gave him her pen as well. "Off you go!" She made shooing motions with her hand and almost giggled at his startled look before he sauntered away.

She had to admire his protectiveness toward his friends and neighbors, but his watching her every second was unnerving. Maybe she should just tell him who she was and why she was here and put an end to the whole watching business. She sighed, admiring the way his jeans hung just so over his fit backside. In truth, she didn't mind watching him right back.

Roger cleared his throat, pulling her out of her denim haze. "So, you gonna organize something or just stare?"

"Kitchen," she said, rooting another pen out of her purse and grabbing her planner.

. . .

Caleb took the box from Lillian and placed it in the cabinet above the refrigerator with the other things Roger didn't use but didn't want to get rid of yet. That particular box held twelve commemorative whiskey glasses from his trip to Tennessee with Mabel decades ago.

It had taken three hours, but they'd finally finished the kitchen. If this was a scam, it was a freaking good one.

Not only had her interactions with Roger been strictly about putting his house in order, it turned out that Lillian Mahoney was great at organization.

She wiped her hands on a dish towel she had hung over the oven handle. "Okay. So, to sum up, the best way to keep this room tidy and efficient is to only keep things you need or love. We've put the glasses and dishes you use the most here, above the dishwasher, so that they are easier to put away." She gave him a look a mother might give a kid. "You're going to promise me you will not use the dishwasher for storage anymore. You are going to run it every time it's full and will put the dishes away so dirty ones don't pile up in the sink."

Roger nodded.

"All the dishwasher pucks are in this container on the counter above it so that you don't have to fish around for them anymore. And no more storing motor oil and antifreeze under the sink, right?"

"Right," Roger said.

She nodded her approval. "Now, we need to make a list of what kind of things you use daily, weekly, and monthly so I can do a check-box shopping list for you. I'll go to your grocery store and organize the list by aisle, so you can follow it in order when you're there."

At this point, Roger looked a little dazed. He'd probably hit the homemaking wall. Caleb looked at Lillian. "How about we take out these boxes of stuff to go to charity and trash and take on another room tomorrow?"

Roger let out a sigh of relief. "That sounds like a good plan. Same time?"

Lillian seemed a little confused but smiled and agreed.

She smiled a lot, and Caleb liked that. He liked her cool control and sharp wit also. He could imagine her being in complete charge of a boardroom full of executives, just like she took charge of this project.

While he might be—reluctantly—starting to believe that she might *not* be running a con on Roger, he couldn't get rid of the niggling feeling she was hiding something. His number-one pet peeve— No, it went way beyond that. The thing that was nonnegotiable for him was lying. Lying was unacceptable. Deceit was his hard no after what he'd been through. One and done for him. No second chances.

"Oh, wait," Roger said. "It's test week!" He walked over to the bag Caleb had brought, carried it to the round, oak breakfast table, and pulled four tin foil–covered plates out.

"What is test week?" Lillian asked.

"Pie!" Roger unwrapped the first of the pieces. "A bunch of churches around the region compete in a blueberry pie contest every year during berry season. It's not as big a deal as the one in Machias, but lots of churches participate."

Roger unwrapped the second piece that looked like it had been sat on. They'd been stacked one on top of the other, so as he pulled the foil off, topping came with it. The remaining pieces were equally abused, but hey, it was pie.

"Each town submits one entry," Caleb explained, pulling three forks out of the now-pristine utensil drawer. "I think these are the final four recipes for Blink's entry this year, though Mom is hoping for more."

"There's a number on each plate," Roger said. "We're

supposed to vote for the best one to represent Blink." He shoved one of the forks Caleb had set on the table toward Lillian. "Dig in!"

Lillian shuffled the plates until they were in number order, then she carefully sculpted out a bite from the side—not the tip, like Caleb always did. As she held that bite in her mouth, she picked at the edge of the crust with her fork, like she was checking out its texture or something.

"You're taking this very seriously," Caleb said.

She held up a finger and chewed deliberately, then swallowed. "Pie is serious." After a sip of coffee, she stood and got her notebook thing from where she'd left it on the counter. She turned to a new page and scribbled. Peeking over, he saw the words, "overly sweet" and "grainy." After another sip of coffee, she did the same with the next piece, more coffee, then the next, making notes each time.

While Roger wolfed down the first piece after Lillian did her evaluation, Caleb picked at the second. "So are you some kind of pie connoisseur?" he kidded.

Her brow furrowed as she scribbled her notes on the fourth piece. "You could say that."

He got the funny feeling she wasn't kidding. Who was this woman who dressed like a boardroom executive and acted like someone from a chef competition? And what the hell was she doing in Blink, Maine, eating pie in an old man's kitchen?

She tore out the paper she'd been writing on. "Here are my notes on the entries for whomever is the organizer." She folded it in half and handed it to Roger, who passed it to Caleb. "When is the contest?"

Caleb shrugged. "A week or so. I really don't know."

She nodded. "Good. They have some time, then." She turned to Caleb. "Boxes?"

"I've arranged for them to be picked up."

"Is there a Goodwill or something nearby?" she asked.

Caleb took another bite of pie and nodded. "You could say that," he echoed.

She stood there awkwardly for a moment, which seemed out of character for her. "Well, I'll see you tomorrow, then. Will you be helping again, Caleb?"

He put his fork down and looked at her. He had work of his own to do, and it didn't look like she was fleecing Roger. "Not sure."

He couldn't read her face at all. Back to the boardroom persona. "Okay," she said. "Thanks for your help today. See you tomorrow, Roger."

Roger nodded and moved on to the next piece of pie, not noticing how well Lillian Mahoney's pants fit across her ass or how spectacular that ass was. Caleb noticed, though.

CHAPTER EIGHT

All in all, it had been a satisfying day. Lillian felt like they'd made good progress at Roger's this morning, though she would like to have at least tackled the stacks of magazines and newspapers before she left. Caleb was probably right, though. Roger seemed to fizzle out after the kitchen, so she shouldn't tax him with more than a few hours a day. She was used to working with her young, enthusiastic team of creators, not octogenarians.

When she got back to the cottage, she'd hooked up her phone to her laptop as a hot spot, attended two video conferences with her team, engaged in some *serious* online shopping, and did more research on the area. No matter how she came at it, Blink made no sense. It had nicer natural features than some of the successful neighboring towns but for some reason had been passed over and forgotten.

"Not my problem," she said, closing her laptop. Her problems were all in New York right now—well, there and on the internet. As prescribed by Erin and her team leaders, she'd stayed away from social media, which was good, because Amanda didn't sell hard liquor.

She smiled at the thought of Amanda. Her new friend had texted her at least half a dozen times today to remind her about her get-together in front of her shop tonight. She'd even called and left an exuberant voicemail message. "Seriously, you have to come!" she chirped in a voice as bright as her clothes. "The theme is, 'roll with it, baby'—isn't that great? It's potluck, but don't worry about it. I know you're not set up yet, so just bring yourself. It's super casual. See you there."

Lillian shook her head with a smile. Her online orders wouldn't arrive until day after tomorrow at the earliest, and since Blink was at the end of the earth, it might take much longer. Super casual wasn't happening. She huffed out an irritated breath. If she had done some of that expert planning she was known for and hadn't lost her cool and skipped town like a fugitive, this wouldn't have happened. She shook her head. She *was* a fugitive, sort of. Right now, the Sharpies were probably sharpening their sticks.

A knock came on the door, and she glanced out the window to see the Handyman Hank truck pulled up in front of her house. It was Cassidy coming to haul off the homicidal sofa, thank God.

"Come on in!" she called through the open window to Cassidy and a young guy with a tool belt slung over his shoulder.

She smiled. She would never just shout, "come on in," back home. Nor would she leave her door unlocked.

"Hey, Lillian. This is my baby brother, Luke," Cassidy said, gesturing to the young man standing in the open doorway.

He nodded at Lillian with a sheepish smile, then flipped his long bangs out of his face and glared at his sister. "You could lose the *baby* part of that intro any day now, Cass."

She reached out and ruffled his bangs, and he slapped

her hand away.

"We're here to pick up the sofa. Brought tools in case we need to disassemble it to get it out the door," Cassidy said while Luke ran his hands through his hair.

"I don't care if you take a chainsaw to it. Just get it out. I don't know what will end me first, the dust or the massive dose of ugly."

Luke strode to the sofa and took a tape measure to the end, measuring horizontally, vertically, and diagonally. "It'll fit out the door as is." He pitched his tool belt on one of the cushions, and a puff of dust rose up, dancing merrily in the light from the open window.

"Good riddance!" Lillian said.

"Nothing a shop vac and a good steam cleaning won't fix," Cassidy said.

Lillian shook her head. "Steam cleaning won't fix the ugly."

"On three." Cassidy shoved her hands under the opposite end of the sofa from her brother. Together, they maneuvered the monstrosity out the door without even rubbing it against the doorframe. Lillian followed them out and recognized the boxes from Roger's kitchen lined up along one side of the truck bed. Chipped and mismatched dishes—the perfect complement to the ugliest sofa ever manufactured.

After they'd slid the sofa in and closed the tailgate, Luke nodded at Lillian again and jumped in the driver's seat.

"Thanks for getting that thing out of my life," Lillian said with a laugh.

Cassidy wiped her hands on the front of her overalls.

"There's a family up the road from us who lost everything they owned in a fire. They'll be thrilled to have it."

And just like that, her self-righteous indignation over an ugly sofa poofed into thin air, leaving a nauseating churn in her stomach.

"Oh, I'm sorry about that," Lillian said.

Cassidy sighed. "Five kids. They're staying with their cousins a town over, but we've almost finished rebuilding their house. Well, I say we, but it's really mostly Caleb and Luke."

Caleb was rebuilding a house for a family—Grumpy Caleb. And Cassidy was collecting items for them. And Lillian was complaining about offensive upholstery aesthetics. Talk about a reality check.

"Let me know how I can help," Lillian said, placing a hand over her churning belly.

Cassidy smiled. No judgment—just kindness. "Thanks. I will. We're hoping to get them back in before school starts at the end of the month." Her brother gave a tiny toot on the horn and shot her a glare through the back window of the truck, and she chuckled. "He wants to get home and shower before we go to Amanda's. You're coming, right?"

Lillian nodded. "Wouldn't dream of missing it."

"That's good, because Amanda's been telling everyone you'll be there, and she's a lot more dangerous than that sofa if she gets upset." She winked. "Just kidding. She'd be really disappointed, though. She's pretty excited."

And oddly, so was Lillian.

Cassidy yanked open the passenger door of the truck and hopped in. "She can't wait to bask in the glory of being the one to introduce everyone in Blink to someone who works for Niles Sharpe." With a wide grin, she closed the truck door.

With, not for, she said in her head. Well, crap. So much for laying low. It appeared Cassidy was right; Amanda was a lot more dangerous than the sofa.

• • •

Lillian had hoped to be the first one to arrive for Amanda's get-together so that she could head off disaster by asking Amanda not to mention Niles, but she missed it by a mile. Evidently, there was a tradition of helping with the setup, and the place buzzed like a beehive when she arrived.

"Oh! You're here," Amanda said with a grin and a bear hug. "I can't wait to introduce you to everyone."

Lillian took a step back and met Amanda's huge brown eyes. Maybe she wasn't too late and could still head it off. "Yeah, uh, about that—"

Sally from the Starfish Diner took that moment to abandon the string of twinkle lights she was hanging between pier posts and run over to hug her as well. "Lillian! How are you liking Blink?"

"It's uh, good. Thanks, I—"

Sally grinned. "I bet it's a lot better than New York."

"Um…"

"Oh, no. I'd love to live in a big city like that," Amanda cut in. "And can you imagine working for Niles Sharpe? Oh, my God, he's hot. How do you stand it working so close with him, Lillian?" She fanned herself with her hand dramatically. "I'd melt."

That was a really good question. Most of the time she *couldn't* stand it. "I—"

"Wait! You work for Niles Sharpe?" A woman she'd never met squealed, dropping a paper lantern to join them.

Glancing around the deck, she noticed the dozen or so people helping with setup had paused to listen in, their expectant faces turned toward her. Perfect. Freaking perfect.

She closed her eyes and took a deep breath through her nose. The cat was out of the bag, and there was no way to put it back in. Time to own this.

"I work *with* Mr. Sharpe, not for him." For some reason, she couldn't help saying that every time. It really irked her that people assumed he was in charge, but hey, she was the one who created that misconception, right? She used his face to sell, and sell it did.

She could almost hear them holding their collective breaths. She sure as heck wasn't going to admit she was the creator and primary owner. Not when she was on the Sharpies' most-wanted list, so she kept it truthful and vague. "Yes. I'm part of the team at Living Sharpe."

*Ooo*s and *ahh*s followed.

The cat might be out of the bag, but she could still lock it in a pet carrier. "But," she said, with what she hoped was a natural-looking smile, "I'm here on vacation, so I'd rather not talk about or even think about my job." She made a childish zipping motion over her lips, hoping that would cement the message. Then, she turned to Amanda, whose drooping shoulders broadcasted disappointment, and said, "Tell me what I can do to help set up."

To Amanda's credit, she put on a good face, smiled, and led her to where a huge cooler of beer and white wine stood open. "You can help by picking a beverage and enjoying yourself."

A plastic cup of wine and a whirlwind of introductions later, Lillian had finally started to relax. Everyone she met seemed genuinely glad she was there. There were forty or so people on the huge deck, which didn't seem like a lot unless you took into account that was roughly 20 percent of the entire population of the town, and they were still trickling in from the wooden sidewalk that hugged the edge of the harbor.

Amanda led her to a small picnic table closest to the water. The ripples on the surface fluttered with the waning yellow tones of the setting sun. "We've almost finished setting up, and the food's about ready, so you just sit here and relax."

With a sigh, Lillian lowered herself onto the side of the bench, then swiveled to put her legs under the table, careful not to snag her pants on the wood. It felt good to get off her feet that had been shoved into pointy, painful shoes most of the day. Her only other option was the pair of yellow boots with red lobsters on them, so pointy and painful it was.

All around her, people laughed and worked together hanging lights around the perimeter and setting out food and paper goods on a long table under the store awning. It played out like a choreographed dance they'd all done over and over together, and as Lillian studied the lopsided tablecloths and mismatched light strings of different shapes, sizes, and types, she couldn't help but smile. She felt like she was sitting in a Norman Rockwell painting or something.

Plates and napkins, obviously left over from people's past picnics and parties, were added to stacks on either end as people laid out food dishes on the long table in everything from Corning Ware, to metal serving dishes, to Fiestaware, to reusable plastic storage containers. The entire mishmash of items created one of the most inviting spreads she'd ever seen.

Wincing at her sore feet as she stood, she wandered closer to the table and took some pics on her phone from different angles. Then she snapped off some shots of the deck itself. Maybe if she studied these pictures, she could figure out what made the setup so appealing and could translate it into something that fit the Living Sharpe brand but evoked the same warmth.

"Hey! You made it," Cassidy said from behind the service table. She was still in her paint-splattered overalls. She set some chocolate-dipped pretzels in a wooden bowl at the end with the desserts. "Isn't the theme great?"

Lillian glanced up at the handmade banner above the table. *Roll with it* was painted in red and then splashed with iridescent glitter that sparkled under the multicolored string lights above it. The food that had been laid out, for the most part, fit the theme. Lobster rolls, egg rolls, jelly rolls, rolled cream cheese appetizers, even cinnamon rolls.

"How do chocolate-dipped pretzels fit the theme?" Lillian asked.

Cassidy placed an unopened bag of pretzels next to

her bowl of dipped ones and grinned. The package read "Rold Gold Pretzels."

"Brilliant!" Lillian said.

"I'd like to take credit, but Luke came up with the idea of the pretzels. I came up with the chocolate part."

"You can never go wrong with chocolate." Lillian held up her glass in salute.

"Or wine," Cassidy said, grabbing a can from the cooler. "Or beer!" She popped the top and tapped it to the edge of Lillian's clear plastic cup. "Or friends."

Something deep in Lillian's chest warmed. "Or friends." She'd only just arrived and had been made to feel completely welcomed by everyone—well, not exactly everyone. Caleb had been far from welcoming, but at least he wasn't outright hostile anymore. Anyway, he wasn't here, so no need to even think about that. She scanned the deck, telling herself that she was not looking for him. Absolutely not. No way.

"Where are you sitting?" Cassidy asked.

Lillian gestured to the table near the water with a yellow and pink patio umbrella draped with a string of tiny white lights. "Join me?"

Cassidy beamed. "Holy cow, it's going to be amazing to not have dinner conversation about arthritis cream or orthopedic shoes for once."

Lillian carefully maneuvered onto the picnic bench, and Cassidy climbed over the bench opposite and settled in, not having to worry about snagging her denim overalls on the rough wood. First thing that had gone into her online shopping cart? Jeans.

After looking around to be sure no one could hear

them, Lillian whispered, "Where are the younger people?"

Cassidy took a big swallow of beer. "These *are* the younger people…well, except a few. We have Amanda, Caleb, two teens, and five little kids—the ones I told you about whose house burned down. Everyone else is much older."

Lillian scanned the crowd. "Why is that?"

Cassidy sighed and followed the trail of a drop of water that had condensed on her beer can with her finger. "There's nothing here for them. No jobs. No reason to stay. And no reason to come back other than to visit parents for holidays and whatnot. It's a dying town."

"You've stayed."

A sad smile crossed Cassidy's face. "I have a reason to stay—for now, anyway." She straightened her back and set her can down, clearly closing that topic. "So, Amanda said you muzzled all convo about He Who Must Not Be Named."

Lillian almost choked on her wine at the Voldemort reference. The way she felt about Niles right now, it wasn't far off. "I certainly did, but I don't think it'll last long."

"Neither do I. I'll put money on someone cornering you for a questioning before the night is out."

Not if Lillian could help it. "How'd you get into the handyman business?"

Cassidy shrugged. "Born into it, I guess. My dad and his dad built most of the houses and structures that are still standing in Blink. When I wasn't in school, I was on jobsites with him." A wistful smile crossed her face. "When I was really little, he would put me in a safe spot at the jobsite and give me a stack of small cut-offs from boards to play with like building blocks. As I got older, I stepped up as his assistant, then a partner, and now, an owner."

"Which is why you stay."

Cassidy looked out over the water as she traced her finger over the top rim of her beer can. "No."

Lillian waited for her to elaborate, but after a few moments of staring at the lobster boats gently rocking in the slips near the boat works building, Cassidy changed the subject instead.

"So, everything at the cottage working okay?"

"Yeah. Some new furniture is arriving on Monday."

Cassidy grinned. "You're staying a while, then!"

Even this morning, the mere thought of spending extra time here would have panicked her; now, she found herself pushing down a weird hollow feeling behind her ribs that felt a lot like regret. That was ridiculous. Leaving this place behind would feel as good as getting rid of that awful sofa. "No. I'm doing it as a thank-you for my sister, Erin. It was nice of her to let me stay, and I want it ready when she visits in the future."

The disappointment on Cassidy's face was obvious. "Oh. Well, text me when it arrives, and Luke and I will help you assemble it and set it up."

"Thanks." She'd arranged for the delivery guys to do that already, but more hands couldn't hurt, and it was a good excuse to hang out with Cassidy. That weird hollow feeling spiraled around in her chest again as she realized she never just hung out with someone back home. She was rarely alone and spent tons of time collaborating with team members, and some of that happened at restaurants or over wine, but all her time was devoted to growing Living Sharpe, not growing friendships.

The table in the far corner broke out in laughter. Easy laughter that came with decades of familiarity. That hollow sensation in her chest intensified. Cassidy looked over her shoulder. "That's Alice, Gus's wife, and James and Fern Cutty. They've been best friends forever."

So Alice was Caleb's mother. Her back was to them, so Lillian couldn't tell if she had the same intense blue eyes as her son. Fern was wearing a bright pink T-shirt and had a sweet, heart-shaped face with graying hair, while James was bald, with little gray patches over his ears that probably extended around the back of his head. Again, she scanned the crowd, convincing herself she was not looking for Caleb.

"How's it going at Roger's?" Cassidy asked.

Good safe topic. "Well, tomorrow's only my second day, but so far, so good."

"He's a great guy. I hate that the big house is sitting empty. They fall apart so fast if they're not lived in." She shrugged. "I get why he moved out, though. He and Mabel only used the kitchen and the second bedroom the last few years, anyway. It was way too much house for their needs. Still, it's a waste. It's the last of the nicer homes still standing." She took a sip of beer.

Lillian thought of the large white Victorian-style house with its wide front porch, which of course made her think of Caleb's smart-ass smirk this morning when he ambushed her on that porch, and that amazing sunrise. "It would make a great bed and breakfast."

Cassidy set her beer can down on the wooden picnic table with a *clunk* and laughed. "With no customers?" She gestured around her, arms wide. "This is Blink, remember?"

Maybe that was why Lillian had the hollow feeling in her chest about leaving. It was like finding a stray dog on the side of the road and leaving it there. Laughter at the table in the corner swelled again. A beautiful, friendly, happy stray dog that she was growing to adore and wanted to help.

"The line's open. Aren't you girls going to go get some dinner?" Sally from the Starfish Diner asked, sliding in next to Lillian with a heaping plate of food.

"Food!" Cassidy cried, almost leaping off the bench. "I'm starving. We finished the last bank of kitchen cabinets at the Lassiter house today, so I missed lunch."

Lillian was pretty sure the Lassiter house was the one that had burned down. She wondered if that was where Caleb went after he left Roger's. She might be looking around the party, but she most certainly was not looking for him. Nope. Not even a little bit.

"Let me know when it's time to stock the Cahill refrigerator and pantry," Sally said.

"Will do." She tapped Lillian on the shoulder. "You coming?" Cassidy asked, gesturing to the food service table.

Lillian eyed the line. So far, nobody had mentioned Niles to her, but she knew that wouldn't last. The crowd scene at the long table wasn't appealing. "Go ahead. I'm going to finish my wine first."

With a shrug, Cassidy strode off with her purposeful gait. Lillian smiled at the wide patches of paint on her backside, where she'd obviously wiped paint-covered hands.

"You settling in okay?" Sally asked, popping the top on a can of Coke.

"I am, thanks."

Sally took a bite of a lobster roll and studied her for a moment. Lillian looked down at the well-worn tabletop, suddenly uncomfortable.

"Not talking about him only makes them want to know about it more, you know," Sally said, wiping her fingers on her napkin. "Is he why you're here?"

Clearly, it made Sally want to know more, too. But she'd asked about *her*, not Niles, which was different.

She took a sip of her wine. "In part, yes."

"I figured." She put her arm around Lillian's shoulders and gave a squeeze. "I'm the resident mom, honorary aunt, fairy godmother, and shoulder to cry on, if you ever need one of those things." And then she released Lillian's shoulders and turned her attention back to her plate.

That was it? No questions, no pushing, no gushing over how hot Niles was? The hollow feeling morphed into a dull ache behind her sternum. "Thanks," she whispered.

Sally placed a paper napkin in front of Lillian and dropped a lobster roll on it. "Share with me until the line is shorter and people are using their tongues to eat instead of wag."

Lillian picked up the roll and took a bite. The lobster was impossibly sweet. She closed her eyes and savored the bite with a little *mmmm*.

"Caught this morning," Sally said. "Makes all the difference."

Which reminded Lillian of the pies she'd tasted at Roger's. She was itching to try out a recipe she'd been working on. "Is there a market or farm where I can buy freshly picked blueberries?"

Sally took a sip of her Coke. "You are in northern Maine in August, which happens to be blueberry season. They are everywhere"—her brow furrowed—"well, except for in Blink, of course."

Of course.

Sally's face lit up. "Caleb Wright's going to Machias tomorrow. Gus told me this morning, and I gave him a list of things to get for me. You could ask him to pick up some blueberries for you."

No way was she going to ask Caleb Wright for a favor. "I kind of wanted to drive around and see this part of Maine for myself. I'll make it into a field trip."

And then, as if Sally saying his name had conjured him, Caleb Wright strode by them with Gus, which, to Lillian's irritation, caused a buzz of adrenaline to zip up her spine. Gus and Caleb joined Alice, Fern, and James at the table in the corner. She heaved out a sigh of relief when he sat with his back to her. It appeared he hadn't noticed her.

She took a sip of wine and watched as he chatted easily with the couple across from him and slipped an arm around his mom's shoulders.

"Dad said yes!" a familiar voice whispered in her left ear. She flinched.

"Bethy, baby!" Sally said.

"Hi, Aunt Sally." Bethany perched on the edge of the bench across from Lillian, her eyes bright. "He's letting me go!" she stage-whispered in a conspiratorial tone, bouncing in her seat. "You were so right. He is letting me go and is gonna pick me up at ten. He just told me a bit ago."

The girl's joy buzzed in the air between them, warming Lillian. "What did Brandon say?"

Still grinning, she said, "I haven't heard back from him yet. I just texted him the news. He's gonna be so happy. We haven't seen each other in forever." She bounced again in her seat. "This is so great. I can't believe Dad said yes."

"I'm happy for you," Lillian said. "Like I tell my team at work, don't give up until you've explored every option, even ones you think are impossible. Nothing's impossible."

Bethany popped to her feet and gave Lillian an awkward hug. "I'm starving." She looked toward the food line and waved at Cassidy and Luke, who were in line together. "See you later."

"Ah, ah, ah…" Sally said, wagging the finger in the universal signal for *don't you dare*, then pointed to her cheek.

With a grin, Bethany gave the woman a kiss on the cheek accompanied with a "mwa!" The familiarity made Lillian's throat tighten. She finished off the last bite of the lobster roll and watched her slip into line between Cassidy and Luke.

"She's a special girl," Sally said.

Lillian noticed that Luke appeared nervous, shifting his weight foot to foot, never meeting Bethany's eyes. Cassidy was oblivious to her brother's discomfort as she heaped her plate high, talking to the woman in front of her in line, but Lillian recognized a crush when she saw it.

She wondered if Bethany did.

"You can't avoid it forever," Sally said. "You're going to have to go through that line. You've already met most of these folks when Amanda paraded you around like a prize pony. What's got you on edge?"

"Nothing." Everything. This wasn't like her. She was the queen of sales pitches and meet and greets. A small-town gathering should be child's play, but instead, she felt like she was entering a battle in *Game of Thrones*. Why was she so emotional? Her stomach growled, and she met Sally's pointed stare. Okay. She could do this. Besides, the line had died down to nothing at this point. She sucked in a deep breath and stood. Showtime.

She was so busy deciding which dishes to try first, she was oblivious to everything else, so she'd worried for nothing. Food was her thing, and there were some interesting twists—or rather rolls—on everyday dishes people had come up with to meet the theme. Living Sharpe should definitely explore a roll-inspired theme feature. Maybe even get people from here to submit recipes.

Stretching to reach a tray of pizza rolls with a set of plastic tongs, Lillian paused as the fine hairs on the nape of her neck prickled with awareness. Caleb. She glanced over at him, standing right next to her in line. Some people had auras, she'd been told. This guy had a full-on storm cloud surrounding him. Whatever. If he got his jollies by following her around, so be it.

She clasped the pizza roll in the tongs and placed it on her plate, feeling his stare on her. "What do you want, Caleb?"

"Dinner."

She glanced up at him, and he was smiling. Actually smiling, and it made him look like an entirely different person. Her heart compressed and did some weird twisty-squeezy thing.

"Who are *you*?" she asked.

After confusion flickered across his face, he said, "Your nemesis, I think."

"That's what I thought, too. But you look happy, and he's—"

"Surly, judgmental, and unfriendly?"

She placed the tongs back with the egg rolls. "Yeah."

"Sometimes people surprise you if you give them a chance," he said.

An odd trickle traversed her spine. Those were the exact words she'd said to… Her eyes searched the deck to find Bethany sitting with Gus, Alice, and the other couple at the far end of the deck. What were their names? Ah, yeah. Fern and James.

"Do you mind if I join you?" he asked, piling several dinner rolls on top of his already-full plate.

She glanced over at her table, only to discover Sally had abandoned her to join four or five other older women two tables down who were laughing and having a great time. She'd met them during the whirlwind of introductions but didn't remember a single name. Why, she wondered, in a place with a fraction of the intensity and activity of home, would she be this distracted?

Oh, right. Probably because of the large, overly suspicious man staring at her right now. Since she couldn't cry off to sit with someone else, she had no choice. "Sure."

Cassidy stood with Luke and Amanda, munching from the plate she'd placed on top of a wide, flat railing surrounding the far corner of the deck. Hopefully she'd come back to the table soon.

He waited for her to slide onto her bench before walking to the other end and scooting in beside her, causing her pulse to pound in her ears. His behavior threw her for several reasons. First, he wasn't scowling; second, he was being polite; and third, he chose the seat next to her when the entire table was open and he should have sat across from her, like a *regular* person. Without a word, he dug into his food, closing his eyes momentarily as he enjoyed the flavor of a rolled taco of some kind. It was like he was getting better-looking the longer she knew him, and she'd thought him hot at first sight.

"You gonna eat or just watch me do it?" he asked.

Honestly, watching him was pretty satisfying, and it appeared to make him uncomfortable, which was an added bonus. She picked up her fork, cut off a bite of pizza roll, popped it in her mouth, and chewed. Her stomach was probably going to hate her for the crazy food combo on her plate, but her taste buds were in heaven.

All around them, people's laughter twinkled like the party lights strung around the deck. The mood wasn't like at a company party or one of the many events thrown at the Living Sharpe house. People were relaxed and unaware of what was going on at the table next to them, unless they were included in the conversations. No sideways looks. No ulterior motives. They were honestly engaged.

The group dynamics fascinated her. The lightness of the party mood wasn't like fizzy champagne bubbles; it was more solid, like beer foam. The people on her Living Sharpe team were close and most had been together for years, but their get-togethers never had this feel. The origin of the difference was a mystery, but she'd love to figure it out and apply it to her business somehow.

"You saving up for winter?" Caleb asked, leaning close.

She could feel the heat rolling off him, and she wanted to lean into it. Instead, she shifted away and swiveled on the bench to look at his face. "I have no idea what you're talking about."

"Wool. My dad says when you are deep in thought, you're woolgathering. You've woolgathered so long, you should have enough to knit a sweater."

She chuckled and picked up her wine. "Sorry."

"No apology necessary," he said. "I kind of like it when you're not telling me off."

She opened her mouth to tell him off but shut it when he winked at her, causing her face to heat.

A burst of laughter came from the table where Gus and Alice were. Bethany was sitting next to Fern and James. Fern appeared to be in her mid-fifties, and James was at least a decade older. No wonder Bethany was having such a hard time. Not only was she stuck in this stagnant place, she was obviously a late-in-life baby to have parents that age. It wasn't hyperbole when she'd said her dad was an old-fashioned old man.

Her phone vibrated in her pocket, and she pulled it out. Erin. Her heart stuttered, hoping everything was okay. She gave Caleb an apologetic smile and stood.

"Sorry. Business call. I'll be right back."

The smile that had been on his face dimmed, and for a moment, she almost hit "decline" on the call just to get the smile back.

She wandered a few yards down the wooden walkway toward the boat works barn, just out of earshot. "Hey, Erin. What's up?"

"Just wanted to give you an update on how things are going. You and I didn't really get to chat during the video conferences. Not only has the negativity across the platforms cooled off, we've seen an uptick in followers and an increase in magazine subscriptions. I guess it's the old 'even bad publicity is good publicity' thing."

"Okay. That's great." And it was, except Lillian really wasn't feeling it at that moment. She glanced over her shoulder to the table to find Caleb watching her. It was rude of her to just get up and leave like that, considering how much effort he was putting into being nice. Heck, she wouldn't blame him if he moved to another table. "Is that all?"

"No, it's not all. Because of that, I convinced Ellen to stay on as our new Social Media Director. You might want to give her a call when we hang up to reinforce the goodwill and officially welcome her on board."

Lillian looked at her phone. "It's eight o'clock on a Friday night, Erin."

"Yeah. She's a 24/7er like we are. She's home working on next week's posts right now."

A 24/7er?

She shot a glance over her shoulder at Caleb, who tipped his beer bottle in salute and took a swallow. His skin was golden, like honey in the warm glow of the string lights and paper lanterns, and all she wanted to do was get off the phone. No way was she going to make a goodwill welcome call on a Friday night. "I'm kind of busy right now. I'll give her a call on Monday morning."

There was a long pause before Erin said, "You okay?"

"Yeah." She ran her fingers through her hair. "I'm at this get-together thing and need to get back to it, you know."

"Oh!" Again, there was a long pause. Lillian could hear the smile in her sister's voice when she said, "Imagine that. You're doing something fun. Miracles never cease. Call me tomorrow." And she ended the call without so much as a goodbye.

Lillian shoved the phone in her pocket, and when she turned, her heart sank. Caleb had left the table. Not that she blamed him. With a sigh, she cautiously picked her way back, making certain not to catch her heel between the boards.

She slumped onto her bench and shoved the remnants of a pinwheel sandwich around the edge of her plate with her fork. It surprised her how disappointed she was that Caleb had bounced.

"Here ya go." A warm, rich voice came from her left as Caleb placed another glass of wine next to her plate.

She almost dropped her fork in surprise. Instead, she cleared her throat. "Thanks. Sorry about the call."

He sat down. "Everything okay?"

"Yes." She took a sip of the wine. Like her first two glasses, it was a cheap chardonnay—a bit too sweet and not her usual fare, but it was cold and hit the spot.

"You gonna eat that?" Caleb asked about the cinnamon roll on her plate.

"Help yourself."

They didn't touch when he took the roll from her plate, but her body came alive as if he'd rubbed his hands all over her. Heart hammering and skin heating, she took another sip of the wine, then set it down. Maybe that was the problem. Maybe she didn't need any more wine.

Caleb cleared his throat. "I'm going to Machias tomorrow. Sally just told me you need some stuff." He took a swig of his beer. "Wanna come with me?"

Not meeting his eyes, she said, "I'm good. Thanks, though." This kinder, gentler Grumpy Guy unnerved her.

"Come with me. I'm already going. You need blueberries, and obviously you need clothes and shoes." He gestured to her business slacks and heels. "Come on. We'll leave early afternoon, after you finish at Roger's. What have you got to lose?"

"Besides my temper?" she asked, taking it back to familiar territory.

He smiled, and her heart did that squeezy thing.

But then his eyes narrowed. "You're a chicken."

"I am not."

Her thigh muscles tightened and she held her breath when he leaned close to her as if he were going to whisper in her ear. So close, she picked up the spicy scent of his aftershave or deodorant or whatever it was. She took a deep, covert inhale to enjoy it.

He paused for a moment, leaned even closer to where she could feel his breath on her ear, then squawked, "*Bawk bawk.*"

Startled, she playfully punched him in the shoulder.

"Lillian!" Amanda called in a booming, too-much-booze voice from a table nearby. She was sitting with a group of women and a couple of men. Lillian recognized the woman who'd asked her about Niles when she arrived. "Come sit with us."

When Lillian didn't jump right up, Amanda came over and pulled her up by the elbow, wine sloshing from the cup in her other hand. "You too, Caleb. Come on!"

Caleb held his hands up in surrender. "No, no, no. Gotta be up really early tomorrow."

Lillian leaned over and whispered in his ear. "Who's the chicken now?"

"Damn right," he said with a sly grin, stacking their paper plates and napkins. He stood, scooped up the trash in one hand and his beer in the other. "I'll meet you at your place at one to head out to Machias. Roger will have had enough by then." He didn't give her a chance to reply before he headed toward the table where his parents sat.

Lillian groaned inwardly as Amanda pulled her to the table of eager people. "Tell us about Niles Sharpe!" one of the women said before she was even seated.

"We're not supposed to talk about that," another said.

Yeah, right, Lillian grouched in her head. She was pretty sure that if they were playing a drinking game where you had to take a shot every time someone said Niles Sharpe, they'd all be passed out under the table in less than an hour.

Her eyes wandered over to the table where Caleb was bidding goodbye to his parents. He stretched, and a tiny bit of skin showed above his jeans as his shirt rode up.

Lillian's mouth went dry. Going with him tomorrow was a huge mistake. She took a swallow of wine and tried to focus on the woman next to her who wanted to talk about arthritis cream.

"Dad, wait!" Bethany called as she jumped up from the table. She gave Fern and James a wave as she ran after Caleb, who was on his way back to the boat barn. As she joined up with him, he slipped an arm around her, and Lillian almost dropped her wine.

Caleb was the father that Bethany had described as the old-fashioned old man who thought people only had sex after dark.

The woman next to her didn't even pause in her glowing review of a product she'd found on Amazon when a silly grin erupted on Lillian's face. She must have thought Lillian found arthritis cream super entertaining.

CHAPTER NINE

"That's a bad idea," Caleb said, eying Lillian's little convertible. "We're picking up groceries and supplies for quite a few people. My truck will be a lot better."

She glanced at his truck with clear disdain. Waving her hand dismissively, she punched a button on her key fob that made her car chirp. "I've fit so much stuff in this car. We've loaded supplies in here that I've been told would take a van." She opened the driver's door. "It's all in the planning. It's like a puzzle. Pack it right, and it'll fit."

As he watched her slide behind the wheel of her fancy car in her fancy clothes…yeah, with those high heels again, he had half a mind to let her win. She was obviously used to winning. It would serve her right.

Still, despite the fact he'd acted like a jerk around her more times than he could count, he wasn't one, really. Not to this level anyway. He wondered if her insistence on driving was due to his mud-splattered truck or her need for control. Maybe both. There was one sure way to tell. He fished in his pocket and pulled out his keyring, then held it out.

"Bethany said you told her to always look for a compromise." He noticed a red flush on the little area above the buttons of her shirt. "So here's a compromise. We take my truck, but you drive."

He could tell she was digging in when she lowered her chin and her lips drew into a thin line.

"My dad is a smart man," Caleb said, jiggling the keys. "From the time I was a little boy, he always told me that selecting the correct tool makes the job easier. My truck is the correct tool today."

Staring straight ahead, she didn't move. He jingled the keys. "Come on. You're driving."

With a dramatic huff, she climbed out of her car and snatched the keys from his hand and stomped to his truck. Yep. It was totally a control thing. He liked that, Caleb decided as he got into the passenger seat and snapped his seat belt.

Machias was not far away. The drive was short and easy. Lillian was easy, too. Not filling every quiet moment with chatter, only breaking the silence with questions about the area. She was completely fascinated by the lowbush blueberry barrens, even pulling over to watch folks hand harvesting on a small family farm with blueberry rakes.

"Have you had lunch yet?" Caleb asked about a mile out of town.

"I'm okay," she said.

"That's not what I asked."

She shot him a quick look before returning her attention to the road. "No. I have not had lunch." She lifted her chin. "But I'm okay."

He laughed. "I'm not okay. I'm starving. Take a right at the first light."

She did, and he guided her to Buddy's Burgers and Shakes. Buddy was a friend of his from high school who married his childhood sweetheart, kind of like Caleb had, only for different reasons and with strikingly different outcomes.

"Caleb!" Buddy said from behind the counter. "Good to see you." The smell of burgers on the grill and French fries filled the small, cozy space.

"Buddy, this is my friend, Lillian Mahoney," Caleb said as he pulled out a chair for her at a table near the window overlooking a tributary to the Machias River.

"Great to meet you, Lillian."

"I hope you like clam chowder," Caleb said to her.

Lillian glanced at the menu handwritten in chalk hanging above the counter that contained nothing but burgers and fries.

"Gonna brag here. My wife, Wendy, makes the best clam chowder in Maine," Buddy said. "She feels stifled by my menu. Chowder is an off-the-menu daily special."

"That's what I want," Caleb said. "And some of her potato rolls."

Lillian smiled at Buddy. "Make that two."

For a few minutes after Buddy left, Lillian stared out the window. She was quiet today. Different.

"Bethany tells me you work for a famous person."

Her eyes shot from the window to his, startled.

"She said you wanted to keep it a secret, but you told Amanda, so by now it's been broadcast throughout the entire Downeast region," he added.

She returned her gaze to the window and sighed in defeat. "I'm the owner and creator of the Living Sharpe enterprise."

Caleb wasn't sure what that really entailed, but he knew what Living Sharpe was. His mom and Fern watched every episode and subscribed to the magazine, too. He studied her face as she stared far away, her brows drawn in worry. He was certain now—this was why she was here, not some con she was running on Roger. She was here because something went wrong at her job.

"Here ya go," Buddy said, placing steaming bowls of chowder in front of them. "Be right back with the bread and some ice water."

She'd said she was the creator and owner of the entire business. Jesus. "You look really young to be the owner of something that big." She looked to be in her late twenties or early thirties.

"I created Niles Sharpe in grad school." She stirred the chowder. "The timing was perfect. A lightning strike. It happened by accident, really." She scooped her spoon into the smooth creamy chowder. "It was when influencers on YouTube were becoming a huge thing. I was getting a Masters in sociology, and our assignment was to try to create a viral video and analyze what made if flop or succeed."

She put the spoon in her mouth and closed her eyes as she savored the bite. He'd never seen anyone enjoy food this much. Hell, he'd never enjoyed someone enjoying food this much. She swallowed, and he was fascinated by the movement of the muscles in her slender neck. She opened her eyes and said, "Wow."

Yeah, kind of what he was thinking. Wow.

She picked off a bit of a roll and popped it in her mouth, giving it a lot more consideration than the average person eating a roll. All the Niles Sharpe stuff Caleb had seen lying around his mom's house had been about food, so that made sense, he supposed.

"You were talking about viral videos," he prompted.

"Oh, yeah." She took another spoonful from her bowl and ate it like a normal person this time. "You're right about the chowder. Probably the best I've ever eaten."

He ate a few spoonfuls of his own and took a bite of roll.

"So, there had been a video about a chocolate chip cookie that went viral a few months before this project, so I decided to use that as a baseline of sorts. I made a video of me making my grandmother's chocolate chip cookie recipe, which was really that same recipe from the viral video."

"So the only difference was you."

She shrugged and stirred her chowder. "And the setting, props, lighting, timing, and reach. A lot of factors drive this kind of thing." She took another bite.

"And?"

"And the video went nowhere. Only a handful of hits and maybe three comments, one of which pointed out I'd ripped off the recipe." She smiled and took another bite.

A woman and two kids came in the door, and Buddy greeted them. Caleb finished off his chowder and wiped the rest of his roll around the inside of the bowl to get the last of it.

"Anyway, I decided to alter the most obvious variable first, the personality, which is what drove most of the viral stations we'd studied." She stared far away like she was remembering it. "I went to the local bar where undergrads hung out to hire someone to act in the video and see if it moved the needle. That's where I found Niles. Well, his name wasn't Niles at the time," she amended.

"He was super attractive. Like, *crazy* good-looking."

Caleb's gut tightened. Suddenly, he didn't like this story.

"Originally, I'd intended to hire a girl, but when I saw him, I thought it would be cool to have someone who you'd picture anywhere but the kitchen present himself as a practiced cook."

Which made Caleb wonder where she'd pictured this guy. An itchy, uncomfortable feeling crept over his neck, and he was grateful when Buddy came by to refill their water glasses and check on them.

"You were in the bar?" Caleb prompted when Buddy wandered off.

She folded her napkin and placed it on the table. "Yeah. So, his appearance was so striking, I just knew I'd hit gold. He agreed to make the video, and we went back to my apartment, and I taught him how to make the cookies. He was still a little wasted, so it took a few tries to get a good video."

He stared at her. "You took a wasted guy to your apartment, but you wouldn't accept a ride from me?"

She laughed and rolled her eyes. "My roommate was there with her boyfriend."

Well, that made him feel a little better. He made a go-ahead motion with his hand, and she continued.

"I posted the video, and in two days, it had taken off. Huge numbers. So big, I couldn't believe it. A guy who looked like a *GQ* model talking about his grandmother's cookies was the key to success. I went back to the bar and found him a week later, made a business proposal, and the rest is history. We now have a large team, a magazine,

TV series, two annual holiday specials, and a bakeware line, all because of the face of a guy I found in a college bar."

"Or because of a woman who recognized a great concept and had the tenacity to follow through on it," he said.

For a moment, she looked surprised, and then she smiled. "Thanks. It was a team effort, really."

He suspected that was BS. Maybe it was a team thing now, but it started with her figuring out the correct formula. It also sounded like the guy getting all the credit might just be window dressing. His mom and Fern went nuts over the way he looked in the magazine and never missed an episode of his show. They'd been talking about him this morning, in fact. There'd been some dustup online about an incident during a morning show. Both women were members of a Facebook fan group and said there was a lot of talk about Lillian and Niles Sharpe's relationship.

He studied her as she stared out the window. Was that why she was here? A falling-out with her lover?

"Can I get you anything else?" Buddy asked.

"Your wife's recipe?" Lillian answered with a brilliant smile.

Yeah, Caleb could totally see this put-together woman with the movie star–perfect Niles Sharpe.

Buddy shook his head. "Wendy won't even share it with me."

"Can't blame a girl for trying," Lillian said, rummaging in that huge shoulder bag of hers. "Could you please give her this and tell her I'd love to talk to her if she has time?"

Buddy stared at the card and then at Lillian. "Wow.

You work for Niles Sharpe?"

"*With*, not for."

Buddy grinned. "That's Wendy's favorite show."

Caleb pulled out his wallet, and Buddy waved him off, saying, "No, man. I still owe you for fixing that broken rudder." He extended his hand, and Caleb shook it. "Good to see you. Tell your parents and Bethany hello. Great to meet you, Lillian."

He pulled out her chair as she stood, but she stayed rooted in place, staring into his eyes, which made his brain go foggy for a moment.

"Bethany seems like a great kid. I only got to talk with her briefly, but I like her."

"She likes you." And so did he, it turned out. "Thanks for helping her with the camping thing. It was a good idea. She's too young for a co-ed overnighter."

"I'm glad it worked out," she said, sliding her bag over her shoulder.

It hadn't worked out yet. Caleb didn't like the little prick his daughter was hot on, and the guy didn't respond after she sent him a text saying her dad was picking her up. As far as he knew, she still hadn't heard from him.

Caleb followed Lillian out the door of Buddy's as she gracefully strode over the cracked parking lot in those ridiculous shoes. She flipped her glossy brown curls over her shoulder and got into the driver's seat of his truck looking as out of place as a diamond watch in a toolbox.

Bethany said that when they were at Amanda's party, Lillian had told her nothing was impossible. He shook his head and opened the passenger door. Some things were completely impossible.

CHAPTER TEN

Lillian couldn't believe she'd told Caleb so much of the story—not the big ruse, exactly, but she'd alluded to it.

He was quiet other than when he gave her directions to a building up a gravel road at the top of a hill.

"What is this place?" she asked, squinting in the sun as she stepped out of the car. The area in front of the huge building was gravel, and she frowned down at her shoes. So silly of her.

"A lumberyard. I'm only picking up one item. You can just wait here," Caleb said, striding toward the building. "I'll be right back."

On one hand, she was irritated to be left behind, but on the other, it was a relief to not pick her way to the building over all that gravel. The place had huge loading doors all down the front, and they were open. Inside, she could see stacks and stacks of lumber. In a matter of minutes, Caleb appeared carrying what looked to be a log as big around and as tall as she was.

Dang, the man was strong. She supposed he had to be, since he worked on boats with his dad. The sun made his short brown hair look golden and his eyes lighter. She huffed out a breath. So, so hot. Not pretty, like Niles. Rugged and athletic and thoroughly male.

The truck dipped when he dropped the log into the bed. Yeah, bringing her car would have been a bad choice. She was glad she lost that battle. In fact, she kind of wished she'd let him drive so she could check out the scenery rather than focus on unfamiliar roads.

The air between them seemed to sizzle when he climbed into the truck. Maybe it was because her hormones had taken notice of the drool-worthy, log-carrying testosterone parade. Maybe it was because he smelled so good and being in a closed vehicle with him was getting more difficult every second.

Maybe it was because she hadn't kissed a man in—she closed her eyes and tried to remember her last kiss and couldn't—in a really long time.

Stop. You are leaving.

There. That did it.

Only it didn't. Kissing someone wasn't a commitment. Heck, to most of her friends, it ranked just a little above a handshake. She glanced over at him. Kissing Caleb Wright would be nothing even close to a little above a handshake.

"You okay?" he asked.

No. She wasn't okay. She was imagining kissing him. Grumpy Guy, for goodness' sake.

"Want me to drive?" he asked.

She started the truck. "Nah, I'm good. Where next?"

Next was the bank. Machias had a branch of her national bank chain, and she was thrilled the manager issued her a temporary card until the next one came, then let her withdraw some cash.

Then she visited a super cool boutique store with casual clothes: boots that weren't decorated with goofy lobsters, pants that didn't snag, and shirts that didn't require dry cleaning. She'd even convinced the shop owner to let her wear the socks and thick-soled leather boots out. They looked silly with her rolled-up dress slacks, but wow, they felt better than her heels.

"I thought you were leaving in a few days," Caleb said from the bench outside the clothing store. He stood and took some of the bags from her. "Looks like you have clothes for months."

She was leaving in a few days, and that thought caused an ache behind her sternum. She took a breath and gave him what she hoped was a believable smile. "I am. I plan to set a trend back home."

He glanced down at her boots, then took in the rest of her outfit and shook his head. "Probably not with that combination."

This time her smile was real, and the one he returned made her mouth go dry. It amazed her how much his face changed when he smiled.

"Watch it, Wright," she warned. "I might start to not hate you."

"Too late," he said with a wink.

Ah, crap. The smile/wink combo was a knockout blow. "Where next?"

He held up a shopping list. "Good thing you put on reasonable shoes."

They stared at each other for a moment. A really weird moment in which she imagined pressing her lips to his full, smiling ones right there in the middle of the sidewalk. Then, his smile faded, and he walked to the truck. As she raised trembling fingers to her lips she'd imagined on his, Lillian realized the *only* thing reasonable about her was her shoes.

CHAPTER ELEVEN

Shit, shit, shit. He'd almost kissed her. And without a doubt, she was right there with him. What a disaster. She was leaving in days.

He yanked open the back door of the truck and placed her bags on the back seat. This was madness. Kissing her was madness. Not kissing her was madness.

She started the engine, and he directed her to the supermarket to stock her up and get some items for Sally and Fern. While he shopped, she wandered the aisles on her own, putting a few things in her basket and writing in her notebook.

Then, they went to the hardware store for Cassidy and the feed store for his mom. Leaning on the truck, he watched with amusement as she visited with a woman about the blueberries she was selling outside the feed store. She had a zillion questions about how they grew and where. How they are harvested and how often.

He had a strong hunch she already knew the answers to these questions but was looking for some bit of insider info she could use for her business somehow. Like a story about how blueberries are harvested for that slick magazine of hers featuring that equally slick guy she'd found in a college bar.

After paying, she handed the woman at the booth her card, and the woman squealed about, yeah—the slick guy that Lillian worked *with*, not *for*.

Grinning, she placed the baskets of berries on the hood of the truck and dug his keys out of her pocket. "Your turn," she said, dropping the keys in his palm. He didn't know if this was significant, like a turning point in her little power struggle with him, or if she was simply sick of driving.

He grabbed the berries and placed them in one of the boxes in the back of his truck so they wouldn't tip over.

As he closed the tailgate, she opened the door and pulled herself up into the truck. And screeched.

Okay, it was probably mean of him to not warn her, but he laughed.

"There's a chicken in a dog crate in the back seat of the truck," she said as if it would be news to him.

"It's a rooster."

"Why is there a rooster in the truck?"

"Because it can't ride in the back bed. Too much wind."

She twisted in her seat and met the rooster's gold eyes. It made a creaking sound and shook its head, causing its comb and wattles to flap. Clamping her jaw shut, she spun back around to face the front. It was like...

"Have you never seen a chicken up close before?" he asked.

"Of course I have. We've done segments on backyard chickens and the variety in the color of eggs, but they weren't in a car with me"—she twisted to check him out again—"staring straight into my soul."

He laughed. "That's Doodle, my mom's rooster. He went to go visit a friend's hens so she can have a new hatch before it gets too cold. The feed store is the drop-off point."

She buckled her seat belt and crossed her arms over her middle. "I have so many pithy comments and jokes right now about this entire rooster-pimping thing, but I'm going to just let it go."

He chuckled, wishing she'd throw out some jokes. It felt good to laugh. He started the truck and pulled out onto the highway. "Don't you wish we had taken your car?"

"You're hilarious," she said.

Doodle evidently agreed, because he chose that moment to cut loose with a spectacular screech.

Lillian covered her mouth and busted into giggles. He loved seeing her like this. Happy and silly, not prickly and defensive. "Why are you here?" he asked. "Is it because of what they're saying online? About you and that guy?"

Her laughter stopped, and she stared at him. *Trust me*, he willed her. Instead, she turned away and stared out the window, and he slowed behind a timber truck. The blueberry barrens had given way to pine forest.

"I have never, nor will I ever have a romantic relationship with Niles Sharpe," she said after a long moment. "Our connection is business only."

His whole body relaxed at her words. Why this mattered, he'd have to figure out later.

"Niles is a dramatic, selfish, hollow person, and yes, he's why I'm here. He blamed me for something publicly, and it was taken the wrong way by his fans. It blew up online, and I was advised to take a vacation from him until he settled down." She brushed some hair from her cheek. "In truth, he needed a break from me, too. I can be pretty intense, I'm told."

"*You?*" His mock surprise did the trick, and she smiled. Her smile was great and caused the skin at the edges of her eyes to crinkle.

The timber truck pulled off on a side road, and he picked up his speed. For several long minutes, they were silent.

"So you're single," he said as he turned off the highway.

His statement must have surprised her, because her brow furrowed as she studied him for a while. Then, she took a deep breath and said, "I prefer to think of myself as unavailable. With my work schedule, I don't have time for anyone or anything else."

"Sounds to me like you need a new job."

He'd expected a smart-ass comeback, but she simply stared out the window as they passed the harbor and turned onto the road leading up the hill.

The whole unavailable-because-of-my-job thing sounded way too rehearsed, and he wondered how many people she'd used it on.

As her cottage came into sight, she shuffled around with her bag, getting ready to leave the truck. Like she couldn't wait to bolt.

He shouldn't have asked her if she was single. Hell, he had no idea why he'd done it. She'd be gone in a couple of days. Maybe that was why. Maybe he'd thought about her day and night since he'd first met her because anything with her had an expiration date. She would go back to her big city and her big life.

He grabbed the remainder of the bags she couldn't carry and followed her up the steps to her place.

"You can just leave them here on the porch," she said.

"I really appreciate you letting me tag along with you today." She never met his eyes, and again, he kicked himself.

He set the boxes down in front of some beat-up porch furniture left over from Emmett's time here, and again he was reminded of a diamond in a toolbox. She was totally out of place here. "I'll go get your blueberries from the back of the truck."

As he walked to his truck, he could feel her eyes on him. What did she see, he wondered. Someone as unavailable as she was? Someone who wanted to kiss her so badly, he could taste her lips in his mind? He moved the box he'd wedged the berries behind and stepped up on the running board to grab them.

"Why were you so mean to me when I first arrived?" she called from the porch.

Berries in hand, he climbed up the steps. She stood on the top one but didn't step aside for him to pass.

"You know why."

Still, she didn't budge. One of her power things, he supposed. He took a deep inhale through his nose, enjoying the smell of her perfume. He couldn't identify the scent other than expensive...and arousing. "Picture this," he started. "A beautiful, well-dressed woman shows up in Blink with no money and runs out of gas conveniently within walking distance of a diner where an elderly widower eats breakfast the same time every day. She then cozies up to this widower and offers to help him. A widower who just happens to be the largest landholder in the county and one of the richest men in the Downeast region. And she offers to do it for free."

She gasped. "Roger?" For a moment, she said nothing else, just stared directly into his eyes. "Roger is the largest landholder in the county?"

A few days ago, he would have thought her surprise was an act. Now, he knew it was genuine. "Roger owns everything in Blink, just about, and lots of stuff outside of it."

She blinked rapidly. "Sad and wrinkled Roger McGuffy?"

"Sad, wrinkled, *rich* Roger McGuffy," Caleb added. "His grandfather was a wealthy timber baron in the late 1800s, and the family kept the mill running until maybe a decade ago."

"Well, now the huge, white Queen Anne Victorian house makes sense," she said. She looked past his shoulder to the harbor below. "He owns the harbor buildings?"

"All but Amanda's mercantile and our place. We also own the slips and land between our place and Amanda's. The rest is his."

"The boarded-up buildings?"

He nodded.

"The undeveloped harbor property on this north side?"

He nodded again. "And the entire forest area behind your cottage and his house."

She shook her head in disbelief. "I get it now," she said. "I understand why you were mean to me. It totally looked like I was trying to scam Roger, but I wasn't."

He shoved his hands in his pockets so he wouldn't reach for her if she came nearer. "I know that now. You coming here had nothing to do with Roger."

A sly smile spread across her face. "My coming here didn't, but my staying here does."

She dialed a number on her phone and tapped her fingers on her thigh as she waited. "Hey, Erin," she said. "Call me when you get this message. I'm staying a while longer." With a grin, she ended the call.

"What are you up to, Lillian Mahoney?"

"You'll have to continue keeping a close eye on me and find out, Caleb Wright."

At that moment, he wanted to keep much more than his eyes on her. Her gaze dropped to his lips, and he knew it was mutual. She planned to stay longer, and a warm sensation filled his chest that felt remarkably like hope.

Then she did something that left him in disbelief: She kissed him. It wasn't a passionate, all-in-including-the-tongue kiss, but it was enough to set him on fire. He was too stunned to do anything but stand there and smolder.

From the truck, Doodle made a noise that sounded like a creaky door. A really loud door.

"I need to drop off everyone's orders," he said.

She gave a resigned nod, then took the berries and set them on the rusty table between the porch chairs.

His heart kicked up as he hovered on total disaster. "Do you have plans tonight?"

He held his breath as she studied him.

"No."

Maybe not a disaster after all. He grinned as that warm area in his chest expanded. "How about a dinner cruise?"

CHAPTER TWELVE

Lillian slipped on her new flats and checked herself in the bathroom mirror. For a night out in New York City, she would have worn a darker lip color, eyeliner, and heavy eye shadow. She smiled at her natural look of mascara and lip gloss. She would have worn more makeup than this no matter where she was going if she were home: work, the gym, or even the grocery store. Her mom had always stressed that she and Erin should "dress for success" and never go out without makeup because, "you never know who you'll run into." Here, in Blink, she knew exactly who she would run into, and with that came freedom.

She looked down at the cotton cardigan and stone-washed jeans she'd bought today and imagined her mom scolding her for letting herself go. Nah. This wasn't letting herself go. It was letting go. Less makeup, less hassle, less worry. Simplicity.

Her breath caught. Maybe that was the key. Erin had told her she was uptight and tense. Of course she was. She was responsible for maintaining a successful lifestyle company—at the expense of her *own* lifestyle. "Simplicity," she said to herself in the mirror. Her life was anything but simple. She needed to find a way to bring this small-town feel back home with her.

She peeked through her front window. Caleb said he'd pick her up at seven for their dinner cruise. She supposed they were going on one of the boats she'd seen advertised on the door of the clothing store in Machias, or maybe they would drive down to Bar Harbor. She didn't really care. She was going on a date with a man for the first time in years. A handsome man.

They got in his truck—she didn't object this time—at seven sharp. He was still wearing jeans, but instead of his faded Maine Mariners T-shirt from earlier today, he was wearing a navy-blue Henley with the sleeves pushed up. It took all her self-control to not stare at him.

"So, did Doodle make it home safely?" she asked as he backed out of her driveway.

"He did. He was happy to see his flock again. I'm sure he's looking forward to chasing the neighborhood cats and dogs and waking everyone up when he starts crowing at three in the morning." He grinned over at her. "He says he would like to go for a ride in your car."

She laughed and threw her hands up in surrender. "Okay. I'll admit it. I was wrong. You were right."

He put a hand to his ear. "I'm sorry. I missed that. What did you say?"

"You'll never hear me say it again," she teased.

"Probably not," he said, sobering a little. Maybe he'd had the exact thought she had: She wouldn't be here that long.

Instead of turning right in the direction of the highway, he headed down toward the harbor, parking next to the boat works barn. Maybe he needed to pick something up before they left Blink.

His adorable dogs must have recognized the sound of his truck, because the minute the truck pulled in, they leaped off a boat tied up at the dock and bounded toward them.

"Should I wait here?" she asked, rubbing down the delighted dogs.

"Not if you want dinner." He whistled, and the dogs ran toward him, then circled back. The big one nudged her hand, urging her to come with them while the little, scruffy one yapped and wagged its tail so fast in a circle it looked like a helicopter propeller.

He gracefully leaped onto the deck of the houseboat she'd seen from her porch and turned, holding out his hand to her. Thankful for his hand and her flat, comfortable shoes, she stepped over the gap between the boat and the dock, and the dogs joined them.

"Welcome aboard," he said.

"It's yours?"

"It is."

From where she was standing, the boat was in pristine shape with a lot more wood than she would have expected. She wasn't a boat person, but she'd gone out with friends a few times, and boats always made her think of plastic and chrome.

There were two life rings on the railing near the front. Printed in clear, block letters was "Bethany Anne."

Her chest warmed inside. He'd named the houseboat after his daughter.

"Beer?" he asked, disappearing through the open side door.

She followed him inside and gasped. It was beautiful. The kitchen was on one side with stainless appliances and quartz counters, and a seating area was on the other side with comfortable chairs around a live-edge tabletop. Beyond that were a sofa and TV. A door, presumably to the bathroom and sleeping area, was at the back.

As she stood there gawking, he placed a cold bottle in her hand. She glanced down at the craft beer from Maine. "Thanks."

"Are you ready for your cruise?"

"You're going to take this out?" She remembered the waves crashing against the rocks at the shore. She pointed toward the mouth of the bay. "Out there?" Her voice was high-pitched and squeaky.

He smiled. "Not this time. It's a hassle to unhook the water and electrical for a trip this short. And the conditions aren't perfect for her right now. We'll take a different boat."

It was hard to categorize this as a boat. "It doesn't look like a boat on the inside," she said. "May I?" She gestured toward the door at the back.

"Of course. I'm going to finish dinner."

Wow. He was going to cook for her. No man had ever cooked for her. Well, in fairness, she never gave anyone the opportunity, and honestly, who would want to? She was the talent behind Niles Sharpe. It would probably be intimidating for most people. She remembered him with that log over his shoulder, sauntering to the car like it was nothing. She doubted anything could intimidate this guy.

Trailing her fingers over the backs of the leather chairs, she passed the TV area and entered the hallway. There was a bathroom on either side of the door. Beyond those were two bedrooms. The one on the left was large, with a king-size bed…on a boat—not a tiny cot. It had a maroon

plaid coverlet, and the same wood from the front of the
boat carried into the furnishings in this room as well,
ceiling included. She didn't go past the threshold. The
room seemed…too intimate. A flash of him in that bed
scorched her brain, and she spun to face the other
bedroom, cheeks hot.

This one had to be Bethany's room. There was a
computer with double screens, a twin bed covered in a
Star Wars comforter, a rolled-up yoga mat in the corner,
and on the inside wall there was an easel. She stepped
into the room and stared open-mouthed at the charcoal
drawing of a lobster boat. On the wall behind the easel
were dozens of watercolors and charcoal sketches. Many
were of people she recognized: Gus, Alice, Fern, and
James were in quite a few, doing everyday things. Bethany
had a great eye for composition—as good as the *Living
Sharpe Magazine* layout designer. On the floor was a
rumpled piece of paper. Lillian flattened it on the bed
and used her palms to smooth it. Caleb stared back from
the paper in black and white, his expression confident.
One corner of his mouth quirked up, and she recognized
his expression. It was the look he'd given her on the
porch of Roger's white house.

She traced two-dimensional Caleb's full lips with a
fingertip and almost screamed when the real deal cleared
his throat in the hallway behind her.

"She crushed it because she was mad at me," he said.
"About the camping trip. Thanks for talking to her about
that. It really helped."

Had she known Bethany was Grumpy Guy's kid, she
might have handled things differently. She was impressed

he welcomed intervention from a stranger. "I'm sure being the parent of a teen is difficult."

He glanced over at the easel. "Being a parent is difficult, period."

A million questions went through her mind, many centered around Bethany's mother, but she couldn't think of a way to bring her up in a tactful manner. Instead, she kept it to safer ground. "She's a really good artist."

"She is," he said with a smile.

Here was the opening to find out something about the mom. "I guess she gets that from her mother?"

A strange look crossed his face that reminded her of how she felt when she said "I work with, not for," about Niles.

"Ready?" he asked, heading back toward the kitchen. "Your dinner cruise awaits."

Yeah, so the topic of Mom was undoubtedly closed.

The cruise was aboard a small, wooden boat with an outboard motor, stored in the boat slip closest to the *Bethany Anne.* From her comfortable, cushioned seat, Lillian ran her fingers over the impossibly smooth wood at the top lip of the boat. The moon was high in the sky, bathing the harbor in a cool, blue light that shimmered on the top of the water like glitter. In the slip at the far end, the enormous sailboat she'd seen from her porch rocked gently as they passed.

The name, *Elizabeth's Wish*, was written in an arc above "Ann Arbor, MI."

"That's a client's boat," Caleb said. "She's almost finished. They should be picking her up next week if Dad gets a part for the motor he's waiting for."

They were moving slow, but still, the shallow ripples caused by their boat made the lobster boats in the slips gently rock and sway after they passed. There were a lot more of them tonight than she'd seen from her porch. Maybe they stayed out all day.

As they reached the mouth of the harbor, the water got rougher. Not terrible, but not placid, like in the harbor. Once outside, Caleb picked up speed, and the nose of the little boat rose. Lillian closed her eyes, enjoying the feel of the wind on her face and the smell of fresh ocean spray. It was like flying. Similar to her convertible but better.

Too soon, he slowed, then stopped. The water was calm here. Around them, buoys bobbed in the water. Some with stripes, some solid, in lots of different sizes and shapes. Lobster traps, she assumed. To their right, tall cliffs rose above the rocky shoreline, and slightly behind them, she recognized the mouth to the harbor. The moon danced and shimmered across the water. "It's beautiful."

"Yes," he said. "Beautiful."

When she looked over at him, he was staring at her. She was glad it was dark so he couldn't see her blush.

"So, dinner," he said, reaching under the seat behind him and pulling out a picnic basket.

Every spring, *Living Sharpe Magazine* did a full feature on picnics and the best foods for mobile fare. Finger sandwiches, cold fried chicken, unusual cheeses, inventive spreads, gourmet olive samplers.

"Peanut butter and jelly sandwiches," he said with a grin, passing her a sandwich wrapped in paper. "I can't cook. Not at all," he said. She eyed the neat package with the ends folded over like it had been gift wrapped. "No plastic baggies on the water," he said, pulling out a cookie tin full of potato chips and then two thermoses from the basket. "Milk. Gotta have milk with peanut butter and jelly."

Her heart squeezed, and it was that moment she realized she liked this man. *A lot*. More than she should, and that was a problem for so many reasons.

Oh, no. No, no, no.

"You okay?" Caleb set his sandwich down on the picnic basket. "Are you allergic to peanuts? Crap, I should have asked."

"Oh, no. No, no, no," she said out loud this time. *Don't panic*, she told herself. *Stay in control. In charge.* This was a mantra she used when going in to pitch projects to network executives or when she had to deal with one of Niles's meltdowns—only it was her own meltdown she was trying to head off this time. "I love peanut butter."

Find a safe topic, she scolded herself. Him as a kid. Yeah, that was safe. "So, you've lived in Blink all your life?" She unwrapped her sandwich, secure she was on solid footing again.

He gave her a wary look, like double-checking she wasn't going to need the Heimlich maneuver or something, then settled back in his seat and picked up his sandwich. "Yeah. Born in the house my parents live in. It's closer to where the city hall used to be, west of the harbor."

"Blink used to have a city hall?"

He took a big bite and nodded. After he chewed and swallowed, he said, "Built by Cassidy's great-grandfather.

Struck by lightning and burned to the ground decades ago. The town was already in decline, and it had been shut down anyway." He unscrewed the top off his thermos and took a swallow. "With the shrinking population and no need for a city council, it was never rebuilt."

"Are there police here?"

He shrugged. "There used to be, but not in a long time. There's not enough population to warrant it. We used to have a mayor, too. Now, the Washington County Sherriff's Office handles issues here, though there really aren't any. We watch out for one another."

Which was why he had been so vigilant in keeping an eye on her.

"This place is great," she said, staring back at the harbor. "I really feel like it can come back." She wanted to tell him about her plans to talk to Roger, but for some reason, she wasn't ready yet.

"It *is* great. I'm afraid, though, that like many small towns all over the country, it's not relevant anymore."

She could help it become relevant. She just knew it. She had a huge platform. The trick was finding a way to bring attention to it to draw people here. That wasn't enough, though. People needed a reason to stay.

He passed her the tin of chips, and she took a few. "Thanks." The saltiness was perfect with the sweet strawberry jelly on the sandwiches. "This is a great boat. The wood is beautiful."

"Thank you," he said with a grin. "I built it."

She looked from the tip of the boat to the motor on the back. "You built this?"

"From scratch, just like you make the dishes in the

food segment on your show."

With satisfaction, she noted he said "you" instead of "Niles." She ran her hand over the wood again, finding his comparison ridiculous. This was a boat, not a cream puff. She couldn't imagine the amount of work that went into something like this.

"I started drawing the plans when I was twelve and began building it in high school. I built the houseboat, too, for the most part. I bought it from a salvage company in Florida after a hurricane trashed it. Took it down to the hull, pretty much."

She stared at him, open-mouthed. Surely he meant he paid to have it restored.

"It took two years, or Bethy and I would have moved into it right away."

No mention of Bethany's mother, she noticed.

"Did Bethany's mom like boats, too?"

A grimace crossed his face. "Oh, yeah. Loved them. Especially the kind with a full crew and a chef."

Well, there was a place she wasn't going to go. She knew bitter when she saw it. "How about Bethany?"

He shrugged. "She likes the water well enough. When she's sick of it or me, she goes to stay with one of the pairs of grandparents. She has her own room at both of their houses."

So his wife had been from Blink, too, if both sets of grandparents were here.

A rumbling came from their left. They'd drifted a bit closer to shore and were still in sight of the harbor.

"That wasn't on the radar," he muttered before shoving the rest of the sandwich in his mouth and chasing it with some milk. "Guess we should get back."

Hiding her disappointment, she wrapped up the remains of her sandwich and put it, along with her napkin and thermos, in the picnic basket.

A bright shaft of lightning flashed to their left, followed quickly by a deafening clap of thunder.

He started the motor. "Too close. You ready?"

She nodded, and he turned the boat and headed back to the harbor. The little boat smacked against the low waves as they neared the harbor. Clearly, he was trying to outrun the rain. They almost made it. Right before they passed between the large buoys marking the entrance of the harbor, the sky opened.

"Holy crap!" she squeaked in surprise. The raindrops were freezing cold, like little stinging needles of ice.

Caleb slowed to a crawl once they passed into the harbor. "No-wake zone," he shouted over the rain.

She put her face down and tucked up tight. So much for a peaceful, relaxing evening on the water.

CHAPTER THIRTEEN

Well, that plan went straight to hell, Caleb thought as he pulled into the boat slip. First, he fed her a substandard PBJ when she probably expected caviar and champagne; then, she was soaked through by a pop-up storm.

All he'd thought about while they were out there was kissing her. He'd run a million scenarios through his head, trying to figure out the best way to make that happen, and then, boom, nature threw buckets of cold water on his plan. Literally. He should have noticed the clouds closing in, but he'd been too busy noticing her.

Scout and Willy had gotten over their pout about not being able to go in the boat—the dogs greeted them enthusiastically when they stepped inside the warm cabin, wiggling and wagging and sniffing. Lillian shivered as she patted their heads. He pitched her a towel, then went to his room to find something for her to wear. He would have grabbed something out of Bethany's closet, but they were shaped differently and he had no idea what would or wouldn't fit. Plus, Bethy hated it when he touched her things. Instead, he rummaged through his chest of drawers and grabbed a sweatshirt and some camping pants with a drawstring waist.

"Feel free to use Bethy's room to change," he said, placing the clothes he'd retrieved on the counter beside her.

"Oh, I'll be fine."

"Change," he said, his voice a little harder than he'd intended. "Nearest doctor is in Machias. Not really worried you'll get sick, but if you do, it's super inconvenient in Blink. Take my word for it." He noticed she was still shivering. "You're miserable." He nodded to the clothes. "Change."

After a moment, she gave in. Why on earth did she resist, he wondered. Probably because she was so used to being in charge and giving orders. Maybe he should have worded it in such a way she thought it was her idea. He'd try that next time. Being told what to do obviously didn't work with this woman. He retreated to his bedroom to get dry himself.

When Lillian emerged, he almost laughed. She looked like Bethy had when she was little and played dress-up. His sweatshirt hung halfway to her knees, and the pants dragged the floor. Her wet clothes were balled up in her hands, along with the towel. She set them on the counter. "Hairbrush?" she asked.

He almost told her there wasn't one. He liked her this way. Totally natural and messy. He'd noticed she'd toned her makeup way down tonight. He liked that, too. "There should be a hairbrush in Bethy's bathroom. The one on the right."

Instead of doing her hair in the bathroom, she carried the brush out with her and flopped onto the sofa, where she was immediately joined by Scout and Willy, jostling each other to get the prime spot closest to her.

"Off," Caleb said, pointing to the floor. With wide-eyed, remorseful looks, both dogs jumped off the sofa and settled as closely as possible to her feet. They weren't allowed on the sofa, and they knew it, but Lillian made them forget the rules. She had the same effect on him.

Starting at the ends, she worked on her hair, brushing out the tangles, and he found himself frozen in place next to the refrigerator. Watching her do this simple, personal task was surprisingly intimate. He gave himself a mental shake and turned his attention back to unloading the picnic basket.

Barefooted, he padded in to join her, but instead of sitting on the sofa next to her, he played it safe, taking up the club chair under the TV. He could look at her this way. He liked looking at her, especially when she wasn't all done up and perfect.

With a slender hand, she flipped open the book on his coffee table.

"Wow," she said. "Amazing." She flipped another page, then ran her finger over one of the glossy photographs. "These old boats in this book are in such great shape."

"Not all of them are old. Most are antique or vintage, but some are fairly new." He moved to sit next to her and turned to the back of the book. "This yacht was completed less than two years ago."

"You're kidding. Look at that staircase. It's like it came out of a nineteenth-century mansion or something. It looks hand carved."

"It is."

"Beautiful."

Beautiful like her. His body felt like it was full of lightning zipping back and forth inside. Moving to sit next to her had been a mistake. He knew his infatuation with her was reckless. She'd go away soon, back to her important, busy, big-city life, and he'd be left here with his boats and bad decisions. At least he had Bethy for another two years—more if he could convince her to go to UMM and live at home. Not a great chance of that. She had her heart set on some art school in Boston and probably had a strong enough portfolio to get a free ride.

Scout put his chin on Lillian's feet and heaved a happy sigh.

"I've always loved dogs," she said. As if Willy understood every word, he gazed up at her adoringly, his tail thumping on the wood floor. "How long have you had them?"

"I found Scout wandering the shoreline five years ago, skinny and scared. He'd probably been dumped or fallen off someone's boat. Willy was Emmett's dog. He couldn't take him when he moved a few years back, so here he is."

Hand still laying over the book in her lap, she studied him, and he forced himself to sit still as that electricity thing kicked up again. "You're a good man, Caleb Wright," she said.

His face heated, and he cleared his throat. "Do you have any pets?"

She shook her head. "Not enough time. My work hours are intense. It wouldn't be fair."

That sounded a lot like her excuse for not dating that she gave on the way back from Machias.

She closed the book and swiveled on the sofa to look at him, tucking one bare foot underneath her. "So your parents are Hemom and Hedad. Are Fern and James Shemom and Shedad?"

"They are."

He could tell she was anxious by the way her fingers tapped on her leg. "Where is Bethany's mom?"

Ah. She finally worked up the nerve to ask. He was surprised Amanda hadn't given her the full story within ten minutes of meeting. It was one of her favorites, complete with betrayal and heartbreak. "I have no idea. I haven't seen her for almost fifteen years. She left when Bethy was barely a year old. Fern and James have been a big part of Bethany's life. I don't know how I would have managed without them or my parents."

She twisted her fingers in her lap. "I'm sor—"

He held up a hand. "Don't. Bethany is the single best thing to ever happen to me. I'll never be sorry."

He put a hand over hers, still twisting in her lap, then placed the other behind her neck. Her hands stilled, and her eyes met his, then lowered to his lips. His entire body hardened. His voice was raspy. "I want to—"

"Yes." She cut him off with a kiss that went from tentative and exploratory to hot and probing in a matter of heartbeats. The kiss could have gone on for minutes or hours. He had no idea because time seemed to slow and tilt, leaving him light-headed.

He slipped his hands under the sweatshirt and up the smooth, warm skin of her back, and he groaned when he realized she wasn't wearing a bra under his borrowed clothes. His heart hammered so hard he was pretty sure he was going to die right there. A good way to go, he decided.

Never breaking the kiss, he glided his fingers over her ribs to the front, his thumbs tracing the underside of her breasts. She ended the kiss, and her head fell back with a moan, then jerked up as her phone rang from the coffee table in front of them.

"That's Erin's ringtone," she said. "I have to answer. I'm so, so sorry."

Not nearly as sorry as he was. He leaned back against the sofa cushions and closed his eyes as she took the call beside him.

"Hey," she said. There was a long interval before she answered, clearly listening to what her sister was saying. "Did he give a reason why?" Again, a long pause, during which she stood and paced the length of the kitchen and back to the sofa. "Is he with you now?" She made a turn and headed back toward the kitchen. "Could you put him on the phone, please?"

Caleb could tell she was angry. Her free hand was balled into a fist at her side, and her eyes were narrowed, staring at nothing as she paced.

"Niles," she said through gritted teeth. "What was our agreement three years ago when we moved into the house on Long Island?"

Wait. She lived with this guy?

There was a short pause while she listened. "Right. No parties. Not even in your guest house. Yet, Erin tells me that you had a heck of a party last night and a woman's bikini bottoms are in the pool and the top to that swimsuit is in my bathroom." Again, she paced. "*My* bathroom, Niles. Erin also says there are beer cans on the tennis courts and the movie room is trashed." Another circuit from the sofa to the end of the kitchen and back while she paced.

Caleb's gut churned. The woman had a big life, all

right. Really big, with tennis courts and a movie room. Why would she hang out in Blink any longer than she had to?

"The same rules apply when I'm gone as when I'm there. Get everything back in place and cleaned up by the time I get home." She stopped and huffed in frustration at whatever he said. "I have no idea when that will be. Not soon enough, evidently. Now put Erin back on the line."

She spoke to the guy like he was a child. Sounded like it was justified, though, if he trashed her place.

Willy and Scout followed Lillian's every move as she paced the galley. "Hey, Er. He'll clean it up. It was only a matter of time, I suppose. Hey, I got your email about meeting with the studio execs. I'm totally open to adding a third holiday special for Valentine's Day, if you think it's a good idea."

As Caleb listened to her, he realized that maybe her story about her work taking too much time for her to date or own a pet was not the load of BS he'd originally thought. She ran a huge company and, from the sound of it, an unruly toddler of a spokesman. He leaned back in the sofa and ran his hands through his hair. What was he doing? He'd sworn to himself he'd never set himself up for hurt again, but here he was, putting himself out there to bleed.

"Set up a time in a few weeks that works for us and the studio." Lillian smiled. "Yeah, me, too. Bye," she said, putting her phone back on the coffee table and sitting down next to him, her thigh against his feeling like a brand. "Sorry about that."

"No problem." He stood, rubbing his hand down his

thigh. "I have a really early day tomorrow. I'll take you home now."

She looked bewildered. She opened her mouth as if to say something but remained silent. Her eyes flitted to her wet clothes on the counter.

"You can get my clothes to me later." His voice sounded as hollow as he felt. He couldn't allow himself to become attached. He needed to back off.

"Okay. I'm working at Mr. McGuffy's in the morning, and the furniture I ordered for Erin's cottage comes in the afternoon."

She was hinting at him coming by, no doubt. He shouldn't. He tried to not let the disappointment show on his face.

Her voice was timid and hesitant. "Wanna join me to watch the sunset from my porch tomorrow?"

"I told my parents I'd join them for dinner," he lied. He should tell her the truth. He should tell her he wasn't ready to feel something for the first time in a long time for someone who wasn't family, only to have them leave.

She studied him, and he knew she was trying to figure out what was going on. She'd never know by looking at his face. He'd had fifteen years to practice hiding his feelings. He was a master.

CHAPTER FOURTEEN

"How did the shopping trip go with the list I made for you?" Lillian asked Roger, who was sitting on the side of his bed, using a magnifying glass to examine a paper from the top of a large stack she'd removed from the corner of his bedroom.

"Great! I found everything I needed and even bought a new kind of coffee creamer. It has cinnamon in it." He set the magnifying glass down on the bed next to him. "Mabel would have loved it. Cinnamon was her favorite. Reminded her of Christmas holidays when we were all together." He placed both hands on his knees as if for support to stay upright.

"All together?" Lillian prompted.

"Yes. Me, Mabel, and Tristan." He looked at her. "My son."

She was hesitant to ask. "Where is Tristan now?"

"Portland. He's a hotshot doctor."

Most people would brag about that, but Roger's tone was demeaning.

"He must be very smart."

"He took after his mother," Roger said, picking the magnifying glass up and resuming his examination of what looked like an ancient car repair receipt. "Smart. It broke Mabel's heart when he decided to practice in Portland instead of set up here, like he'd planned. Said there wasn't enough business to make it worthwhile."

Lillian set down the garbage bag she'd been filling with useless items from under the nightstand. This was a segue to what she'd been dying to talk to him about.

"Your son is right. Blink appears to be disappearing," she said.

He waved his hand like he was fighting off a gnat or fly. "Nah. It's been here for a long time. It'll be here for a long time more."

She wiped the dust off her hands onto her jeans and pushed to her feet. "I disagree. It will only be here until the last person who lives here right now leaves or dies. Nobody new is coming in."

"People have been saying that for decades, and yet, we're still here. We don't need new people."

"The demise of a town is a slow process. It doesn't happen overnight." She hated to twist the knife, but from his nonstop headshaking, she could tell he'd had this conversation before and was completely closed to a discussion. "Roger, listen to me. Blink's death is like Mabel's cancer. Slow and invisible at first, then worse and worse until…"

He closed his eyes and stopped shaking his head. Maybe he was listening now.

"But it doesn't have to be like that. It can be stopped and even reversed. You can stop it."

"How?"

"Sell some of the property you own. Let it go so that someone can build and bring in new business."

"You sound like Tristan. The answer is no. Walmart will come in and ruin everything."

"You can vet buyers. Stipulate no third-party or

corporate buyers," she said.

"What keeps an individual from turning right around and selling to Walmart after they buy from me? I'll tell you what: *nothing*."

She let out an exasperated huff. "Remember when you said that your son wouldn't come set up a doctor's office here because there wasn't enough business? Well, there sure isn't enough business to open a Walmart. That's not even within the realm of possibilities."

"Blink needs to stay Blink, not try to be something it's not."

"Blink is a sick, dying town." She put her hand on his shoulder. "Is that what you think it should try to be?" He pretended to look at his paper, but she knew he was only avoiding having to reply. "*You* can help it. Only you…" She bit her bottom lip. "And maybe me."

That got his attention. He lowered the magnifying glass to his lap. "How can you help?"

"I don't know yet. But you've seen what I can do with a house. You should see what I can do with large-scale planning. I'll figure something out." She took his hand. "Don't you see? This is a great town full of great people. We can't just let it disappear."

"We." He patted her hand, keeping it between his. "You sound like you plan to stay."

For a moment, she found herself holding her breath. What was wrong with her? There was nothing to hesitate over. No scenario in which that was even a consideration. She slid her hand from his and began dropping the papers he'd separated out as trash into the garbage bag. "No. I can't. I have a business to run in New York, but I can help Blink from there."

He gave her a disappointed look, then shook his head. "You're expecting people to do something you aren't willing to do yourself."

"You don't understand." Honestly, neither did she.

"Don't kid yourself. I understand better than anyone around here." He sounded a little angry, but mostly, he sounded tired.

"Think about what I said." She twisted the top of the garbage bag and put a twist tie on it. "If you sell some of that property, new businesses will move in."

He shook his head. "Nobody moves to Blink. They move away. I'm not gonna sell a square inch. What you're talking about is impossible."

By the stubborn set of his jaw and his closed-off body position, Lillian knew she'd hit a wall for today. He needed time to think on it, and she needed time to come up with a strategy.

"I'll see you tomorrow," she said.

Like a kid released from his seat for recess, Roger stood and made a line straight for his recliner in front of the TV. "I'm not selling," he shot over his shoulder.

"Nothing is impossible," she whispered to herself as she shuffled down the front steps to head home. She stopped in her tracks and gritted her teeth. No. Not to head *home*. To head to Erin's vacation cottage.

• • •

"You didn't expect to have furniture delivered without us, did you?" Amanda asked from Lillian's front porch.

Us? Heart racing, she looked past her to see Cassidy and Luke pulling up in front of the house. No big dirty pickup truck. No strong man who kissed like the world was on fire. Swallowing her disappointment, she smiled and stepped aside for her guests.

"It doesn't come until three," Lillian said.

"That'll give us time to eat these!" Cassidy took a box from Luke and placed it on the kitchen counter, then flipped it open to reveal chocolate cupcakes. "These are a moving-in-day gift from Sally."

"I'm not moving in," she responded a little too vehemently. She didn't see their expressions, but instead pulled four dessert plates from the cabinet and set them, along with a roll of paper towels, on the counter next to the cupcakes. "I'm just making it nicer for my sister as a thank-you for letting me stay here."

She turned to find Luke stiffly seated in one of the two chairs in the place, both wood and both beaten up. Cassidy and Amanda were shoulder to shoulder, wearing identical looks of disappointment. "I am staying here for a little while longer than expected, though."

The women's faces brightened. Luke flipped his hair out of his eyes and stared out the window as if willing the delivery guys to hurry up so he could get out of there.

She pulled a tin of coffee beans she'd bought in Machias yesterday out of the pantry. "There's water and soda in the fridge. Anyone want coffee with their cupcake?" Chocolate and coffee was her favorite combination, and she could use both right now after her almost sleepless night.

"Ooo! You have a coffeemaker now!" Cassidy said,

moving closer to check it out.

"I do. Thank goodness for Williams-Sonoma's home delivery and expedited shipping." She poured some of the beans in the grinder and breathed in deep when it roared to life, sending the aroma of heaven itself into the air. "You guys really didn't have to come help."

"We didn't have to; we wanted to," Cassidy said.

She added water to the basin on the coffeemaker and turned it on, not remembering a time in her adult life when someone helped her out who didn't work for her. She swallowed hard, keeping her back to them.

"So, how did the trip to town with Caleb go?" Cassidy asked.

Lillian shot her a look. She hadn't talked to Cassidy about that. Amanda was giving her a knowing grin as bright as her yellow blouse with flowing sleeves. Sally had known about the trip, though, and Cassidy and Amanda had been by there to get the cupcakes, so…

Small towns. Sheesh.

She opened the refrigerator and pulled out the milk, then stood on her tiptoes to reach the bag of sugar. She'd ordered a set of counter cannisters, as well as dishes and cookware from the Living Sharpe collection, but they hadn't arrived yet. "The shopping was fine. My feet feel great, and there's coffee in this house now." She wiggled her toes in her comfy hiking boots and pulled out four mismatched coffee cups that came with the house.

"And how did your little boat outing go last night?" Amanda asked in a singsong voice.

Now that, she hadn't told anyone about. She turned and raised an eyebrow at Amanda, who didn't even bother to blush.

"I live above the store. My evenings consist of Netflix and watching Caleb mope around." She waggled her eyebrows. "Only he wasn't moping last night."

Oh, for Pete's sake. Just how much had she seen? Feeling the heat crawling up her neck, she turned and started rinsing out the coffee cups.

She filled one and placed it next to the milk and sugar. "Help yourselves." Then filled another.

Amanda made a whoop sound. When Lillian turned to deliver another cup of coffee, Amanda had her hand out, palm up in front of Cassidy.

"You owe me five, Cass. Put 'er there."

"How do you know?" Cassidy asked.

"Look at her face. Red as a lobster. I win. Pay up."

Cassidy dug in the pocket of her splattered overalls and pulled out a jumble of wadded-up bills, then slapped a five in Amanda's palm.

Lillian leaned back against the counter and stared at them. "Hold on. I must have missed something. Wanna fill me in?"

Amanda held the five-dollar bill by two corners and wiggled it. "I bet Cass you and Caleb would be hooking up before the end of the week." She held the bill up in triumph. "You guys didn't even make it to Tuesday." She waved the bill like a flag.

Lillian shot a self-conscious look at Luke, who was in the exact same position, staring out the window, apparently oblivious. Eyes heavenward, she heaved a long, weary sigh, like her kindergarten teacher used to do. The same sigh she used on Niles when he was being ridiculous—a sigh she used a lot.

With a sly grin, Cassidy held out her palm, and Amanda handed the bill back. "Easy come, easy go," she said, shoving it back into her overall pocket.

"It's only Tuesday," Amanda said, pulling a paper towel off the roll and grabbing a cupcake. "Still plenty of time."

If Erin hadn't called, Amanda would be five dollars richer, most likely. But with how weird Caleb had acted, maybe not.

"You want some coffee, Luke?" Lillian asked, desperate to change the subject.

"No thanks."

He hadn't made eye contact with her, and she wondered if something was wrong. Hanging out with his big sister and two other women had to be pretty awful for a teen.

"Lose the pout, Luky," Cassidy said. "It won't change anything."

He didn't break his stare out the window.

Cassidy added a huge spoon of sugar to her coffee and stirred. "Luke is unhappy because he wanted to go paint some cabinets in the Lassiter house because *someone* will be there with her father, but I'd already committed him here, and we follow through."

She'd been disappointed when Caleb hadn't offered to help her today, but now she knew it was because he and Bethany were working to get the house finished in time for school. That still didn't explain the hot-to-cold reaction he'd had after their kiss.

Luke shifted in his chair, not removing his gaze from the window. Poor kid. The yearning was all over his drawn features. She totally got that.

"I've paid the delivery guys to do setup. I really don't need Luke for this," Lillian said.

For the first time, he looked away from the window and gave his sister a hopeful look.

"Let him take the truck. I'll give you a ride home, Cass," Amanda said, peeling the wrapper off her cupcake.

With an indulgent sigh, Cassidy dug keys out of the overall pocket over her chest and held them out, looped over one finger, like a lure for a fish.

Luke took the bait from his sister's finger with a grin, kissed her on the cheek, and grabbed a cupcake before heading out the door like a completely different person.

"Ah, young love." Amanda put a hand over her heart with a melodramatic flutter of her eyelashes.

Cassidy sighed. "Poor kid. He really likes her, but she's crazy about some other guy from their school."

"Brandon," Lillian said.

Cassidy looked surprised. "Yeah. That's him. Evidently a real jerk. It's ripping Luke up, but he can't seem to stay away from her."

"Maybe the contrast between him and jerk boy will turn things in Luke's favor," Amanda offered.

After a moment of standing awkwardly in the kitchen, Lillian said, "I'd offer you guys a seat, but there are only one and a half chairs."

Cassidy toasted her with her coffee cup—a ghastly thing with Garfield on it. "Hey! That's the number of brain cells my brother has right now."

Lillian could relate to that, too. She'd been distracted all day. After Caleb had dropped her off last night, she couldn't sleep, so she surfed travel and cooking sites for inspiration for upcoming features. She couldn't figure out what had happened to turn him off like a faucet. She got off the phone, and *bam*. The door to lust land slammed closed. Maybe the call had given him time to cool off long enough to decide he didn't want a short-term fling—though that seemed unlikely. She couldn't figure him out. Maybe Amanda and Cassidy could help.

"Did you guys know Caleb's wife?" Yep. There it was. All in now, but she had to get some answers. He didn't seem to want to talk about his ex, and she couldn't help but think it was the key to what happened last night.

They looked at each other, then back at her.

"I was raised in Connecticut by my mom. I visited my dad here during the summers but never knew Ashley. I was away at college when all the drama went down," Amanda said.

"I was a clueless little kid in grade school," Cassidy said.

Amanda gave her a glare, and Cassidy shrugged with a smirk.

"What was the drama?" Lillian asked, checking the time on her phone. The furniture was late. Of course it was. This was Blink.

Amanda took a big breath, and Lillian leaned back against the counter, knowing Amanda was going to do what she did best: tell a story.

"Caleb and Ashley were high-school sweethearts. He was a year older than she was, and he was crazy about her." She took a long, contemplative sip of coffee, which Lillian suspected was a strategy to build suspense and keep her audience on the edge of their seats. It worked.

"And?" Lillian prompted.

She smiled over the rim of her cup. "And they got pregnant the summer before her junior year."

Lillian thought back to what Bethany had said on the beach: *He's afraid I'm gonna end up like him.* She was the same age Ashley had been when she got pregnant. Lillian's chest pinched deep inside.

"The families circled the wagons. Celebrated the good side of it. The parents had been friends forever and tried to make it as positive as possible for Ashley and Caleb. They had a nice little wedding in the church and moved in with Ashley's parents."

Cassidy poured another cup of coffee. "Sally told me they had to drop out of school and Caleb lost his scholarship."

"Why did they have to drop out of school?" Lillian asked, placing her empty coffee cup in the sink.

Amanda gave her a disbelieving look. "Pregnant in a high school with students from several small towns wouldn't fly."

Lillian could see that being an issue in a place like this.

"She stayed home, and he drove to Machias every day to work with a furniture builder in the morning, and then back here to work for his dad in the afternoon. After Bethany was born, he stopped building furniture and started doing body repairs on boats while his dad worked on motors. Eventually, he started doing some major jobs, rebuilding and fabricating vintage pieces for boats his dad worked on. His dad encouraged him to pursue that in a big way, buying him a bunch of fancy tools, and it paid off."

"Oh, my God. His work is amazing. Have you seen his portfolio?" Cassidy asked. "He's done restoration on famous yachts all down the East Coast. He had a really cool book of his work printed up to show prospective clients."

"The one on his coffee table?" she asked with a churn in her belly.

She beamed. "Yeah. He does beautiful work."

That was his *portfolio*. Those amazing staircases, railings, ceilings, and ship interiors were his work. With a groan, she covered her face with her hands. She'd asked him if Bethany got her artistic genes from her mom. She groaned again.

"Aaaannnyway," Amanda said, reclaiming her limelight. "Clients come to him now, well, most of the time, unless their boats are too big, but he used to always have to travel to work on them when he first started making a name for himself. Ashley would beg to go with him, so he took her, and they left the baby with the four grandparents."

That made sense. Ashley was little more than a child herself. Full-time mom was probably difficult, especially if her husband was going away for extended periods of time.

"That's where the story gets kind of hazy," Cassidy cut in. "Nobody talks about it. All we know is on one of those trips, Ashley met a rich yacht owner out of New York City when Caleb went to bid on a restoration job. A few months later, the guy sailed here so that Caleb could do some minor work, and when he left, Ashley went with him."

"Sally says Caleb's never been the same," Amanda added.

Lillian put a hand over her fluttering heart. "Wait. She just left her baby?"

Amanda leaned back against the pantry door. "She did. Granted Caleb sole custody in the divorce papers he received by courier. I don't think he's seen her since she sailed off into the sunset with Daddy Warbucks."

Lillian lowered herself onto the only working chair.

"It crushed her parents," Amanda said. "Sally doesn't think she's in touch with them. I don't know how someone can do that. Just dust everyone off and leave."

For a moment, Lillian found it hard to draw air into her lungs. She placed her hand over her chest and drew in a slow, painful breath.

"Oh, look. Your furniture is here," Cassidy said, bouncing to the door and yanking it open.

"This'll be cool!" Amanda set her coffee cup down on the counter. "It's sort of like being in one of your *Living Sharpe* episodes where Niles totally updates a space by rearranging the furniture."

Lillian sighed. Niles couldn't update his phone, much less a living space. "Yeah, cool."

With a forced smile, Lillian stepped outside to greet the delivery team so that she could make the cottage all cozy just in time to go back to New York. To dust everyone off and leave, just like Ashley.

CHAPTER FIFTEEN

The morning sun streamed into the cottage, making the new furniture glow like it was under the Living Sharpe camera lights. The shabby little cottage looked like a different place now.

"Thanks for coming by to check out the oven, Cassidy," Lillian said.

"No problem. I'm sorry I couldn't do anything about it. I'm *not* sorry I'm here, though. The pie is delicious, uneven oven heating or not. The pie committee will flip over this."

"Wait until you taste this next one." Lillian opened the oven and turned the pie ninety degrees. She'd been spoiled by the state-of-the-art Living Sharpe kitchen, and this situation was less than ideal, and it wasn't only the oven setting her back. Sadly, the dishes and cookware hadn't arrived yet, so Lillian was still having to make do with what had been left behind. At least she'd had the forethought to buy pie pans when she was in Machias.

She stretched her stiff back and yawned. She'd had another sleepless night, despite the new king-size bed, tossing and turning, wondering when she'd see Caleb again. After hearing about Ashley, she had a pretty good idea why he'd backed off after the kiss at his houseboat several days ago.

Lillian brushed the flour off her hands on her apron. "I can't believe Roger stood me up again today," she grumbled. "He's a complete chicken. He called off my coming over yesterday and this morning to finish his organization project because he knows I'll want to discuss listing some of his properties for sale."

"You suggested land-hoarder McGuffy turn loose property?" She gave Lillian a high five.

"I did. So far, he's not hot on the idea. I need to prove to him there is interest in the area. That's why I need the perfect blueberry pie. If Blink wins the contest this weekend—"

"Then we get to host it next year, and loads of people will visit!" Cassidy continued, face glowing like the sunlit furniture. Her smile faded. "But there's nothing here to visit."

Lillian stopped scrubbing the mixing bowl and gave her a sly smile. "There will be if I can convince Roger to sell some of the property in time to make improvements before next year's contest. Especially the empty businesses at the harbor." She rinsed the bowl and put it in the drying rack.

"Convincing him is going to be hard. Roger's hung on to those properties his whole life, acquiring everything he could get his hands on as businesses and families moved out." Cassidy dried the mixing bowl and set it on the shelf next to the measuring cups.

"But why does he collect properties if he's going to just let them sit idle? It's like he doesn't really want them, but he doesn't want anyone else to have them because, God forbid…Walmart!"

Cassidy chuckled. "You nailed it. I mean, look at his main house. I've offered to work on it hundreds of times in the last five years. That super cool historic house needs to have some repairs before it's lost, but he'd rather let it collapse than change or sell it. I'm amazed you got him to throw away that stuff from his guest house."

"He's not a hoarder; he was just disorganized. He was overwhelmed." Now that she thought about it, she realized that was the underlying problem—he was overwhelmed by change. He'd been a bit resistant once they got out of the kitchen and started organizing things that were uniquely his. She had to convince him the change would not disrupt his life but enhance it. Maybe it was uncertainty that got to him. She needed to convince him that selling the properties would save the town—that the change was good and would enhance him. How?

Cassidy poked one of the pies on the counter with a fork. "I don't know why you rejected these. I think they're delicious."

Lillian grabbed the hand towel and wiped Cassidy's cheek. "Blueberry juice or something." She opened the oven and rotated the pie another quarter turn. Too bad the new oven wasn't here yet. Opening the door all the time was not ideal. "I think this attempt will be better than the first two tries. I added a touch of cinnamon, and this crust should be more appropriate."

"Appropriate? That word is for Sunday-school clothes, not pies." Cassidy tapped the previous pie's crust with her fork, and it flaked away. "I think this one is more than appropriate."

Lillian smiled and gestured to the oven. "That's because you haven't tasted this one yet. This style of crust is finer and more delicate."

"The only difference I noticed was you added ice water when you made dough this time."

Lillian hung a dish towel over the rack at the end of the counter. "The measurements and mixing technique are different with a pâte brisée, and so is the outcome. Trust me."

Cassidy shrugged. "Pie crust is pie crust."

"That's like saying paint is paint. Don't certain types work better in certain applications?"

She rolled her eyes. "Of course."

"Same exact thing. Pie crusts are varied and specific. This isn't a fill-the-belly pie. It's a win-a-contest pie." And save-a-town pie. Just the thought of what was at stake made her stomach churn.

If her new oven didn't arrive in the next few days, she'd need to use someone else's to bake the contest pies for Saturday's contest. First, though, she needed to get her pie in front of the pie committee.

The timer went off on her phone, and she cracked the oven door. "Perfect." She slipped on oven mitts and removed the pie, bumped the oven door closed with her hip, and placed the pie on a cooling rack.

"I think this is the best-smelling house in the universe," Cassidy said, turning off the oven. She took a deep breath through her nose, then gasped. "Uh-oh."

Lillian turned to see what was wrong and followed her gaze out the window. A large dinosaur of a car had pulled in behind Cassidy's truck. "Who is it?"

"It's the church ladies. You might want to head this off on the porch. Once this army infiltrates, they never leave." She shook her head and made a *tsk*ing sound. "Yeah.

Definitely head them off on the porch. From the look on Fran's face, it's not a social call."

Who was Fran, and why would Lillian need to head something or someone off?

Lillian pulled her apron from around her neck and hung it on a hook near the refrigerator, watching through the window as four women got out of the car. She recognized Caleb's mother, Alice, but the others hadn't been at Amanda's get-together on the deck. She knew Alice was on the pie committee, so maybe this would be a good thing.

Cassidy opened the front door and signaled to follow her outside. Completely confused, Lillian stepped out on the porch.

"Are you Lillian Mahoney?" the one Cassidy had called Fran asked. She was a tall woman with a tall hairstyle wearing a shirt with vertical stripes, giving her the illusion of even more height. Two women flanked her, and Alice stood behind them, taking an almost apologetic stance with her shoulders slumped and hands twisting in front of her. This Fran person must be the leader of the pack. No, not a pack. More of a gaggle.

"I am." Lillian forced a smile.

"You have some nerve," a bony lady in a green dress to Fran's right said. The dress looked like something out of an old eighties sitcom with a big belt and lots of pleats.

"My pie crust is *not* mealy," a round woman to Fran's left almost shouted, face flushing until it resembled the color of her pink blouse.

"And mine is not too sweet. Seamus says it's perfect," green sitcom lady said.

The only one who hadn't spoken yet was Alice, Caleb's mother. Still lurking behind them, she had a worried look on her face as she watched her companions. Perhaps she would be an ally.

Lillian almost laughed. At least she knew what their agenda was. These were the women whose pies she'd tasted and critiqued at Roger's. Obviously, when they'd asked Roger for feedback on testing day, they hadn't really wanted it. They only wanted praise. This could work to her advantage, though. She needed to get her pie in a position for contest consideration, and it appeared the very people to do that had invaded her porch like culinary warriors.

"Just because you work for Niles Sharpe doesn't make you an expert on cooking," Fran said.

"With, not for," Lillian replied woodenly. And it most certainly *did* make her an expert, but she kept that to herself. They were already irritated.

"Especially when you sabotaged him after you've been lovers for so long," the skinny woman in green said.

Lillian was shocked to hear what was written in so many social media comments. It seemed even more horrible when said out loud. The tops of her ears grew hot.

"The Sharpies are circulating a petition online to get you fired," Fran said.

Okay. Now that pissed her off, and the heat spread from the tops of her ears to the top of her head. Lillian pressed her lips shut to keep from lashing out. Everything in her wanted to tell them off, but she couldn't. She had to think of Living Sharpe and what was best for Blink.

Going ballistic on these women was not the best tactic. *When someone hurts you, kill them with kindness*, her mom always said. It was time to slay with pie.

"I appreciate you dropping by and look forward to getting to know you better," she said in a level voice that betrayed the bomb of anger ticking in her brain. "Why don't you come inside and have some coffee?"

All of them exchanged surprised glances except for Alice, who smiled and led the way, greeting Lillian and Cassidy on her way in.

Lillian gestured to the new seating area that consisted of two sofas facing each other and a large, comfortable chair on each end, completing a square. In the middle was a two-tiered round glass coffee table. "Please make yourselves comfortable. I'll make a fresh pot of coffee."

Cassidy was giving her a "now you've done it" look as she passed, but Lillian disagreed. All ugly comments stopped once they were invited inside, though that might have been the result of the smell of fresh-baked pie rather than her invitation. Whatever the reason, the looming battle on her front porch had been stopped dead in its tracks.

As she started the coffeemaker, she glanced up to find them craning their necks to see into the kitchen. Cassidy wandered in, brow arched.

"Will you pull six of the least chipped plates out for me?" Lillian asked as she selected coffee cups that had the least obnoxious designs on them, which ruled out the one that was a gag gift of some kind with the handle on the inside, as well as the one with topless hula dancers on it. Then, she put small slices of her most recent pie on each plate and set forks with each serving. After handing two to Cassidy, she picked up two more and led the way to the women.

"I would be grateful if you would agree to participate in a tasting for me. I welcome your critiques as you welcomed mine," she said as she and Cassidy set the warm slices down in front of each woman. As if stunned, they shared looks and picked up their forks.

Lillian was pretty sure that their shock was because they'd launched a surprise attack, planning to catch her off guard, and instead were ambushed right back.

As if seeking permission, they waited for Fran to take her bite first. More looks were shared as they chewed.

Alice was the first to speak. "This is, hands down, the best blueberry pie I have ever tasted."

The others nodded in agreement, still appearing a little stunned.

Cassidy was leaning against the kitchen doorframe eating hers. "You're right. All pie crusts are not created equal. This is better than your last try."

"The coffee is ready if anyone would like some," Lillian said.

"So, is this Niles Sharpe's recipe?" the bony woman in green asked, setting her plate on the table and standing.

Hiding the fact Niles didn't have the culinary skills to scramble eggs was important, but there had never been an attempt made to hide who created content on the show. "No. It's mine. All recipes on the show and in the magazine are created or discovered by me."

The woman looked skeptical but nodded, then poured a cup of coffee.

After everyone sat back down, Lillian lowered onto a sofa next to Alice. "Thoughts?" she asked them. They'd had plenty of thoughts on their way in, but they seemed hesitant to comment now.

"I agree with Alice," Fran said. "This is the best blueberry pie I've ever tasted."

Agreement went up from around the room. For a few minutes, they ate and drank in silence. It was uncomfortable, but Lillian wanted them to ask for her help with the contest. She didn't want it to be her idea.

She decided to clear the air regarding the online accusations while she waited for them to gather the nerve. "I do not work for Niles Sharpe. I work with him. I am not in a romantic or physical relationship with him, nor have I ever been. And I wouldn't want to be."

The woman in pink said, "But I saw the recording on the Sharpies fan page."

"I'm sorry. I don't know your name," Lillian said.

"Oh, I'm Charlotte."

"Nice to meet you, Charlotte. Niles thought I had mixed up the order of the ingredients laid out for the show, but he was mistaken. He added the ingredients in the wrong order. Everyone makes mistakes. Even Niles Sharpe." *Especially* Niles Sharpe.

The woman in green spoke this time. "I saw on the recording that he asked how you could sabotage him after five years together." She blushed when Lillian didn't reply except to cock an eyebrow. "Oh, my name is Doris."

"I'm glad to meet you, Doris. In that clip, Niles was referring to five years working together. Nothing more." She scanned the room, making eye contact with each woman. "As for the petition. I am the owner and creator of Living Sharpe, LLC. I'm the very top person. The boss." She added that last bit just in case it hadn't been clear enough. After a dramatic pause, she said, "I fire people. I cannot be fired."

"I told you that you were making a mistake," Alice said to her friends. "Short tempers make for long regrets."

"It's all good," Lillian said. "I'm glad you were here to test out my pie."

Cassidy snorted from the kitchen at this ridiculous statement, and Lillian fought the urge to turn and glare at her—or laugh.

"This pie is much better than the one we entered last year," Doris said.

"That was yours, Doris," Fran said.

"I know. This one is better." Doris took another bite.

Alice was the one to finally step up and ask. "It feels crass to ask after we barged in here slinging insults and accusations, but would you be willing to share your recipe with us so that we can enter it in the contest this year? Blink has never even finaled in the decades we've entered."

"That's because we only have one church and therefore one entry. Other towns, like Bar Harbor, have dozens," Doris said defensively.

"We've lost because we didn't enter a pie that tastes like this one," Alice said. She placed her plate on the coffee table and swiveled to face Lillian. "If you say no, I'd understand. We showed up like a bunch of harpies." She gave her friends a narrow-eyed glare. The surprise attack clearly wasn't her idea. "But we would be grateful if you could help us out."

"I'll do better than that. If someone will provide an oven that bakes evenly, I'll make them for you. Anyone who wants to help is welcome to join me." She held a hand up palm out. "But there's a stipulation." It appeared they were holding their breaths, waiting for her to lay out the catch. "You cannot mention me or Living Sharpe to anyone in conjunction with this contest. I want the credit to go to the town of Blink and its citizens." She wanted all attention on this town.

They exchanged glances, then after a nod from Fran, Alice said, "Sally lets us use the diner every year. It has a big kitchen and a really good oven."

This whole thing had gone better than planned. Now, if she could just convince Roger as easily. Lillian stood and took her cup to the kitchen. "That's perfect. Just let me know the schedule." She waited for them to take her lead, but they stayed seated. Cassidy gave her an *I told you so* smirk complete with arched eyebrow. "You'll need dynamite to blast them out now," she whispered as Lillian passed her on the way to the sink.

She sighed. Subtlety wasn't going to work. "I appreciate you coming by to see me. I need to join some conference calls with my team in a few minutes." That wasn't exactly true. Because of her schedule helping Roger, her meetings happened in the afternoon.

Alice stood and took her plate and cup to the kitchen, but the others remained seated. Fran and Doris even started a conversation about the defects of last year's winning pie. Dang. Dynamite was right.

She strode to the front door and opened it. "I'll see

you soon." Surely, they didn't think *she* was the one leaving.

"Time to go," Alice said. "The woman has things to do besides entertain us."

Lillian could almost hear the kaboom of Alice's dynamite. With a mom like her, it was little wonder Caleb turned out to be such a great guy.

Crap. Why did everything have to circle back to Caleb?

The women filed out. With a sigh of relief, Lillian shut the door, leaning back against it until the sound of the car's motor faded away.

Cassidy flopped onto her back on one of the sofas. "Girl. I'm in awe. The pie committee is the thing of legends. Warriors, all."

Now it was Lillian's turn to snort. "More like pains in the backside. Now, I need to get this pie in front of Roger, since he's one of the tasters."

Cassidy sat up. "That's easy. He and the guys had set up camp at table two in the diner this morning." She cast Lillian a knowing look. "Along with Caleb Wright."

"Field trip," Lillian said, picking up what was left of the pie and grabbing her purse. "Come on, Cassidy. Have pie, will travel."

CHAPTER SIXTEEN

Caleb put his hand over his coffee cup when Sally came to top them off for the millionth time. He glanced at his watch and grimaced. Luke should be done with the floors in the Lassiter place by now. He couldn't go in until the varnish dried.

"So I told her, I said, Doris honey, you have the best pie in Washington County. Don't let anyone tell you otherwise." Seamus nodded, pleased with himself. Then he leaned forward and whispered, "But the New York lady is right. Her pies are too sweet."

Gus patted Seamus's round belly. "Don't keep you from eating them, though."

Roger, seated in the booth next to Caleb, had been quiet most of the morning. He should have been home working with Lillian right now. He wondered if the old man was feeling sick. A tingle of dread zipped down his spine. Maybe *Lillian* was sick. He knew from Luke that her furniture was delivered Monday, but he hadn't seen her since he dropped her off Saturday after that phone call...and that kiss. Damn. That kiss. The trickle of dread was eclipsed by heat blooming in his body when he remembered the way she felt in his arms.

"What do you think, Caleb?"

He shook his head to clear it. Hell, he didn't even know who had asked a question, much less what they'd asked. "I'm sorry. I was thinking about a project." Yeah, one with long legs and a killer smile that could kiss like the devil.

He was saved from the awkward moment when the bells on the diner door rattled and clanged. Like a choreographed dance, everyone in the place—which would be Sally and the four of them sitting at this booth—turned to see who had entered.

"Hey, Sally!" Cassidy called out as she held the door open with her foot so that Lillian, hands full with a dish covered by a cloth, could enter.

Caleb turned back around. He was totally at war. He wanted to see her, talk to her, but at the same time, he wished he was somewhere else. Though, if he were being honest with himself, where he was seemed just fine as that expensive-smelling perfume she wore hit his nose coupled with blueberry pie. Double whammy.

Roger was fiddling with the sugar packets in the little square container in the middle of the table. It looked to Caleb like he wished he was somewhere else, too. Maybe he and Lillian had a falling-out.

"Roger. You are just the man I wanted to see," Lillian said.

Caleb had a weird dropping sensation, secretly wishing she'd said that to him instead.

The smell of her perfume intensified as she neared. So did the scent of fresh-baked blueberry pie.

He didn't look at her face as she set a half-empty pie pan on the table. "I need you to taste sample number five for this year's contest." Cassidy strode up with a stack of plates and a fistful of forks.

Lillian set a piece of pie and a fork in front of him.

"What about us?" Gus asked.

"Good morning," she said. "I'd love to have more opinions." She served up three more pieces and set them in front of Gus, Seamus, and him. He could feel her looking at him, but he kept his eyes on the table.

His dad was the first one to taste it. He shoved a huge bite in his mouth. "Mmmmmffff!" he said, giving a thumbs-up.

Seamus took a bite and made a big show of chewing and considering. He swallowed, then took a chug of water. "Too sweet," he said. Then he guffawed and slapped his palms on the table, causing the silverware to rattle. "Just kidding. It's great." He eyed the two remaining pieces still in the pan. "Is that all you brought?"

Caleb took a bite of his piece and was stunned. He'd lived in Maine all his life. He'd tried blueberry everything, but this was a standout. The crust was crunchy in parts, and it had a little zing. Some spice. Cinnamon, maybe? "Did you make this?"

"I did."

He glanced up. It was the first time he'd met her eyes since she'd walked in the diner. Big mistake. "It's exceptional," he said. Just like everything about her. She looked away. He picked up his cold coffee and set it back down without taking a sip. When he glanced up, his father was watching him from across the table.

"Roger?" she prompted.

Staring at the oddly interesting sugar packets, Roger said, "You won't change my mind."

Yeah, there was obviously some rift between them.

Lillian huffed. "The only thing I'm trying to change

is the pie that gets submitted to the contest, Roger McGuffy. Five judges from every church have to vote, I'm told. You are judge number five."

"I made my selection last week. It stands."

Lillian's lips drew tight as she glared at him. Roger's eyes narrowed as he glared right back. Caleb almost laughed. Two of the hardest headed people on the planet were in a standoff about a piece of pie.

Sally strode up, took a fork, and cut off a bite of Roger's piece. "Mmm. Lillian. That's a winner."

As if she hadn't heard Sally, Lillian didn't break her stare off with Old Man McGuffy. "Go ahead, Roger, and keep that piece of pie all to yourself. Let it go unused and untouched until it shrivels and becomes worthless."

Caleb had a feeling she wasn't talking about pie. He also had a feeling Roger would get up and leave if he weren't trapped in the booth between him and the wall.

"I never change my mind once I've made it," he said, pushing the piece of pie away.

With a sound that reminded Caleb of a growling bear, Lillian stomped out of the building, leaving the bells on the door clattering in her wake.

"She's my ride," Cassidy said, giving Sally a kiss on the cheek as she headed for the door.

"Friends don't let friends drive angry," Sally called after her.

Gus whistled. "Hoo-eee. That one's got a temper," he said.

"I like a woman with a temper," Seamus replied, serving himself another piece of pie. "And I like a woman who can cook."

She was a lot more than that, Caleb knew. She was smart and funny. And she was leaving.

As if nothing had happened, Roger rubbed his hands together as if warming them up, then picked up his fork and pulled the plate toward him. Like Lillian had done when she'd tested the pies at his place, he took a bite from the side of the piece, not the tip. Eyes closed, he savored the piece.

"It's good, isn't it?" Seamus asked.

Roger opened his eyes. "I think I need to go home now."

Caleb stood so that he could slide out of the booth. "You want a ride?"

The old man shook his head and held up his car keys with a smile. "Lillian found my car keys. She installed a hook by my door for them."

"She also taught you how to change clothes!" Seamus teased.

He put a bill on the diner counter and patted it. "She has taught me a lot of things." He stared off into space for a moment, then shuffled out the door.

"He's acting strange," Gus said.

"I'll go check on him later today," Caleb said. "I'm heading to work." He'd hidden in the diner long enough. Even if Luke wasn't done with the floors in the Lassiter place yet, he could do a final walk-through of the *Elizabeth's Wish*. He'd hung out here, in the diner, figuring he'd be safe from Amanda's probing questions and innuendo and less likely to bump into Lillian. Instead, he'd put himself right in her path, though it hadn't been him she'd come to see. It had been Roger.

Again, he wondered what that was all about. Maybe the old man would tell him when he swung by there tonight...passing right by Lillian's cottage.

CHAPTER SEVENTEEN

Lillian shook her hair out of her face and continued her climb up the side of the hill overlooking the beach where she'd met Bethany. The hill that Roger Freaking Miser McGuffy owned, no doubt.

Winded, she sat, catching her breath, and took in the glorious view of the deep blue water that seemed to go on forever. In the distance, lobster boats dotted the surface. She took a cleansing breath of fresh sea air into her lungs. Something she couldn't do back home. Honestly, something she wouldn't take the time to do back home, even if she had fresh sea air to breathe.

It's like she never had time for herself. All her life, she'd reached for success. From being the top cookie seller in her scout troupe, to being high school class president, to owning Living Sharpe, she'd been on a nonstop climb. It was hard to think that her first big failure would involve this tiny town nobody had ever heard of.

And now, nobody ever would, thanks to Scrooge McGuffy.

She'd thought the pie would do the trick. That he'd realize they could win the contest and interest could be generated by hosting next year's event. People would see how great this place was and want to stay.

But there had to be something here for people to see, first. In her mind, she imagined storefronts ringing a bustling harbor and maybe a restaurant.

She sighed and pushed her sunglasses up on her nose. Nothing would happen if Roger wouldn't sell the properties. She had to find a way to convince him.

From up here she could see the far side of the harbor as well as the beach. Caleb's truck was parked next to the Wright Boat Works building, and his dogs were asleep on the wooden walkway near the big sailboat he'd said he was working on. She wondered if he was in there right now. Maybe he'd know a way to convince Roger—that is, if he stopped avoiding her and started talking to her again.

Her phone rang, and she slipped it out of her pocket. "Hey, Amanda," she answered.

"What are you doing up there on that rock? Are you stalking Caleb?"

"What? No!" She switched the phone to her other ear. "Are you spying on me?"

"Can you see my store?"

She looked down at the weathered buildings on her side of the harbor. "Yes."

"If you can see Miller Mercantile, I can see you."

"Do you just stare out your window all day like a creeper?"

She laughed. "There's not a lot else to do around here. Nobody's come in all morning."

"You want some company? My first meeting with my team isn't until three today. I've already reviewed the agenda and proposals."

"I'd love it."

"Be right there." How weird it was to have friends

outside of Living Sharpe. People who didn't want something from her other than conversation. People who wanted to be with her for *her*—and somehow, that made her feel more powerful and valuable than running a wildly successful company ever had.

. . .

Caleb saw Lillian heading down the walk to Amanda's place from the deck of the *Elizabeth's Wish*, where he was doing a final make-ready before her owner came to pick her up this afternoon. Traitors that they were, Scout and Willy bounded down the boardwalk to act as welcoming committee. His gut twisted with regret when she kneeled down and loved on both of them.

"You're not broken, you know," his dad said from somewhere behind him. Nosy old coot.

"Didn't think I was." He knew he was.

His dad leaned against the railing. "I watched you at the diner. If you could've made yourself invisible, you would've. You're running away."

"That's ridiculous. What would I run from?"

"It looks to me like you're running from Lillian."

Not just a nosy old coot—nosy and *perceptive*. "You need new glasses if that's what it looks like."

He met Caleb's eyes, face stern. "You and Ashley were kids. You're a grown-ass man now."

And he felt every second of that grown-ass part. "This has nothing to do with Ashley."

"Keep telling yourself that, son."

He ran a frustrated hand through his hair. "What's

your point, Dad?"

"You're pushing that woman away."

He was.

"Why? Because she's going back to New York? That can be worked around. In two years, Bethany heads off to college. Two years isn't that long, and it gives you and Lillian plenty of time to figure out what you want and where you want to be."

He didn't want to be anywhere but here, and there was no way Lillian could live in a place like this. It was pointless. "Our friendship isn't like that."

"And it never will be if you don't put yourself out there. There's nothing in this world worth having that doesn't come with risks." His father shoved his hands in his pockets. "What's that saying your mom always quotes?"

"The early bird gets the worm."

His father laughed. "No. It's better to have loved and lost than to have never loved at all."

Caleb had loved and lost once already and knew his father's words were spot-on. He'd had some good times with Ashley, and he had Bethany because of it, which far outweighed the pain of the loss.

Maybe his dad was right. Putting the brakes on his relationship with Lillian accomplished nothing but frustration. They liked spending time together, so why not have fun while they could? He'd be careful to never lose sight of what this was—temporary—and then there was no way he could get hurt.

His father's lips quirked. He always could read Caleb's thoughts. "She makes a mean pie." After a long pause, he added, "Your mom likes her."

"So do I." His attention strayed to Amanda's place, where he could see Lillian at a table through the window.

Following his gaze, his dad gave Caleb a pat on the shoulder. "Glad you changed your mind. Go down there and make it right between you, then. Digging in is only good if you're a clam."

CHAPTER EIGHTEEN

"Here comes trouble, as they say," Amanda whispered, looking past Lillian out the window.

"I'd like to know who 'they' are," Lillian said, taking a sip of Dr Pepper. "They say lots of things—mostly garbage." She wanted to turn and see what trouble was coming but quashed the urge, not wanting to look eager. *Eager?* Yeah, she was. She wanted desperately for it to be Caleb but knew it could be anyone in Blink.

"Did you guys have an argument or something? Caleb's been grouchy."

Her heart surged. It *was* Caleb. It took everything in her to not turn around or grin, but instead, she maintained her detached, unaffected demeanor. "Isn't grouchy his only mode?"

"Grouchi*er*."

Lillian shifted in her chair to look at Caleb storming toward them like a raincloud, all intensity and purpose. He was wearing the same thing he'd had on when he'd ignored her at the diner: the blue shirt with the Wright Boat Works logo on it and blue jeans.

"Hey, Caleb," Amanda said. "You here to murder someone or just smash the place up?"

His brow furrowed like he didn't have a clue why she'd ask that. "May I speak with you?" he asked Lillian.

"Sure." She gestured to the chair between her and Amanda.

He glanced at Amanda, clothed in a bright pink blouse with beaded cords dangling from the bottom, and then over his shoulder at the door. "Somewhere else?"

She considered needling him a little bit by insisting they stay, but he seemed genuinely uncomfortable. "Sure." She stood and picked up her can of Dr Pepper.

"Don't go far, kids," Amanda called. "Stay where I can see you."

Caleb stared at Amanda like she'd sprouted another head or something.

"It's called teasing, Caleb," Amanda said. "You know, a joke. Fun. You should try it sometime."

With a shake of his head, Caleb held the door open, and, fighting a smile, Lillian exited.

Her first inclination was to light into him about ignoring her at the diner, but when she glanced over, he looked troubled. "Okay. What's up, Atlas? Holding up the weight of the world on your shoulders has to get tiring."

His face shifted as several emotions played across it. Concern? Uncertainty? Then, determination. "I owe you an apology."

Hoo boy. His voice sounded like Erin's when she was going to deliver some bad news. Lillian took a sip of her drink.

"I'm ordinarily a pretty relaxed and transparent person," he said.

To her credit, she kept a straight face. Relaxed and transparent were not words she'd use to describe Caleb Wright. Sexy? Maddening? Confusing? Yeah. Those.

"When Ashley left me and Bethany behind like gum she'd scraped off the bottom of her shoe, I vowed I'd never open myself up for hurt like that again." He stopped and stared out over the harbor to the undeveloped side below Erin's cottage and Roger's huge white house.

Lillian leaned against one of the tall poles lining this side of the walkway and watched him. It was clear he was struggling, but she didn't know if it was because of the message or the memories.

"I find it hard to warm up to people and let them in."

Understatement, but okay. She took another sip of her drink.

"You know my thoughts about why you were here when you first arrived." He ran a hand through his short hair. "Then, I watched you with Roger and decided I'd been wrong about you." He looked over at her. "I don't have to tell you what happened from there. We both know there is something between us, chemistry-wise. I let my guard down for the first time in ages. We…" He closed his eyes and opened them again. "We almost…"

Deep breath. The guy had been wounded and abandoned with a baby to raise. She suspected the whole grumpy demeanor was a defense he used to keep people at arm's length. For a while on his sofa, he'd let down the armor that he'd built around himself for a decade and a half, and it spooked him. It made sense.

A gull flew overhead with a loud screech and landed on a piling close to the houseboat, and the dogs charged toward it. "I'm a grown, independent woman," she said. "I know who I am and what I want. I want to spend time with you, Caleb. Neither of us have any misconceptions about my leaving. If that scares you, I understand. But if it doesn't…"

The dogs barked and jumped under the piling where the seagull ignored them. After a few more moments of enthusiastic barking, the bird gave up and flew away.

"I like you, Lillian Mahoney," Caleb said, shoving his hands into his pockets. "It's been a long time since I've felt anything for a woman, and here I am, attracted to someone who has an expiration date."

A whistle came from the deck of the big sailboat. Gus waved both hands over his head. Next to him was a man wearing a dress shirt and tie.

"That's my client ready for his walk-through." He stared at her as if looking into her thoughts. "I apologize for avoiding you the last couple of days."

She smiled. "Done and gone." Like she would be soon. Again, that coil tightened in her chest. "My offer to watch the sunset from my porch still stands."

He took a deep breath, studied her for a long moment, then slowly grinned. "Yeah. I think I'll take you up on it."

Her heart pitter-pattered. Dang. The man should smile more often. The back view wasn't bad, either, she conceded as he strode down the dock toward the *Elizabeth's Wish*, his dogs loping at his feet.

Amanda was practically pressed to the glass of her store as Lillian approached, not even attempting to pretend she hadn't been watching them.

"And?" she asked, beaded earrings swinging below her dark curls.

"I'll never tell," she said. "I have to go. My first online conference starts at three."

"Wanna join me and Cassidy for wine on the deck tonight?"

"Thanks for the invite. Ordinarily I'd say yes, but I have a lot of work to do this evening."

Like wait for sunset on her porch, hoping to make Amanda five dollars richer.

CHAPTER NINETEEN

Caleb pulled up in front of Roger's guest house about thirty minutes before sunset. Plenty of time to make sure the old guy was okay before heading over to Lillian's porch. Maybe he could find out what the tension was between Roger and Lillian.

From the porch, he could hear the TV blaring. Roger would benefit from hearing aids. Maybe he'd mention that to Lillian so she could help him with that before she left.

He put a hand over the pain in his sternum. He hated this feeling that almost crippled him when he thought about her.

There was a large, bradded envelope addressed to Roger from a law firm on the doormat, so he picked it up, then knocked on the door. Roger didn't answer. He probably couldn't hear the pounding over the TV. After several more attempts, Caleb opened the unlocked door and stepped inside. "Roger?" he shouted.

"E! Choose E!" Roger hollered at the TV.

"No, there is not a K," the host of *Wheel of Fortune* said.

Caleb walked around the edge of the room so that Roger could see him from a distance and wouldn't be spooked.

"E!" he shouted again.

"Roger!" Caleb called, waving his arms.

Not showing any surprise at all, Roger held up his finger, indicating he should wait a moment.

"Sorry, no Q," the host said.

"Who in their right mind chooses the letter Q if there is no U and they haven't revealed the E?" Roger said. "Buncha dummies!"

Caleb set the envelope on the coffee table in front of Roger. This was going to be a little while.

While waiting for the bonus round to end, Caleb wandered the house. Lillian had worked miracles. On the refrigerator, there was a calendar with a medication chart and grocery list that Roger could check off as he ran out of things. The list even had corresponding grocery store aisle numbers, and, he noticed, it moved from the left side of the store to the right in order with frozen foods near the end. Roger's car key hung on a hook by the door over an umbrella stand and next to a coatrack, where several types of coats and hats hung. The woman was amazing.

The ending theme song played, and Caleb moved back into the TV room, where Roger was pushing up from his recliner. "Mabel could have won that show if she'd gone on it," he said, turning off the TV with the remote. "I bet Lillian could win it, too."

No doubt, she could. "How's it going?"

He looked confused. "Fine. Why?"

Roger was smart. Being honest was by far the best strategy. "You acted like maybe you weren't feeling well at the diner, and I was told you'd put Lillian off, not letting her come help you," Caleb said.

Roger nodded. "All true. I'm fine. Want a beer?"

"No, thanks."

The old man stared at him like he was a bug under glass. "Why do you stay in Blink?"

That was a weird question. "My folks are here, and so's my daughter."

That appeared to frustrate him. "What about after your daughter leaves? Because she will, you know. They all leave. Will you stay then?"

Caleb put his hand on the back of the sofa nearest him. "Yes."

"Why?" The guy's eyes were intense—almost challenging.

"I grew up here. My parents are here. My business is here."

"Your parents won't be here forever. You can work on boats anywhere."

Caleb didn't understand the reason for this line of questioning at all. Something was really eating at the guy.

Roger walked to the kitchen, snagged two cans of beer from the fridge, and returned to the TV room. "Cassidy stays because of her dad. Luke stays because of Cassidy. I have no earthly idea why Amanda Miller stays here. She's gotta be losing money hand over fist. That family you're helping—"

"The Lassiters."

"Yeah. David's kin." He handed Caleb one of the beers and popped the top on his own. "They stay because Junior works in the mill nearby and they got the land from his daddy." He shook his head. "They're still trying to pay off the remainder of what David Senior owed when he died. They're too broke to go anywhere else with all those kids."

"Why all this concern over why people stay?" Caleb asked, opening his beer.

"Just been thinking, that's all." He sat in a chair across from the sofa. "As much as I can tell, there's no single thing that keeps people here, but there are definite things that cause them to leave."

Caleb waited, but the guy simply sipped his beer pensively. Oh, no. He wasn't going to just lob that ball up in the air and not spike it. "And those are?"

He ticked them off on his fingers. "They leave to seek financial gain, adventure, and comfort."

That seemed solid. Maybe the guy was having an old-age meltdown of some kind that was causing this whole questioning-Blink's-existence business.

"Seems to me, that's what would attract people to stay here, too, not just leave, if we offered those things." He met Caleb's eyes. "If Lillian's pie wins, people will come here next year."

He nodded.

Roger looked tired as he rested back in the chair. "She wants me to list the harbor properties for sale."

Well, that would explain the tension between them. He kept his face expressionless.

Roger leaned forward. "What do you think are the chances of someone buying and rehabbing one of those businesses in time to attract people to move here?"

About zero. "I have no idea."

"Yeah, you do."

Caleb took a swallow of beer.

"Winning a pie contest will only get people here from places right nearby. They already live in the area—that won't attract any new residents. Successful towns like Booth Bay and Bar Harbor have strong tourism campaigns. We have no way of doing that, even if we had something worth visiting." He shook his head. "I like Lillian, but once she goes back to New York, we'll be the last thing on her mind. She'll forget all about us like everyone else does."

Every time he thought about her leaving, Caleb's chest ached. This was no exception.

"I'm not inclined to sell the property. No point in it." He upended his beer, then gave a satisfied belch. "Thanks for dropping by."

That was it? Honestly, he was more concerned about Roger now than he was back at the diner. He stood and moved to the front door. "Lillian coming by tomorrow to help you out?"

Roger nodded, following him to the door. "She is. You should drop in."

"I can't. I'll be working on the Lassiter house."

"Good to know." He smiled, saluted him with his empty beer, and shut the door.

Why, Caleb wondered as he got into his truck, did he feel like he'd just gotten played by Old Man McGuffy?

· · ·

Lillian chased the bite of smoky aged cheddar with a sip of wine.

"That was delicious," Caleb said, popping the last olive

in his mouth before sitting back in her new porch swing and rubbing his stomach.

She'd thrown the charcuterie board together at the last minute when she'd seen him pull up at Roger's—a frustrating task with limited kitchen supplies. "Thanks for bringing the wine," she said, pouring herself a second glass.

"I can't take credit for that." He placed his arm over the back of the swing behind her. "Amanda sent it."

Lillian smiled. That woman really wanted to win that bet. The sun had set about thirty minutes ago, and now the moon was rising, making the surface of the water twinkle like dancing diamonds. This truly was a magical place. She was going to miss it.

And there went that coil tightening in her chest again.

"So, I spoke with Roger this evening," he said.

"I saw your truck over there. Is everything okay?"

He sighed and trailed his fingers absently over her shoulder. "I think so. He mentioned you had pushed him to sell the harbor properties."

"I *suggested*. I didn't push. Not yet, anyway."

He set the swing into motion, gently rocking. "Don't waste your time."

She sat forward and put her feet on the ground, stopping the swing with a jolt. She was too stunned to even come up with a suitable response. After a moment and a couple of deep breaths, she said, "Why would saving Blink be a waste of time?"

"Trying to convince Old Man McGuffy to turn loose of property is a waste of time. Saving Blink is impossible."

She opened her mouth to argue, but he put a finger to

her lips. She'd seen the finger-over-the-lips move done in movies, but nobody had ever done it to her before. If she had her way, nobody ever would again. She pushed his hand away. "Don't try to silence me, Caleb Wright. I only get louder."

He covered his face with his hands and took a deep breath. "Hear me out first."

"Fine." Like a pouting child, she crossed her arms over her chest and sat back in the swing, giving a hard kick to set it into motion.

"The people who come here for the pie contest next year if Blink wins—"

"*When* Blink wins."

"*When* Blink wins, will be residents of local communities. They won't have any desire at all to move here. They already live nearby. It'll be like opening your house to neighbors."

"Yes, but it's good if there are businesses in place. They will gain customers, perhaps long-term ones if it is a unique service. And perhaps news will spread by word of mouth."

"He won't sell those properties on the hopes of a single day of success. And nobody is going to buy a business where they will certainly fail."

She knew this was all true, and it wasn't news. "I have a longer-range plan."

This time he was the one to stop the swing. When she looked over at him, he was searching her face.

"I have several upcoming episodes that will feature photos and mentions of Blink."

The swing began to rock again. Clearly, he wasn't impressed.

"Living Sharpe has a massive base. We have a lot of reach with our products and features," she said.

"I'm sure you do." He put his arm over the back of the bench again. "I'll leave that between you and Roger. I just wanted to tell you what he'd said so you'd be prepared. I don't have a boat in this race."

"But you do. Wright Boat Works and Miller Mercantile have a lot to gain by the harbor being developed."

"That's true for the mercantile, for sure, but I know Roger McGuffy, and a no from him is no."

She needed everyone on board if she was going to find a way to get through Roger's thick skull and make a difference here, especially since she would be doing most of it from another state. It was urgent she get Caleb's cooperation.

A chill ran down her spine as Caleb ran his fingers over the bare skin of her shoulder. Discussing Roger lost its urgency when he touched her like this.

An owl hooted nearby, and another answered from somewhere in the distance. "I understand why you love this place," she said. "It's natural. Honest." Like him. "It has no pretense."

He trailed his fingers over her upper arm, leaving warmth in their path. "All things to admire," he said.

For a while, they rocked as he rhythmically stroked her arm, causing her entire body to heat.

"What are we doing?" she whispered, as much to herself as to him.

His fingers stilled. "I don't know."

Neither did she, and it scared her. She liked this man. Really liked him. Probably more than any man she'd ever met. And she wanted him. But for some reason, at this moment, the stakes seemed too high. Like there'd be no going back.

She stood. "I have to be at Roger's pretty early. I still have some work to do before I go to sleep."

He rose and picked up the battered wooden cutting board she'd used to stage their snack. "Let me help you clean up."

If he came into her house, she was pretty sure he wouldn't leave until tomorrow, and she was all jumbled up inside. Earlier today, she'd been like, oh, yeah, casual, brief affair? No biggie. But now she felt like she was standing on top of a cliff about to make a life-altering leap. "I'll get it," she said, taking the board from him and setting it back on the table. "Thanks for sharing the sunset with me."

His gaze dropped to her mouth, and she found herself wetting her lips.

"I really want to kiss you," he said.

"I really want you to."

So he did. For a long, long time, with roaming hands and dancing tongues until she was sure she'd pass out from the sheer intensity of his touch. Finally, he pulled away, cool air rushing against her flushed skin where they'd touched.

"I'll see you tomorrow," he said with a nip to her earlobe that made her knees wobble.

"Bye." Her voice was ridiculously breathy, but dang the man could kiss.

After his truck was out of sight, she scooped up the board and napkins from the table and took them to the kitchen, returning to collect the wine bottle and glasses. As she reached for the bottle, she noticed Roger in the kitchen window of his guest house tucked into the moon shadow of the huge Victorian home. She couldn't see more than his silhouette from this distance, but she waved. He waved back.

CHAPTER TWENTY

Roger was waiting out front with a sweater in his lap when Lillian arrived. He stood. "We are going on a little trip today, Miss Mahoney. Would you mind if we took your car? I haven't ridden in a convertible since I was your age."

She stopped on the bottom step. "Sure. I'll go get it."

"I'll come with you," he said. "A walk will do me good."

This was different. Ordinarily, he was complaining about aches and pains and how hard it was to walk. Today, he seemed almost spry.

"My father loved this hillside," he said, gesturing to the area of pines stretching above her cottage. "When I was a boy, he said he'd build cabins for me and my siblings on this hillside so we could all be together."

"Did you have a big family?" she asked.

"No. It was only me. They wanted more children, but it never happened. They kept trying and hoping, though. Then, they set their sights on grandkids, but I was a big disappointment. Met Mabel when I was in my late forties." He waggled his eyebrows. "A younger woman. I was fifty-four when Tristan was born."

That meant his doctor son was quite young.

"Don't do it," he said, still looking up at the pine trees.

"What?"

"Don't wait until you're old to finally live." He stopped and paused until she met his eyes. "Don't waste yourself on a job or a goal. Give your love and talent to someone who can love you back."

Whoa. Roger was in a pensive mood today. She gave him what she hoped was an appreciative smile and not a grimace.

"I'm serious," he said when they reached her car. "You have helped me immensely. You've given me your time and expertise, and I want to give you something in return. I know you're a successful businesswoman and you don't need financial compensation, but you do need advice."

"I do?" She didn't know whether she should be touched or offended.

"You do. You are utterly lost, Lillian Mahoney."

She should be offended, she decided. She was the most put-together person she knew. Everyone said so.

He opened the door and got in the car, running his hand fondly over Bessie's dash. "Nice," he said. "But it's not practical. You'll need to trade this car for something more suited for the snow up here."

Good thing that wouldn't be an issue in New York and Long Island and the paved roads between. She gritted her teeth and forced a smile. "Where to?"

• • •

"Car, mommy! Car, car, car!" one of the Lassiter kids shrieked so loudly, Caleb bumped his head on the bottom of the drawer he was working on.

Rubbing the back of his skull, Caleb smiled, remembering how excited Bethany would get when a car would pull into the parking lot near the shop. He wiped his hands on his jeans and shoved the screwdriver back into his toolbelt. He tested the drawer, happy with his adjustment to the rollers.

Two other kids had joined the first as they hopped with excitement at the big window he'd installed only last week.

The littlest one, Tommy, used his chubby fingers to pull up on the windowsill to see out. "Red car go zoom!" He tottered back to the ugly sofa, grabbed one of the Hot Wheels toys Luke had given him, and ran back to the window, rolling the car over the recently dried paint, shouting, "Zoom! Zoom!"

Their mother, Glory, joined them, wiping her hands on a dish towel over her shoulder. "I wonder who that is with Mr. McGuffy?" She smoothed her straight black hair with her hands and brushed off the front of her shirt.

If Tommy knew his colors, then Caleb was certain who it was, and his heart kicked up at the thought. The woman did a real number on him.

"I want all of you on your best behavior," Glory warned her exuberant pack of kids, who were squealing and jumping up and down at the prospect of visitors. "Settle down, or I'm not opening the door." That got the older ones' attention, but not the two littlest, who were still bouncing like bunnies. "Sit on the sofa," their mother ordered, hands on her hips. She'd used that universal tool employed by all moms: the *I-mean-business* voice. It worked.

Caleb moved to where he had a view of the driveway. Lillian was giving Roger a hand climbing out of her low convertible. The top was down, and her hair had been blown around, leaving it wild and free—a far cry from her usual look. Gone were the spindly heels and tailored clothes, replaced by hiking boots and blue jeans. Like she belonged here.

But she didn't. She's leaving, he reminded himself.

Glory opened the door, glancing back to give her squirming kids another mom favorite: the *don't-you-dare-move* look.

"Mr. McGuffy! What a surprise. Please come in," Glory said.

"This is a friend of mine, Lillian Mahoney," he said.

The women shook hands, and the visitors stepped inside.

"These are my children." Glory gestured to the five wiggling kids on the sofa. "Clara, Dana, Lucy, David, and Tommy."

"I'm Tommy!" the littlest shouted.

"We're on our best behavior," David said.

Mr. McGuffy shuffled to the sofa to greet the children, and Caleb recognized the envelope from last night as he placed it on an end table next to the sofa. "You're Clara?" he asked.

"Yessir," the girl of about ten or eleven answered.

"You must be named after your grandmother," he said. The girl nodded. "She was a good woman. Do you like lollipops?"

"I like lollipops!" Tommy shrieked. David gave him an elbow to the ribs.

Roger winked at Glory and gave the three girls lollipops after asking about their favorite colors and being assured they were going to work hard in school.

"You're David," Roger said.

The little boy held up three fingers. "My daddy is also David. I'm David three!"

"You and your father are named after your grandfather, David Lassiter." The boy nodded. "He was a dear friend of mine," Roger said. "He worked very hard. So does your father. Do you work very hard?"

"Yessir," the boy said, puffing out his chest.

"What do you want to be when you grow up?" Roger asked.

"I want to work in the mill with my dad, and when he owns the mill, I want to be a foreman like he is now."

Caleb had to look away for a moment. Their father was a foreman at a huge, corporate-owned timber mill twenty miles away. He would never own the mill. He would never advance further than his current job, which, despite the title, hardly fed his family. Yet his kid wanted to follow in his footsteps. That would change, of course, and little David would move away to get a better job, unless, like his father, he started a family right out of high school and had to do what it took to survive.

"I'm Tommy, and this is my new car Luke gave me, see?" He held up the battered toy for Roger's inspection.

"A very fine car." He handed David and Tommy lollipops. Tommy ripped his open and shoved it in his mouth right away.

"May we open them, Momma?" Clara asked, giving her littlest brother a glare.

Glory nodded. "You may. Wrappers in the trash. Please go outside to play while we visit, kids."

In a whirlwind of pent-up energy and excitement, the

five children hopped, bounced, and skipped their way out of the room, dumping lollipop wrappers in the trash can at the back door on the way out.

It was like the house held its breath in the silence left behind when the children were gone.

"Wow. You have your hands full," Lillian said. "They are lovely kids."

Glory's taut face relaxed. "I'll be glad when school starts and I can get settled in. Everyone has been so fantastic." Her eyes brimmed with tears. "This will be our first night in the new house. I..." She closed her eyes and took a deep breath. "I don't know what we would have done if..." She acted like she'd heard something in the backyard. "Excuse me for a moment. I need to check on the kids." She ran out the back door.

"She's pretty emotional," Caleb said, stating the obvious. "She keeps it together in front of the kids, but she's gone weepy on me a few times today when we were alone."

"That's understandable," Roger said. "They'd be homeless right now." He patted Caleb on the shoulder. "You did good." From his rapid blinking, it appeared Roger was choked up himself. "Gonna go look around." He shuffled out of view into the kitchen.

The air seemed to charge when they were alone. Not with the frenetic energy of the children but with something more direct.

"Good morning," Caleb said, taking a step closer to her.

She smiled and brushed some hair back off her forehead. "Good morning. This place is really nice. You built it?"

It was pretty basic. Nothing fancy, but it was well-built and clean. "I had a lot of help, and the residents of Blink raised the funds, but yes. I did a good part of the work," he said.

She looked him up and down. "And here I thought you were just eye candy."

"Only if you have a sweet tooth." He hadn't known what to expect after the kiss on her porch, but he and his rapidly heating body loved her teasing.

She put her hands on her hips. "Why, Grumpy Caleb. If I didn't know better, I'd think you had a sense of humor."

"I have a lot of things. Wanna see?"

Blush flushed from her neck all the way to where her hairline began. He loved this side of her. All-business Lillian liked a good flirt. He was happy to oblige. "Grumpy Caleb?"

"That shoe seems to fit," she said as she strode toward the kitchen with a grin. He followed.

Instead of checking out the house, Roger was staring out the window at the kids playing with Caleb's dogs and climbing trees. Beyond them, Glory was wiping her eyes with her dish towel.

Lillian opened a drawer, then another and another. Then opened cabinets like she was looking for something, then opened the cabinet next to the refrigerator. "These are the dishes from Roger's house."

Caleb nodded. "She received some pots from her cousins, too. Glory says they're all set."

Lillian looked in the refrigerator and pantry, then pulled out her phone.

"They're good kids," Roger said, still staring out the window. "I should have come by before now. I just got hung up in my own life, what with Mabel's cancer and then the funeral. I lost sight of things."

"That's understandable," Caleb said.

He noticed Lillian was frantically typing on her phone, face tight with concentration.

"I hadn't known Junior was in such trouble, or I'd have done something. I figured that big company paid him fine," Roger said.

"You contributed most of the money for the materials for the rebuild," Caleb said. "And you paid for insurance on this one."

"The other house should have been insured. I had no idea." Roger shook his head. "They were left with debt on the land and no place to live when the house burned down. It's a miracle none of those kids were killed."

The fire had been from a space heater shorting out when the house was empty. Glory was at the school bus stop with all the kids, waiting to send the three oldest off, and David Jr. had already left for work. The house didn't have heat, so they were using an old space heater. Glory said she had turned it off, but Tommy, who was crawling at the time, was fascinated with buttons and knobs. David said he saw him playing with it before they left, but that might have had nothing to do with it. By the time the volunteer fire department from the next town over arrived, there was nothing left but ashes. With no insurance, no further inquiry was necessary.

"So did you just come by to check out the work?" Caleb asked. Roger had been a little off the last few days, and his presence here was out of character.

"That and to drop off some paperwork for Glory and Junior."

Lillian looked up from her phone long enough to give them a smile that made his heart skip a little. "Want to see the rest of the house?" he asked. "The bedrooms and playroom are upstairs."

"Sure. You coming, Roger?" she asked.

He was looking at them with a strange expression on his face. The same one he gave before closing the door on Caleb last night. "No. You two go ahead. My knees and all."

Halfway up the stairs, Lillian muttered, "His knees were fine when he insisted on walking to my car from his house this morning. He's up to something."

She followed him down the hallway, glancing into the rooms on both sides of the long hall. He stopped at the big room at the end. "This is being used as the master right now, and the playroom is downstairs, but I built it so that when the kids were old enough, they could swap the use of spaces. Master down and playroom and kids' bedrooms up."

"That's a great idea," she said. "You're brilliant."

He knew better, but her saying it made him want to preen like his mom's rooster. "Thanks. It's a big improvement over the house that burned. This one is six bedrooms—small ones—and three baths. The last house was three bedrooms and one bath with only a small living area and no playroom."

"I'll say it again. You're a good man, Caleb Wright," she said, reaching out to stroke his cheek.

Her touch lit him on fire, and he pulled her against him. She let out a squeak at the contact with his toolbelt.

"There are so many jokes I could crack right now." She glanced down and flicked his hammer with her finger, then covered her mouth as she giggled. A door closed downstairs, followed by the joyful chatter of kids. She looked over her shoulder towards the stairs and then back at him. "No time to show me your handyman skills right now. We should get downstairs."

"The doors lock," he whispered in her ear.

"I take it back. You're not brilliant. You're impossible." After a brief peck on the lips, she pushed him away and hurried down the stairs.

Impossible. That was the right word. He was in an impossible situation. His best move would be to pull the plug on his attraction to this woman. She was leaving. And so, evidently, had his senses. He was going to get hurt. Bad. This wasn't like Ashley, who had ripped his heart out and he hadn't seen it coming. He had advance warning this time, and still, he was forging ahead, flirting and hoping and... He shook his head. It would be worth it. He'd regret not being with her if he took the safe path. Having her for a week was better than not having her at all.

He found them in the living room. Everyone had circled around Roger again, who was passing out another round of lollipops, clearly loving the attention. After he made it around the circle, he picked up the bradded envelope he'd laid on the end table.

"This is for you and your husband, my dear," he said to Glory. "I want you to promise me you will put it in a safe place and will not open it until Junior gets home. Will you do that?"

She took the packet from his hand. "Yes. I promise." As if to prove it, she opened one of the empty cabinets and placed it on the top shelf.

"Mr. McGuffy," she said as he made his way to the door. "Thank you for coming to see us." She put her hands on little David's shoulders. "When the house burned down, I thought we were going to have to leave Blink. And that was worse than losing the house." She gestured to the window. "David says we're like those trees. Our roots go way down deep. Too deep to even burn out."

He nodded and followed Lillian out the door. "I feel the same way."

From the porch, Caleb watched them drive off in the convertible, Roger waving to the kids as Lillian's hair whipped wildly around her face.

Yesterday, Roger had asked him why he stayed, and now he understood. Glory had said it perfectly. His roots went way down. Too deep to even burn out.

CHAPTER TWENTY-ONE

Lillian wasn't ordinarily an emotional person, but something about being at that house had pulled up all kinds of feelings she wasn't sure how to deal with.

She glanced over to see Roger smiling away, like he had a big secret. The little tufts of hair lining his bald head were dancing around in the wind as they traveled up the road east of the harbor leading to a heavily wooded area. "You going to tell me where we're going?"

"We're taking a trip down memory lane," he said. "Take a left at the next road. It's coming right up."

She slowed and turned onto the narrow, blacktop road that dead-ended at a gate. Roger pulled a ring of keys out of his pocket and got out of the car.

"Bad knees my butt," she muttered as he unlocked the gate and gestured for her to drive through.

He left the gate open behind them. She pulled into a parking lot in front of a large, metal building. There were several other buildings nearby, all of them boarded up with faded "no trespassing" signs on them.

Above the door of the closest one, there was a battered sign that read McGuffy Mill. She glanced over at him. He was looking at her, not the building.

"We used to employ thirty-five to fifty men, depending on the season. That doesn't include drivers who delivered the product or woodsmen who supplied us. I figure the mill helped support near a hundred people, maybe more."

Caleb had told her his family were timber barons. There probably weren't thirty-five men of working age in Blink anymore.

"Today, the big corporations dominate the market and most of the equipment is fully automated, making it easy to run a mill with a fraction of the manpower and a much higher output."

"Is that why this mill is closed?" she asked.

He shook his head. "No. It's closed because of spite… and foolishness." He looked down at his age-spotted hands, then patted his knees. "I've seen enough. Take me home now."

Putting the car in gear, she gave herself a mental shake. She felt like the Ghost of Christmas Past taking Scrooge for a tour. What was up with this guy? She'd planned to talk to him about his harbor properties today, but with his odd behavior, she decided to put that off.

"So, we're almost finished with your house organization," she said. In truth, they were completely finished, but she was reluctant to let go. This old man had grown on her over the course of the makeover. Especially after seeing him with the Lassiter kids today. He clearly loved children. She wondered if his son, Tristan, was married or had any kids.

"Maybe we should tackle the main house," he said.

Part of her was thrilled by that suggestion. The other part knew it wasn't possible. "That's a big project. You know that I have to leave soon. I have a business to run," she said.

"For twenty years, I basically ran a business from the diner," he said. "Has your business suffered from your absence? I know you have meeting after meeting with your people through that computer of yours after you leave my house."

"It's not the same," she said, slowing to take the turn toward the harbor.

"You're right. It's probably better." He made a har-umph sound. "Better for you, anyway."

In truth, Living Sharpe seemed to be rolling along just fine without her, which kind of stung. At the start, she did everything, but now she had layout designers, food stagers, photographers, scriptwriters, researchers, and the most important thing, her sister, who did the hardest job in addition to lots of other things. She managed the unmanageable Niles.

For just a moment...no, less than a moment. For a nanosecond, she imagined staying. Staying in this beautiful place with its warm, loving people—and one large, grumpy man—but then reality prevailed. Even amazing Erin would burn out eventually. In fact, the last few times they'd spoken privately, she'd seemed stressed. Niles was probably doing a number on her patience. Lillian had to return home, and she needed to do it sooner rather than later.

When she hit the T at the harbor, she turned left, up the road to Roger's. She noticed he was craning his neck to see the harbor.

"That sailboat from Michigan is gone. I suppose Caleb and Gus finished it."

She nodded, still a little raw from his remark that being here was better for her than being back home, realizing the reason that had made her uncomfortable is that it was probably accurate. She did feel better here. Better than she had in years.

"He likes you," Roger said. When she didn't respond, he added, "Caleb Wright," as if she didn't know who he was talking about. Of course, she knew who he was talking about, and she was certain he had faked the knee thing at the Lassiter house so they'd be alone together. He'd also insisted she take him to the Lassiters' for some reason she suspected was bigger than putting her and Caleb together. And then there was the Ghost of Christmas Past field trip to the abandoned mill.

She pulled up in front of the main house and killed the engine. When he reached to open the door, she hit the lock button. "What are you up to, Roger McGuffy?"

"Getting out of your car," he answered innocently. "Nothing more."

"Mmm-hmm," she said. "And I'm the Easter Bunny." She hit the unlock button, and he got out before she could get around to help him. The bit when they had pulled up in front of the Lassiters' had been a ruse, too.

He closed the car door and gave her a wave over his shoulder. "I'll see you tomorrow."

"I'm onto you, Roger," she called. "Playing up the feeble-old-man bit doesn't work on me. Your mind is a sharp as it's ever been, and I know you're up to something."

He waved again and disappeared into his house. The coward.

For a minute, she relaxed in the driver's seat, eyes closed, enjoying the sun warming her skin. August in Maine was perfect. Highs in the seventies, lows in the fifties—about ten degrees cooler than back home. At home, she would be sitting out at her pool—

Yeah, right. She'd never once used the pool. She'd never used any of the bells and whistles of the huge Long Island estate. She'd enjoyed as much leisure there as she did when she was working from her apartment in Manhattan. Maybe she should sell that apartment. She couldn't imagine ever living there again, and it wasn't worth keeping it for the two dozen or so nights she spent there when meeting with Manhattan-based contacts. Honestly, she could sell the estate, too. They could build a stage kitchen and living area and film there. She could downsize.

"Simplify," she said out loud.

She'd thought that getting bigger and going grander and looking the part were essential to her success and that her success was what would make her happy. And it did, to some degree. But maybe she was confusing satisfaction with happiness.

"Oh, my God. Stop!" she scolded herself. Roger was getting to her. Caleb was getting to her. This place with its roots too deep to burn was getting to her. She yanked her car door open and stomped to the house, pulling out her phone.

"Hey, Erin. Let's brainstorm for next year's Christmas special. How about something like Mistletoe in Manhattan? A big-city angle of some kind." Anything but the heartbreaking pull of a small town. When she turned to close the door, the sun was shining off the water in the harbor, making it look like a sapphire set in the stony hollow of the cove. On the walkway near the houseboat, Scout and Willy were on seagull patrol, and leaning against one of the tall poles stood Caleb, arms folded over his ribs, face turned up in her direction.

That coil in her chest was going to break if it wound any tighter. "Yeah, a celebration of big-city life," she said to her sister as she closed the door.

CHAPTER TWENTY-TWO

"She says she's in a meeting," Amanda said, filing her neon green nails at one of the tables on the deck outside her store.

Caleb stared out over the water, pretending he wasn't acutely interested.

"Tell her to hurry up." Cassidy threw a piece of cracker to a gull.

"Stop that," Amanda said, taking the sleeve of crackers from her. "I know your house isn't on the water, but that's a no-no." She pointed up at the gull, squawking and circling. "Flying poop machines."

Scout and Willy barked furiously at the bird, who would have given them the middle finger if it had fingers. Caleb had to give the dogs points for effort. They never gave up on hassling the gulls. Just like he never gave up wishing for something he couldn't have. She was leaving. Case in point: Amanda and Cassidy were planning Lillian's going-away party and wanted her opinion.

"I think we should have an NYC theme," Cassidy said. "Play Frank Sinatra, serve pizza. Give her a taste-of-home send-off."

"We don't even know what day she's leaving yet," Amanda said, holding her hand out to check out her ghastly green nails. Why did she do that? Make herself so...bright.

"When is she leaving, Caleb?" Cassidy asked.

"How would I know?"

Both women groaned and gave each other that look that says *men = worthless*.

"Because you're..." Amanda made a baffling helicopter motion with her arms, causing her numerous bracelets to clatter. "You know."

He had no clue what her flailing meant. He wasn't sure he wanted to.

"Because you're hot on her and she's hot right back," Cassidy said.

That. Yes. He didn't answer, knowing that would get under Amanda's skin like nothing else could. He liked Amanda. She was funny and genuinely loved Blink and its people. She was also great fun to tease because she could dish it out as well as take it.

Cassidy was a bit stiffer, probably because she was dealing with her dad's illness. Handyman Hank was anything but handy these days, and it was taking a toll on his bubbly daughter. Still, she was here, enjoying herself with Amanda, which meant the home healthcare nurse was working out. It also freed up Luke, who was having to grow up way too fast.

"Oh, wait. She just texted back. Meeting ended. She's on her way down, now," Amanda said. She pointed a green-tipped finger at him and swirled it around. "Go change."

He looked down at himself. His clothes weren't dirty. "Why?"

"Because you look like *you*," Amanda said.

"Because you're in work clothes and should dress up to catch her eye," Cassidy clarified.

He arched an eyebrow. "I've already caught her eye."

Both women squealed and high-fived.

No matter how long he lived, he'd never understand this kind of behavior. Bethany made him know this deep down. He'd never get it. Never.

"Go change into something *not* blue," Amanda ordered. "We'll put the spaghetti on. Bring back beer if you have any."

"Yes ma'am," he called back.

"And bring Bethany if she's there," Cassidy added.

"She's with Shemom and Shedad," he said.

Pulling on a not-blue shirt—a red one he'd gotten from a client with the name of a fishing boat emblazoned across the back—he noticed Bethany had left her door open. In neat stacks on her bed, she'd laid out supplies for her "camping" trip tomorrow in which, he reminded himself with relief, she wouldn't stay overnight. She'd offered to take items for dinner, and she'd organized plasticware, plates, napkins, and cups on her bed. Two six-packs of soda and chips were on the kitchen counter, along with bread and condiments for hot dogs, which he assumed were in the refrigerator. There were also marshmallows, chocolate bars, and graham crackers. She and her grandparents had been busy.

He knew she was still disappointed at not staying overnight, but this was a good compromise Lillian had orchestrated.

Lillian. He wondered how long after she left she'd still permeate his life like fog, penetrating everything, even his relationship with his daughter. He grabbed a six-pack of Bud from the fridge.

"Caleb!" Amanda called. "Hurry up! There's an emergency!"

Adrenaline spiked, making his muscles tense and his heart race. Beer in hand, he ran for the deck in front of the mercantile. "What's wrong?" he asked, finding Amanda, Cassidy, and Lillian casually seated at a table.

"Beer emergency," Amanda said, holding her hand out. "I broke a nail."

. . .

Lillian's breath caught when Caleb charged out of his houseboat, expression intense and concerned, looking like he was going to put out a fire—with beer.

"Are you kidding me?" he asked, breathing deep.

"This is serious." Amanda turned her hand to show Caleb the broken nail.

"Hi, Lillian," he said, ignoring Amanda. "Beer?" He pulled one out of the plastic ring and handed it to her. Then handed one to Cassidy.

"What about me?" Amanda asked.

"With a situation that serious, Amanda"—he waved at her hand—"I don't think you should drink. You need to keep a clear head."

"You're about to *lose* your head, buster. Hand me a beer. I don't want to break another nail punching you."

Lillian studied him as he coaxed a beer free and teased Amanda with it by pulling it back every time she reached for it. He had a sense of humor and a playful side, and she found it attractive. Too attractive. It was easier when he was hot Grumpy Guy she wanted to kiss. Now he was multifaceted, charming, generous, humorous, hot Grumpy Guy she wanted to keep.

Keep. Nope. She was leaving. Soon. There could only be kissing. No keeping.

Amanda grabbed the beer and popped the top using a plastic spoon. "What's all this?" She gestured to the papers Lillian had placed on the table along with several packs of gum she'd borrowed from the sales counter.

She grinned and arranged the papers in order, placing a pack of gum on each one to hold it in place in the sea breeze. Only four pages so far, but it was a beginning. Eventually, she'd send them a bound notebook detailing all aspects of the event, like she did for Living Sharpe.

She needed Amanda and Cassidy to be her boots on the ground here. Planning something this size was quite a task. "It's the start of a proposal for next year's pie contest Blink will host."

"We haven't won yet," Amanda said, examining her chipped nail.

"We will." Cassidy lifted her beer in salute to Lillian. "No doubt about it."

Caleb was leaning against the deck railing, watching his dogs sniffing something near the boat slips.

Lillian nodded and placed the final page, weighing it down with a pack of Juicy Fruit. "Traditionally, I'm told, there is a bake sale hosted by the winning church and music and then, of course, the contest. I think we need to take it further to attract more people."

She pointed to the page where she'd sketched out the harbor. "Instead of hosting it at the church, we'll host it here, at the harbor."

Amanda made a *tsk*ing sound. "That's not going to go over well with Fran and her posse of church ladies."

Lillian gave her a sly smile. "That's where you come in. You, Amanda Miller, are going to be the venue director."

Amanda gave her a skeptical look. "Again, we have to win first."

"*Again*, we're *going* to win," Cassidy said. "You didn't get a taste of that pie, or you'd understand. Right, Caleb?"

Caleb nodded. "It's a helluva pie."

Face warming with a delighted blush, Lillian pointed to a spot on the hand-drawn map of the harbor. "We can host the judging in this big open area in front of Wright Boat Works." She glanced over at Amanda. "The church ladies can be in charge of that, which will mitigate the venue issue to some degree, I hope." Lillian opened her arms wide to indicate Amanda's large deck. "And this area can serve as a public meeting and dining space with extra seating provided by rented tables and chairs. We'll use Amanda's bright pink and yellow umbrellas and get some matching tablecloths."

"Extra seating? For an event in Blink?" Amanda opened one of the packs of gum and unwrapped a piece. "Keep dreaming big, Lillian."

"Big dreams yield big results." She had to get Amanda to buy into this. The woman knew everyone here and had a lot of influence. "It's the only way we're going to save this town, and dammit, that's what we're going to do." She surprised herself by slamming a hand down on the table.

There was an awkward beat of silence.

"Well, if anyone can do it, it's the creator of Living

Sharpe," Amanda said.

Lillian rubbed her stinging hand on her thigh. "I can't do it alone."

"I'm in," Cassidy said, lifting an eyebrow at Amanda.

"Okay," Amanda said. "I'm venue director. But I want a T-shirt that says 'director' so I can boss people around." She popped the piece of gum in her mouth.

Caleb snorted. "You boss everyone around anyway."

"What's Caleb's role in this?" Cassidy asked.

"Whatever I tell him to do," Amanda answered, chomping her gum with delight.

"I can do anything that requires tools or paint," Cassidy offered.

"That's going to come in super useful," Lillian said, pointing at her drawing of the harbor again.

Caleb wandered over and studied the drawing from over her shoulder, making her body hum with a warm buzz.

Lillian cleared her throat. "We'll have vendors, like at a fair, so we can get a much bigger crowd. We can place them in the parking lot and along the flatter places around the harbor walkway here and here." She indicated the locations on the map, and she noticed Caleb studying the places she'd indicated, as if he were picturing it in his head. "We charge the vendors enough to cover the cost of the tent and table rentals."

"What about those eyesores?" Cassidy asked, pointing to the two dilapidated stores next to the mercantile. "All the pink and yellow umbrellas and tablecloths in the county won't distract from those."

Lillian looked at the boarded-up structures and sighed,

all her excitement about her plans draining through the bottoms of her feet.

"We could always pass them off as haunted houses or maybe dress them up to look like something out of an old western ghost town set," Cassidy said with a laugh. "They are pretty awful, and probably dangerous if we are going to have people walking around near them. Maybe we could cordon them off with safety tape." She stood and put her empty beer can in the recycling bin at the corner of the deck next to the trash can. "Abandoned buildings are not much of an inducement to get people to visit or move here, though, if that's the goal."

"That's a little tougher," Lillian said. "I'm hoping to somehow convince Roger McGuffy to sell them. Maybe if he won't sell them, he'll consider rehabbing and renting them out. I still have a little time to work on him before I leave." Not much time, she thought as her chest ached inside. She stacked her papers up and placed them in her purse.

Amanda stood. "Speaking of which, we're throwing a going-away party for you. Surprise! When is your last day? We should do it on a Friday night since that's the town's usual party day. What is the last Friday before you leave?"

Her heart hammered, and her breath caught in panic. She'd talked to Erin about this less than an hour ago. This was not a trick question or an unknown. It was a done deal written in her planner. She was leaving next Saturday afternoon, immediately after the pie contest winner was announced. She should be able to just say this. She *would* say this. She'd say *next Friday* right now.

"I don't know."

Oh, crap.

"Well, that's not helpful," Amanda said.

No. It wasn't. Not at all.

When she looked up at Caleb, the intensity in his eyes made her feel restless, like her skin was too tight. She'd said she'd hang around for dinner when she texted Amanda during her Living Sharpe meeting, but there was no way she could do it now. Not even for Cassidy and Amanda. From the way Caleb had begun pacing, she was pretty sure he felt the same way. Today had been too much. Roger, the Lassiters, and now this. Too much. It was like New York and Blink were playing tug-of-war with her heart and were about to rip it in two.

Confident, organized, in-control Lillian Mahoney was being laid low by a vanishing town. A town she was desperately trying to save and a man she wasn't ready to let go of yet.

"I have to go to the cottage," she said, standing abruptly. "I know I said I'd stay, but I can't." At least she still knew when to fold her cards and walk away. And walk away she did. Caleb's dogs padded alongside her, wagging and bouncing all the way to the car. When she opened the door, they jumped in. Perfect. Paw prints on the white leather.

She heard Roger's voice in her head. *It's not practical. You'll need to trade this car for something more suited for the snow up here.*

Closing her eyes, she took a breath through her nose as Blink took the advantage in the tug-of-war.

"Dammit," she said. Both dogs froze, heads down, tails

tucked. She sighed. "Not you. Me."

"Looks like you have company," Caleb said from immediately behind her. "Do you want more?"

So much more. She felt like she was living inside an hourglass that was almost empty. She wanted to treasure every grain of sand she had left. "Yes."

He snapped his fingers and pointed to the houseboat. "Go on home." After longing looks at Lillian and another snap of his fingers, they obeyed. He waited until they had jumped on the deck of the boat. "They have a dog door in from the back of the cabin. There's always food and water. They'll be fine."

The scent of him filled her car—laundry detergent and mint and sea air. The interior seemed to shrink and be filled completely with him.

For a long moment, they stared at each other, and then he took her hand. "Your ideas to help Blink are pretty amazing." She held her breath as he rubbed his thumb over the top of her hand, leaving a trail of heat. "*You* are amazing," he said.

Her panic from earlier subsided, replaced with a feeling of resolve and rightness and overwhelming need.

The drive to her house was silent. They didn't need words. Words weren't necessary when they pulled up outside, or when they entered the cottage, or when they made their way to her bedroom, leaving a trail of clothes behind them.

CHAPTER TWENTY-THREE

Lillian hadn't woken up with a man in her bed in…ever. In fact, she'd never woken up with a man in her bed. Sleeping over was way too intimate, and she'd never allowed it. Until last night.

Tossing her car keys on the counter, she opened the cupboard and pulled out the coffee beans. Her behavior was completely out of character. She put the beans in the grinder. Everything she'd done had been out of character since she'd gotten here. She flipped the switch, and the grinder rumbled. That kiss they'd shared a few minutes ago when she'd dropped him off at his houseboat was way out of character.

Maybe out of character was really her *true* character and she didn't know it until now.

"Oh, for Pete's sake," she muttered, pouring the ground coffee into the basket. She liked who she was here. Not the freaked-out bits like when she'd bolted from Amanda's deck last night, but she liked who she was the rest of the time. More relaxed. More… She thought about last night with Caleb and cleared her throat. Yeah, more that. She liked who she was with him.

She started the coffeemaker and shuffled to the bathroom to get ready to go to Roger's. The woman in the mirror was a total stranger with wild hair and red cheeks caused by abrasion from Caleb's whiskers. And her bathrobe was inside out. Perfect. She'd driven him home like that. She almost laughed. Perfectly put together Lillian Mahoney was a complete inside-out mess, and she didn't care.

Getting herself together was going to take way too much work to attempt it before caffeine, so instead, she wandered to the porch to watch the sunrise until the pot finished brewing.

From the kitchen counter, her phone rang. With a groan, she shuffled into the house.

"Hey, Erin," she said, pouring a cup of coffee in a chipped mug with a lobster under a beach umbrella that said, "Crustacean Vacation."

"You didn't answer last night. Is everything okay?" They had an agreement they would never ignore each other's calls. Erin was the last thing on the mind once she and Caleb had hit the house last night. She hadn't even heard it ringing. She smiled at how that could have happened.

She shuffled back out to the porch. "Sorry. I didn't take my phone to the bedroom last night. I guess I slept through it." Well, the first bit was true, anyway.

The sun was just peeking over the water, sending shafts of gold over the reflective surface.

"So, I've been thinking about these ideas you've been sending."

She checked the time on her phone screen. "Erin. It's not even six o'clock yet. What are you thinking about other than sleep?"

"The same thing you are. Work."

Yeah. Further proof she was behaving way out of character. Work was the last thing on her mind.

"Anyway," her sister continued. "I like this small-town

focus in the ideas you've sent. I really liked the pictures from the party you went to. But the team is concerned that it is too out of character for the brand we've developed."

Lillian rolled her eyes. Out of character. Imagine that. "I think it'll work." It had to work. She had to get some mentions of Blink in there to draw attention to it. She needed to have something to prove to Roger that the town could generate interest. Heck, she'd develop those two empty shops on the harbor herself.

Wait a minute. That wasn't a half-bad idea.

"The team is pretty sure what you sent us won't fly. It's too superficial and not immersive like the rest of our stories and features."

Lillian took a sip of coffee, knowing full well that a proposal was coming. Everyone on her team knew that hard noes didn't happen. There was always a compromise.

The sunrise had become infused with a rich amber that warmed the tones of the harbor, making it look like a postcard taken through a sepia filter. Maybe buying those properties herself wasn't the ticket. Managing the remodels and outfitting long distance would be challenging. She'd be better off finding a suitable local buyer for them.

"Are you still there?" Erin asked.

"Yes. You were saying my idea won't fly."

She gave an exasperated huff. Erin never huffed. "Niles says if you don't come home this weekend, he's going to quit."

She sat upright in the swing, almost spilling her coffee. "That's your compromise for my idea?"

She sighed. "No. That's the real reason I called at this ridiculous hour and why I called last night. He's serious. Evidently, I'm a more controlling bitch than you are—his words, not mine."

A loud ringing started in her ears. "This weekend? Today is Friday, Erin. I'd have to leave tomorrow." Panic started to rise. Real panic that closed her throat and made her stomach churn. She thought she had at least one more week. "I can't. I'm not done here. There's too much to do."

"We're going to lose him."

Gripping the porch post, she caught her breath. "I can't leave. There's a house I'm organizing for an old guy named Roger. And yesterday, I ordered a full kitchen and six bedrooms' worth of furniture for a family who lost everything, and there's a very important pie contest that this town has never won but stands a very good chance of winning this year because I found the perfect recipe, and Amanda and Cassidy want to throw a going-away party for me, and there's..." The coil around her heart had become a relentless vise. *There's Caleb.*

The sun had fully risen over the beautiful, pitiful, partially developed harbor, highlighting every boarded-up window on the two abandoned buildings while at the same time causing the water to glow like a gemstone.

"I can't leave yet." There was no compromise on this. "I need another week. Tell Niles one more week, like you and I talked about."

There was a long pause, and for a second, Lillian thought the connection had dropped.

"I'll see what I can do," Erin said.

• • •

Lillian stared at the handwritten note on a page from the sticky pad she had bought for Roger so he could leave instructions for the mailman and gritted her teeth.

L: Have to cancel today. R

No way. He was not getting away with this again. She wasn't in the mood. Not after the meltdown she'd had on the phone with her sister.

Snatching the note from where she'd slapped it on Bessie's dash, she stormed into the diner, leaving the bells on the door clanking in her wake. He was where she'd expected him to be: cozied up with his cohorts, Seamus and Harry, hiding behind a cup of coffee. Well, there'd be no hiding this time.

"I need to talk to you, Roger McGuffy."

He looked up and actually had the audacity to smile. "Lillian. I see you received my invitation."

She was so outraged, she sputtered sounds like the seagulls at the harbor made.

"If you gentlemen don't mind, Lillian and I have an appointment," he said in a congenial tone to his friends as he stood.

She had an appointment to throw him through a window about now. But instead of committing a highly satisfying act of violence, she followed him to the booth in the corner she'd sat in when she first arrived in Blink. He gave her the seat facing the diner, which mollified her fractionally.

"Hi, Lillian," Sally said, placing a cup of coffee in front

of her as if she hadn't stormed in here like a battleship to war. "Would you like some breakfast?" She took Roger's coffee cup and replaced it with a fresh one.

Her stomach growled. She and Caleb had shared a sandwich at her cottage last night, and goodness knew they'd more than worked that off. A buzzing warmth spiraled through her belly, and she pushed thoughts of last night away. "Yes, thanks. I'd love some breakfast." She removed a menu from a clip at the end of the table and selected something called the Lumberjack Special without even reading what it was. The name seemed about right for her mood.

"You must be hungry," Sally said.

"Very," Lillian said, stirring half a packet of sugar in her coffee.

Roger gave her a sly grin as he added two packs of sugar to his cup. "I saw you drive Caleb home this morning."

Sally's eyes grew huge, and she gasped. "I'll just go get your breakfast started," she said, hustling off.

"Roger!" Lillian hissed. "This is a small town. Word spreads like wildfire."

He stirred his cup. "You ashamed or something?"

"Of course not."

"Then let people talk." He took a sip of his coffee, made a face, and added another sugar packet. "People have been tiptoeing around that boy since the Cutty girl took up with that yacht man. Time for the nonsense to stop. Time for him to stop brooding. Time for them to stop feeling sorry for him."

"And just what do you think people will say about me

when this gets around?"

He met her eyes directly with his faded gray ones. "You're leaving. What do you care?"

Ouch. She sat back and stirred her coffee. On one hand, he was right. On the other, she felt like he was goading her.

"What do you want, Roger?"

"I want to talk business. Mabel told me I shouldn't bring work home, so I figured the diner could be our office today. I'm tired of putting my house in order, anyway." He took a sip of his coffee. "Let's put Blink in order instead."

She could hardly believe it. He was finally going to talk about listing some of his properties. The muscles in her shoulders relaxed, and she leaned back in the booth. "You really got me thinking the other day when you talked about attracting people to the area," he said.

Yes!

"Here ya go, hon," Sally said, placing a gigantic plate of food in front of her. A truly enormous plate of food. Enough for three or four people. Or one lumberjack. "I'll be right back with the pancakes and syrup."

Before she could stop her and tell her to not bother, Sally scurried off.

"I hope you're hungry." Lillian gestured to her plate. "Three eggs plus three kinds of meat and a biscuit is about three times more than I need."

"Plus pancakes!" Roger said. "I've had breakfast, though."

She cut off a bite of egg. "You were talking about attracting people to Blink."

"Yes, well…" He looked over his shoulder, then at his watch. "I'm going to reopen the mill."

Bite of egg forgotten, she lowered her fork. This was not at all what she'd expected. A business like that would be good, of course, offering locals employment, but she wasn't sure it would grow Blink rather than just draw workers to commute from nearby towns. They needed to work from the inside out.

"Are you going to sell the harbor properties?" she asked.

"Here ya go." Sally set the pancakes on the table. "I brought maple, but I have sugar-free if you need it."

"This is great, Sally. Thanks."

Roger glanced at his watch again, then peered out the window at the parking lot.

"Are you waiting on someone?" she asked.

"I am." He grinned. "And here they are."

She followed his gaze out the window to see Caleb and another man about to enter the building. Roger stood. "I need to talk to David Jr. in private." He gestured to her boatload of breakfast. "We'll go to the counter. Don't leave."

She opened her mouth but closed it when Caleb strode in with wet hair and a fresh shave. She rubbed the tender spot on her cheek as her body roared to life. Man, oh, man. Just seeing the guy caused fireworks.

"Hey," he said.

"Hi." Her voice was light and high. Oh, great. Time for the morning-after silly shyness and blushes. "I hope you're hungry." She gestured to the table.

"The Lumberjack Special. Well done." He sat on the

same side of the booth, which forced her to scoot over to give him room.

Self-consciously, she shot a glance around to see if anyone was watching them. Sally was talking to Roger and the guy she knew to be David Lassiter Jr. at the counter, and Seamus and Harry chatted in their regular booth.

She jumped when his warm hand slid over her thigh.

"You're wound up tight," he said, pulling her closer. "Everything okay?"

It was much better now. His touch was like a balm. "Yes." She laced her fingers through his over her thigh.

Glancing up, she found Sally was watching them with a proud, satisfied look on her face that reminded her of her mom's face when she or Erin were in grade-school plays. Roger and David were still deep in conversation.

She and Caleb polished off a lumberjack's worth of eggs, sausage, and ham. He ate with total focus and zeal, sort of like he... As she popped the last bite of bacon in her mouth, she blushed and shifted in her seat.

"Me too," he said, squeezing his fingers. "We should have stayed in bed this morning. We'll get out of here soon."

Great. He was a mind reader, too. And she went from restless to overheated just like that.

He nodded to Roger and David. "That won't take too long."

She hated being an outsider like this. "What's going on?"

"I figured you knew, since you're probably the reason for Old Man McGuffy's recent behavior." He took a big bite of biscuit and released her hand to wipe butter from the corner of his mouth with his napkin. He stared at her face. "You don't know."

"Bingo."

"That document he gave to Glory yesterday?"

She nodded and sipped her coffee.

He set the napkin on the table. "It's the deed to the property their house is on. Roger evidently paid it off, and they hold the title free and clear. No more mortgage payments. Roger texted me this morning and asked me to bring David in for a meeting. No idea about what."

Lillian had a pretty good idea. "He's reopening his lumber mill."

"McGuffy?"

She nodded.

He stared over at Roger and David, who were vigorously shaking hands. "Well, that's news. It was a shock when he shut it down in the first place. It was doing fine, by everyone's accounts. It's like he just got sick of working or something."

Closed because of spite...and foolishness, he'd said. "I'd bet it was more than that." And she was going to find out.

"When we're done here, let's go back to the cottage," he whispered in her ear. "I have some things that need organizing."

"Why, Caleb Wright," she said with mock surprise. "I have it on the best authority that you are an old-fashioned old man who thinks people can only fool around after dark," she whispered back.

He held both hands up in surrender. "I don't want to

know who said that, though I have my suspicions, and I don't want to know how it came up in conversation. But know this: I fully intend to put that rumor to rest as soon as possible, and I'm not letting you out of my sight before then."

She shivered when he ran his hand up her thigh. "You brought David here. How's he getting home if you're not letting me out of your sight?"

"His wife. She had the car to take the kids to the store this morning before he had to leave for his shift, which starts later on Fridays and Saturdays. Ordinarily he keeps the kids while she goes, but obviously, today was different." He gestured to Roger and David, who were still deep in conversation, standing at the counter. This time, they man-hugged instead of shaking hands, complete with pats on the back.

David stayed at the counter, and Roger returned to their table. "Now for you," Roger said, pointing a finger at Lillian. "Tell me what you are going to do to bring people to Blink in the kinds of numbers that would warrant restoring the harbor buildings and listing other property for sale."

"First, tell me what just happened over there. I think it's related."

He gave a self-satisfied smile. "I just made Junior my partner in the mill. I cover the cost of getting the equipment operational, and he recruits from people he knows through his daddy's and his lifetime working in mills to get it up and running. Together, I think we have the supply side covered. I haven't been out of the business long enough for everyone to die off yet." He winked. "We split fifty-fifty until the mill has made a profit for two years. Then, it's his—with conditions, of course."

She had to consciously keep her jaw from dropping open. He'd basically given a lumber mill to the Lassiters.

"What are the conditions?" Caleb asked. "Since you mentioned it, I figured you wanted me to ask."

"I like you, Caleb Wright." Roger leaned back in the booth, looking satisfied. "There are two conditions. It must stay family-owned by a local resident. No out-of-towners. No corporate buyers. And it has to offer products for use in Blink, whether for business or residential, at cost, until the population exceeds one thousand residents."

This time, her jaw did fall open.

He gestured to Lillian. "Your turn."

"How long before the mill is up and running?" she asked.

"He's giving notice at his job today. We're meeting at our mill on Sunday to do an assessment. Outside estimate is two months, maybe less for short runs of limited products. Enough to get things going around here construction-wise. It will take longer to get enough employees to be fully functional."

She slipped her planner out of her purse and flipped to the annual calendar. As the page settled, her breath caught at the red star on next Saturday's square. "Pie contest" was written next to it, and under that was scrawled, "Return home." One week left here. Maybe less if Niles didn't back down on his demand that she be home this weekend.

She tapped her pencil on the page, looking at her year. Filming would start back up in September, and the team didn't like her ideas with regard to brand consistency, which applied to the magazine, too. Begrudgingly, she had to agree with them. It was like putting Polaroids in with professional shots. Even with a photographer sent out, it wouldn't have the polish of their staged work with a full team.

What she needed was the full team...

And Niles.

Her heart stuttered. She didn't need to send pieces of Blink to New York. She needed to bring New York to Blink. And she could even meet Niles's demand that she be back to work in person this weekend.

Roger cleared his throat. "So tell me—"

She held up a finger. "Wait." She traced her pencil over the pie contest, ticking off all the features she had proposed. Three days to set up and do shorter segments, maybe two more to stage bigger shoots.

She grinned and pulled out her phone. They weren't going to have a few mentions of Blink. The first three episodes would be filmed on location, and they would rival any tourism campaign bigger towns around here launched. On top of that, they'd air after sufficient time for the harbor properties to be sold and rehabbed and the mill to be fully operational.

She put the phone to her ear, grabbed Caleb's hand, and winked at Roger. "Hey, Erin. I need someone to arrange a plane ticket for Niles and a rental car for him out of Bangor tomorrow. Then, I need you to call an emergency meeting of the full creative and production staff at the first convenient time today and bring me in online."

"Oh, thank God you're going to get Niles out of my hair," Erin said. "I'll put out an email now about a meeting. Sounds like you've had an ah-ha moment."

"I have." She looked over into Caleb's ocean-blue eyes. "Several."

CHAPTER TWENTY-FOUR

"Okay, so we're on board with going on location to Washington County, Maine," Erin said from the computer screen. In the background, Lillian could see the team packed into the conference room. "Niles will be flying out tomorrow morning to work with Lillian to prep until we get there. We'll load up a truck with equipment, and I'll arrange for the Living Sharpe bus to take those of you able to leave your families for a week. With a group this large, it's more practical than flying, since the location is not close to an airport and we will have a lot of gear. I'll send out an email when I have the schedule finalized. Thank you for coming on such short notice, everybody."

"Thank you, everyone," Lillian said, waving at her screen as it went black.

She closed her laptop and padded barefooted to her bedroom to return it to its home on top of her dresser. She took in a deep breath. The room still smelled faintly of Caleb, who'd left to finish up at the Lassiters' after making good on his promise to prove he wasn't an old-fashioned old man.

She took off her dressy silk blouse and hung it in the closet, then pulled on a loose sweatshirt that went much better with the yoga pants she had on than the dress shirt had. She was kind of liking this video-conferencing business. She only had to worry about her top half for most of the meetings. She wondered if she'd ever get used to heels again.

Her phone rang. "Hey Erin. I think that went pretty well, don't you?"

"Yes." She didn't sound nearly as excited as Lillian was. "But?"

"After we hung up, there were questions."

Lillian sat on the bed that looked like a tornado had hit it. It sort of had. Caleb was a force of nature. She smiled and laid back in the middle of the disaster zone. "And?"

"You have to come back, Lils."

Erin's ability to know Lillian's mind was eerie sometimes.

"That's the plan."

"Is it?"

The air seemed thick and hard to breathe. She sat up and opened the window. "What's this about, Er?"

"Ellen said there was a post on one of the social media platforms from someone who says they live in Blink and that they knew the rumors about you and Niles were false because you're dating a hunky guy who lives on a boat."

She lowered herself to the bed again and grabbed a fistful of sheet, her mind reeling. And here she'd been worried about the people in Blink finding out. This was much worse.

"Are you?" Erin asked.

She wasn't sure what the question was. "Coming home?"

"Dating a hunky guy who lives on a boat."

She stood. Then sat again. This was it. This was the

moment when she could tell her sister that she wanted to work remotely. That at this time in her life, time away had made her happy and she wasn't ready to come back yet... maybe at all.

"You can't stay there," Erin said. "The team is falling apart. Not in a dramatic way, but the edges are fraying, and the morale is low. Everyone wants to know when you're coming back, and there's grumbling. It's not just Niles. And I'm going to be honest, I need you back. This was not what I signed up for. I don't want to run this business. And I won't."

Lillian vacillated between wanting to cry and throw up. With this plan to film on-site, she'd thought she'd found a way to make everyone happy and also help save Blink. She'd imagined having them all meet at a remote site once a year to kick-start the season's filming and meet face-to-face, then they'd do remote the rest of the year and she would not be tied to New York. Lots of business-es operated remotely just fine.

"Okay," her sister said. "I'll lay it out this way. We'll go to the expense and trouble to have our employees leave their families to come there so that you can feature this town for whatever reason, but in return, you are going to agree to come back home the day we end shooting and step back into your job. Do we have a deal?"

Lillian knew Erin wasn't bluffing. She'd never indicated she would leave before. Things must be unraveling pretty bad for her to lay out an ultimatum. And she knew her sister was right. It was Lillian's company, after all. Lillian owed it to her team to be responsible.

She wiped away a tear with the sleeve of her sweat-shirt. "Yes. We have a deal. You guys come film those segments, and I'll come back home."

She would return to New York to help save Blink. It was totally worth it. This situation was always supposed to be temporary. She pressed a hand to her sternum. She was pretty sure this pain wasn't temporary.

• • •

Caleb paced the deck of the *Bethany Anne* while its namesake wailed and sobbed inside. When she was little, he could hold her and rock her to calm her down. He was clueless what to do now that she was sixteen.

He wished he'd had the foresight to close the windows to spare everyone within a mile radius eardrum damage. He was aware that Amanda was watching from her deck, but he hadn't asked for her help. She didn't know about the camping situation, and honestly, he wasn't sure if her take on things would help or hurt. All he wanted was to soothe his heartbroken daughter and maybe punch a punk named Brandon. Bethy hadn't told him anything other than she wasn't going camping, and then there was a lot of crying.

Lillian pulled into the lot, and his adrenaline immediately leveled off. She would know what to do.

"Thanks for coming on short notice like this," he said as she stepped onboard.

She waved him off. "Where is she?"

A particularly loud volley of wails came from inside, and she brushed past him and into the cabin. He followed.

"Bethany?" she called, rapping on her door with her knuckles. "It's Lillian."

The sobbing stopped. "Oh my God! Did my dad call you?"

"May I come in?"

After a long pause, the door cracked open, then swung wide. Lillian entered. Bethany's face was puffy and red as she stuck her head out to shoot him a lethal glare before slamming the door. He threw his arms up. Just great. Now *he* was the bad guy.

For a moment, he lingered in the hallway, but eventually he returned to the deck, where he didn't feel as trapped and helpless.

"I can't believe he called you." Bethany's voice came through her open window. He moved closer.

"He's worried."

"He'd never understand."

"That's why he called me."

There were several seconds of silence that felt like a year. At least the wailing had stopped. He slid down the wall and sat on the deck under Bethany's window to listen. Hell, maybe he could learn something about how to help his daughter.

"It's Dad's fault," Bethany said in a wavering voice.

"Okay," Lillian answered calmly.

Okay? Caleb covered his face.

"If he had let me spend the night, none of this would have happened."

"I'm sure you're right."

Caleb couldn't believe it. Lillian was agreeing instead of defending him. Maybe Amanda would have been the better choice to calm Bethany down—though, he had to admit, the waterworks had completely stopped. Maybe that was the goal. Unruffle the feathers first.

His daughter let out a frustrated breath. "Maybe it's a good thing." Her bed creaked like she'd flopped down onto it. "I mean, Brandon was really mean in his text."

The bed creaked again. Caleb assumed Lillian had sat on the bed with his daughter.

"I'm sorry," Lillian said.

Sorry? Caleb gritted his teeth. He would have asked what the text said. Maybe even grabbed her phone to read it himself.

Scout stuck his head around the front of the cabin, probably checking to see if the coast was clear after all the wailing. He patted his thigh, and Scout, with Willy in his wake, padded over and sat next to him, one on each side.

"Brandon said that if I wasn't spending the night, don't bother." She sniffed. "He said I was boring."

"You're right. That's mean."

Bethy broke down in sobs again, then said, "He said he was sick of no and Pricilla Lundt was going instead." The sobs turned to wails. "Prissy won't say no."

Caleb wanted to get up and go hunt Brandon down and teach him what no really meant, but he was too pissed to move. He had no idea what he would have said to this news. Maybe it was a good thing Bethany had closed him out—he'd have totally messed this up. He was curious what Lillian would come up with.

For a long time, Bethany cried and Lillian said nothing, which confirmed what he already knew: women were weird and he'd never understand them.

"You know what I want to do?" Lillian asked.

Bethany sniffled. "What?"

"I want to put poison ivy in their sleeping bags."

There was a snort, then Bethany giggled.

"I want to safety pin their tent flap zipper so they can't get out," Bethy said.

The laughter faded after a while, and Lillian said, "I'm pretty sure he wasn't a good fit for you. He didn't even bother to come see you even though he has a car."

"That's what Luke says."

Willy put his head on Caleb's knee, and he rubbed the dog's pointy ears.

"Luke also says Brandon goes out with lots of girls and brags to the guys what he does with them."

Caleb was pretty sure he didn't want to hear this. He was pretty sure Brandon didn't want him to hear it, either, because his head was about to explode.

"I like Luke," Lillian said.

"I do, too. I even thought about going out with him when he asked me one time, but we're really different, you know? I'm going to go away to school, and he's going to stay here. It's not worth it."

"That's over a year away, isn't it?"

"Yeah."

Lillian took an audible breath, then sighed. "I really like your dad."

That got Caleb's attention. His fingers stilled on Willy's head.

"I know. He likes you, too."

"And I'm leaving in a week."

The bed squeaked. "I wish you could stay, but I get it. Who would choose to stay here?"

Caleb closed his eyes. He hated this feeling of dread. He wanted her to stay, too.

"My point is that sometimes a ticking clock makes time more meaningful. Your dad and I are making the most of the limited time we have. Maybe you should look at Luke the same way. Just a thought."

There was another prolonged period of silence.

"Brandon's a jerk," Bethany said finally. "He doesn't deserve a girlfriend like me. I'm glad this happened."

So was Caleb. Silently, he stood, wandered into the kitchen, and started throwing supplies in a bag, now determined to make good use of limited time—not only with Lillian, but with his daughter, and this was a good place to start.

Bethany's door opened. Her face was still blotchy, but instead of glaring at him, she gave him a watery smile.

He put the can of beans down on the counter and took her in his arms. Just like when she was little, she wrapped her arms around him in a bear hug and buried her face in his shirt.

• • •

Lillian leaned against the doorframe as Caleb embraced his daughter. She was pretty sure she wouldn't have been able to remain upright otherwise. The dogs circled them excitedly, wagging like crazy, and she swallowed hard. It was probably a good thing Niles would be here tomorrow to distract her. She was losing her heart to this town and its people. Especially the man hugging his daughter to him like the world was ending. The pain in her chest felt like it was, but she knew this was just the beginning. She was better for being here. She'd go back to her life with a different outlook and a more simplistic approach—and a broken heart. She took a deep breath and lifted her chin. Like she'd told Bethany, she needed to make the most of the time with him.

Caleb had a big canvas bag on the counter that appeared to be full of food. She peeked inside to find cans of beans, bags of chips, and what looked like makings for hot dogs.

"I know Bethy is free this evening," Caleb said, giving his daughter a final squeeze before releasing her. "What are your plans, Lillian?"

Bethany was looking up at her dad in expectation, and he grinned at her. "We're going camping on the beach," he said. "We're not letting all this food and beautiful weather go to waste."

Bethany beamed. "Come on, Lillian! It'll be fun. We have a bunch of tents."

"There's enough food for ten people. Let's invite Amanda and Cassidy." Caleb pulled several packs of hot dogs out of the fridge. "How do you feel about inviting your grandparents to join us at the beach for a cookout? I know they'll go home to sleep, but the more the merrier."

"That sounds great," Bethany said. She bit her lip and gave Lillian a look. "What about Luke? It would be rude to invite Cassidy without him, probably."

"I completely agree," Lillian said. This was nothing like

the Brandon situation. There would be chaperones everywhere. Caleb was obviously a step ahead of her. He winked at her over his shoulder and said, "Sure, give him a call, Bethy. I'll contact the grandparents."

"I'll text Cassidy and Amanda," Lillian said. "I need to deal with Amanda anyway. She's blowing up my phone with texts asking what's going on."

Bethany looked out the far window. "Nah. She's okay. She hasn't pulled out the binoculars yet. That's when you know she's serious."

CHAPTER TWENTY-FIVE

Lillian leaned back in the canvas camp chair and folded her arms over her belly. She couldn't remember the last time she'd eaten so much junk food in one sitting. "I have no regrets," she said. "Although that second s'more might have me retracting that statement in a few hours."

She was seated between Amanda and Cassidy, both of whom were toasting marshmallows. Caleb's parents, Gus and Alice, were talking to Fern, James, and Caleb on the other side of the fire, which had burned down to a cozy size but had been one step short of an inferno when Caleb and his dad had started it.

Over the flames, Fern smiled at her, and Lillian smiled back. Caleb had held her hand and made it abundantly clear that they were a couple all night, and his ex's mother seemed happy about it. So much love here. Acceptance and support. She wanted this. To live like this.

"So, is Niles Sharpe really coming tomorrow?" Amanda asked.

Lillian rolled her eyes. "What, is there a gossip hotline in Blink going straight to Miller Mercantile?"

"Yes," Amanda and Cassidy said at the same time.

Down the beach, Bethany and Luke strolled side by side. Not touching, but close.

"Yes. Niles will arrive tomorrow before noon."

Amanda bounced in her seat, which set her earrings in motion. The mirrored disco balls threw little points of orange from the flames across the side of her neck. On most people, they would look awful, but Amanda pulled them off as if they were the height of fashion, along with the pink camouflage sweater—her camping outfit, as she told them. "I'm so excited. Where's he staying?"

"With me, of course."

Amanda and Cassidy exchanged a look.

"What?" Lillian asked.

"This is Blink," Cassidy answered.

"And?"

"Well, it will look bad with the online rumors and all," Amanda explained.

Oh, for Pete's sake. He wasn't even here yet, and Niles was already causing trouble.

"I have two bedrooms. He's coming here to work. I need to keep him on task." And out of trouble. "He stays with me." She didn't mean to sound so pissy, but this was ridiculous.

Amanda blew out her marshmallow, which had caught on fire. "What will Caleb say?"

Lillian startled when Caleb's deep voice came from behind her. "About what?"

"About Niles staying in my second bedroom," Lillian answered.

"I'd say events like this afternoon would need to move to my place instead of yours." He leaned over and kissed her cheek, making her insides twist.

"Ooooo, five bucks, Cassidy!" Amanda squealed.

Cassidy, for once, was not wearing paint-splattered overalls. Pulling up the bottom of her sweatshirt, she slipped a bill out of her front jeans pocket and slapped it into Amanda's hand. "So, you're staying!" she said with a grin.

Lillian's heart stuttered. She shot a glance at Caleb, who arched an eyebrow, then turned to Cassidy. "Uh. No. I can't."

The fire didn't seem to put out enough heat anymore. Lillian grew cold all over. She folded her arms over her middle and hugged herself.

The moon was high overhead, illuminating the beach enough for the two large tents to cast shadows. The bigger one was for the girls, and Caleb and Luke would take the other. Lillian wished now that she'd declined the camping part. For a place that was so simple, things were starting to get complicated, and she imagined it would only get worse.

"Walk with me," Caleb said, holding out his hand.

She slipped her hand into his, and warmth traveled up her arm.

"Thanks for your help with Bethany earlier. I had no idea how to handle that. Everything I said made it worse."

She stepped over a piece of driftwood and pulled her favorite jacket tighter to keep out the chill from the light wind off the water. "My pleasure. Sometimes we're too close to someone to be objective. A fresh set of eyes and ears sometimes helps. Being woman to woman was an advantage, too."

The wind had died down, and the waves that had slapped against the rocky beach now lapped rhythmically. They walked in silence, and her heart slowed as nature pulled her in. She would miss this. And this man beside her.

They passed a large jutting section of rock, and he pulled her into the moon shadow it created. He wrapped her in an embrace, like a warm blanket, making her body hum all over. Then he kissed her long and deep, turning the warm blanket into flames. After a kiss thorough enough to make her want to rip off her clothes, he pulled back and took her face in his hands. She could barely make out his features in the darkness of their hiding place. He gave her one more kiss, gentle this time, and released her.

He took her hand and led her out of the shadows and onto the beach again. She'd expected him to turn back toward camp, but he didn't. Something sparkled in the moonlight in front of them. She leaned down and picked it up.

"Sea glass," he said.

She turned the smooth, translucent piece over in her hand and then shoved it in her jacket pocket.

He started to stroll again but abruptly stopped. He opened his mouth to speak but simply exhaled and stared out over the water. "I swore to myself I wasn't going to do this," he said. "I told myself that things happen the way they are supposed to happen and can't be forced." He dropped her hand. "I know you have a business to run, and it has to be run out of New York. I also know you are going to leave. That you have to leave—but I don't want to look back on this for the rest of my life wondering what would have happened if I…" He ran a hand over his face and let out a frustrated breath. "I don't want to wonder if things would have been different if I had let you know how I feel."

Oh, no. No, no, no. She looked back toward the campsite, wanting to run. This was hard enough as it was. Her heart fluttered like a bird trapped in her rib cage.

"I can't leave Blink," he said. "I have Bethany and my parents and—"

"Stop," she said, doing that finger-over-his-lips thing she had hated so much, but she had to shut him up.

He pulled her into his arms and kissed her again, then stepped back, breathing heavily, and studied her face. "Stay," he whispered. "I want you to stay."

For a moment, the world stopped. She stared up into his clear blue eyes and allowed everything to fall away except the two of them on this beautiful beach bathed in moonlight—allowing herself, for a fraction of a second, to picture herself with this man with no ticking clock hanging over their heads.

Too soon, the world sharpened back into focus.

"I can't," she said.

He pulled her against his chest and the steady, comforting sound of his heartbeat. "I know."

CHAPTER TWENTY-SIX

"Here he comes!" a woman screamed from the crowd that had formed in front of the cottage. Lillian bit back a groan and glanced over at Caleb leaning against the railing at the far end of her porch. He winked, and some of the tension in her shoulders slipped away. Niles dropping on her little bit of heaven like a bomb was bad enough, but an impromptu army of Sharpies made it even worse.

"There he is!" another woman shouted.

Where had all these people come from? There were at least twenty women in front of her house, their cars parked along the road. Niles was going to love this. His ego would inflate so big, his head wouldn't fit through doors. As if he wasn't bad enough already.

A little blue car rounded the bend in the road, and cheers went up.

"Oh, for heaven's sake," Lillian muttered when Amanda squealed and stood up so fast she almost toppled Lillian out of the porch swing. She pushed to her feet, and the swing hit her in the back of the knees.

"VIPs!" Amanda called. "Follow me! This way."

VIPs? Clutching the porch-swing chain, Lillian stepped aside as half a dozen frenzied women clutching *Living Sharpe* magazines followed Amanda into the cottage.

"You should have sold tickets," Cassidy said with a grin,

lowering herself onto the swing.

"I should have put up an electric fence," Lillian muttered, watching Amanda organize her followers in the living room like she was staging a photo shoot.

Another wave of squeals went up when Niles stepped out of what appeared to be a Ford Focus. His usual crisp shirt was limp, and his slacks had wrinkles on the front. He pushed his sunglasses up on his head like a movie star and waved at his adoring fans, his smile dimming when they moved to close in. Lillian almost felt sorry for him.

"I've got this," Amanda said, dashing down the porch steps, her multicolored paisley caftan fanning behind her like a superhero cape.

In shocked amusement, Lillian held her breath as Amanda, Niles in tow behind her, cut a path through the women like one of those icebreaker ships Lillian had seen on Discovery Channel, leading him safe and sound into the cottage, where her VIP tableau awaited.

"That's it!" Amanda shouted from the door to the women outside. "Mr. Sharpe will be at my party on the deck next Friday. Go home." And she closed the door.

The women grumbled and dispersed as Lillian, still clutching the porch-swing chain, stared from the closed door to the little blue car to Caleb, who looked like he was going to bust out laughing any second.

"Pretty sure a shock collar for Amanda would have been more effective than an electric fence," Cassidy said from the swing.

"What just happened here?" Lillian asked.

"I think Amanda appointed herself personal bodyguard for Niles Sharpe," Cassidy said, straight-faced.

"She was making a list of who should have VIP status last night at the campfire."

Lillian peeked in through the window. Except for Amanda, nobody in that room was under sixty. She recognized Doris, who was again wearing her green dress, and Charlotte, this time in blue instead of pink, and Sally. Niles was seated between two elderly ladies, both wearing hats, looking like he was one breath away from passing out from fear.

Lillian scanned the porch and sat down, relieved that Cassidy and Caleb were the only ones left to witness her devolve into fits of giggles.

• • •

Caleb hadn't expected the arrival of the infamous Niles Sharpe to be quite so entertaining. Neither had Lillian, evidently, because she'd laughed so hard she was holding her ribs.

She was still gasping for breath when the door opened and Niles stepped out. "Help me," he said.

"Hi, Niles. Glad you made it." She covered her mouth to hide her smile. Caleb half expected her to fall into a laughing fit again in front of the poor guy. He looked haggard, like he'd traveled days from overseas and not a couple of hours from another state.

"This isn't funny, Lillian. They're asking me cooking questions."

She quit trying to hide her smile and grinned openly at him.

Niles took a deep breath. "I had to sit in economy

class on the plane because there weren't any seats in first or business. *Economy*, Lillian. The only rental available was"—he gestured to the little blue car—"*that*, and now I'm being asked cooking questions by women older than my mother."

That did it. Caleb laughed with her this time, and the guy flushed red.

"Uncool, Lillian," he said. "Did you set this up to get me back for the online scandal? Because I apologized. Erin even made me put the apology in writing."

The hairs on the nape of Caleb's neck tingled in irritation. The guy acted like a middle schooler. A spoiled-rotten middle schooler.

Composed, Lillian held up a hand. "No, Niles." Her face became serious. "I did not set this up. These are your real fans. The young women you usually see are fans of the way you *look*. These women are your true fans. They admire you as a person and value what you do, not just what you look like."

He peeked in through the window. "Really?"

"Yes," she said. "I promise."

Caleb's jaw clenched. She indulged his spoiled behavior. Unbelievable.

Lillian gestured to Cassidy. "This is Cassidy James, and that's Caleb Wright."

He greeted Cassidy and shook Caleb's hand. At least the guy had a decent handshake. Caleb wasn't impressed by much else.

Niles cleared his throat. "Will you come back in with me, Lillian? They're asking things I can't answer."

This was ridiculous. Niles wasn't a little kid who

needed his mommy to go with him. This was wrong. From everything he knew about this guy, he relied entirely on Lillian for success. It showed.

"Yes," she said. "I'll go in with you."

And dammit, she was enabling him.

Caleb touched her elbow. "Can I talk to you for a moment?"

Amanda flung the door open and, like a heat-seeking missile, found Niles and grabbed his hand. "You need to autograph the VIPs' magazines."

Niles shot Lillian a terrified look as Amanda pulled him back into the cottage.

"I have to go run interference for Niles. Can it wait?" she asked.

This behavior between Lillian and Niles had obviously been going on a while. A little longer wouldn't matter. "Sure."

He didn't follow them inside; instead, he sat next to Cassidy on the porch swing. "You're not going in to get the amazing Niles Sharpe to sign your magazine or your body somewhere?" His voice sounded bitter, even to his own ears.

"Jealous much?" Cassidy said with a smirk.

He shook his head, staring over the sunlit harbor below. "Not at all. I feel bad for the guy—and Lillian, too."

"He's not exactly what I expected," Cassidy said. "In the shows, he seems so charming and confident."

That was Lillian's work. All of it. "Not your type, huh?"

"I like my guys with a little more going on, you know?" Cassidy shrugged. "He seems insecure. A guy that looks like that should *not* be insecure."

Unless he was in way over his head and couldn't find his way to the surface. This guy needed a life ring.

"I'm going inside. You coming?" he asked.

"Nah. I'm heading home. Nurse leaves at one today."

"Your dad okay?" he asked.

She gave a noncommittal shrug.

"Are *you* okay, Cassidy?"

She met his eyes and then looked away. "Sure."

She'd always closed off when he'd mentioned this subject. Next time he saw Luke, he'd make certain they didn't need anything.

"He didn't recognize me this morning," she whispered. "It was the first time."

She'd never acknowledged what was wrong with her father before, though he'd pieced it together. Caleb closed his eyes against the ache in his chest. He couldn't imagine how much it hurt. Hank and Cassidy had been so close.

She took a deep breath. "It's almost time. He made me promise." She picked at a paint spot on her overalls. "I promised I wouldn't let his friends see him like this and I would keep him home until he wasn't himself anymore."

There was a highly regarded memory care facility in Machias. "Hope House?"

She nodded. "It will be best for him. And Luke."

She was too young to have to be a caretaker and mother figure. Her own mother had died soon after Luke was born. "Does Amanda know?"

"Had you ever heard anything about Dad's illness outside of what I tell you?"

"No."

She snorted. "There's your answer. Amanda doesn't know."

"I'll keep it close." He tapped his chest.

"Dad would appreciate it," she said.

"I'm always here, you know," he said. "It's unhealthy to not have someone to talk to. Someone to help you through things." Who knew where he'd be today if his and Ashley's parents hadn't been there for him and Bethany when Ashley left.

"Thanks, Caleb," Cassidy said. "I really am okay. Luke's okay, too, now that he has Bethany to distract him." Her expression had relaxed, and she looked more herself, but her brow furrowed. "What about you? You okay? With Lillian's leaving, I mean."

His throat tightened. No. He was not okay. He might never be okay, but he didn't really have a choice. His life was here, in Blink; hers was not.

"I'm good," he lied.

She gave him a doubtful look but then smiled. "Cool. Well, like you say, I'm here, you know."

"Thanks."

"Gotta go." She grinned, then, in her usual bouncy way, headed down the steps two at a time.

Behind, he could hear women's voices, broken occasionally by Niles's smooth tones. Something in him knew that as much as he wanted to hammer on Niles for being such a leech, the guy could probably use someone to talk to, too. Maybe rather than having a conversation about it with Lillian, he should talk to Niles instead.

When he entered the living room, his first inclination was to turn right back around. There was a quilt thrown over the coffee table, and Sally was pointing out something on it to Niles, whose eyes had completely glazed over like Bethany's did when he got carried away on eighteenth-century shipbuilding techniques. The guy needed a rescue.

"How about a beer, Niles?" he said.

The shocked looks from the women and the livid expression on Lillian's face had him rethinking the offer, but he held firm.

Amanda looked disappointed but was clearly determined to remain self-appointed drill sergeant as she folded up the quilt and shoved it at one of the hat-wearing women flanking Niles, then stood. "So, everyone who contributes twenty dollars to the Quilts at Christmas fundraiser will get to attend tomorrow morning's Noms with Niles breakfast at the Starfish Diner."

"Noms with Niles?" Lillian said—well, more like squeaked.

"Every year, we make lap quilts for the residents of the county women's shelter," Doris explained.

"I offered my diner for Amanda's breakfast event, hoping to raise the money for enough quilts to go around this year. We came up short last Christmas," Sally said.

Lillian closed her eyes, and her expression softened from anger to acceptance. Caleb knew this was hard on someone who was used to setting the schedule and having people follow it to the letter. He also knew she had a good heart and would never deny a charity like Quilts for Christmas.

Amanda was collecting bills from the women. "Tell your friends. They can pay at the door. It covers breakfast as well as access to our visitor." She shoved the bills in the pocket of the godawful thing she was wearing. "Is nine o'clock good for you, Mr. Sharpe?"

Niles, still a little glassy-eyed, turned to Lillian. "Is it?"

"Nine works, but all of you have to leave now. Mr. Sharpe and I have some business to take care of. Thanks for coming by."

Reluctantly, the women gathered their magazines and cookbooks and things made of yarn and fabric and left. Amanda started to sit as if she were exempt, but Sally pinched her arm, and she yelped, raising her green-tipped fingers to rub the spot.

"You and I have some planning to do for that breakfast tomorrow, Amanda Miller," Sally said. "I'm sure Lillian will let you know if she needs your help."

"Bye, Niles... I mean Mr. Sharpe," Amanda said, looking over her shoulder as Sally practically pushed her out the door.

Niles waved, still dazed. He'd clearly hit the wall. Caleb didn't blame him.

"How 'bout that beer, Niles?" Caleb said, closing the door behind Sally and Amanda.

"Not now," Lillian said. "I need to get Niles up to speed on wild blueberry harvesting and crop rotation. Tomorrow, we'll focus on the segment on the lobster industry."

"Not now, but thanks," Niles said, mimicking Lillian's answer.

"Okay, I'll be back at five."

"We have a lot to do, Caleb. Five is early for us to go anywhere."

"May I speak with you, Lillian?" he asked. "I know

you're busy, but it's important."

She sighed and dropped a file on the coffee table in front of Niles. "That's the overview of next week's schedule."

Niles didn't even reach for the file as they stepped out onto the patio. Caleb shut the door.

"He can't leave right now," she said, hands on her hips. "It takes a long time to get him up to speed on things, and I only have a couple of days before the team gets here."

He held both hands up. "You are extraordinary at what you do. You have created a successful business from scratch using your mind and talent for leadership."

This seemed to take some of the heat out of her, and she relaxed her stance to lean on the porch railing.

He walked to her, wrapping his hands around her waist. "Like I said, you are extraordinary." He tilted his head toward the front door. "That guy is not."

She stiffened.

"And he's out-of-his-brain exhausted. Have you looked at him? You'd be wasting your time trying to get any meaningful work done with him. He looks like he was out partying all night before flying here."

She shrugged. "He probably was. You say he's not extraordinary, but he's pretty good at that."

"Because he doesn't have a reason to be good at anything else."

She pulled away. "He has lots of reasons. All of them green."

"But he's getting paid anyway. Why would he improve? He needs a reason other than money."

Her eyes narrowed. "You don't know anything about it, Caleb."

"You're right. I know very little about your business, but I know a bit about being a man, and I think I understand that man." He pointed a finger at the door. "When I thanked you for pulling Bethany out of that wailing fit about Brandon, you told me that sometimes people were too close to a situation to be objective. That an outside eye was helpful. Let me be that outside eye."

She was leaning against the railing again, skeptical expression on her face, arms folded over her chest. "You think you can help Niles?"

He nodded. "I know I can if he'll listen."

She snorted. "Good luck with that."

"He's tired and beat down right now. This is the perfect time for me to talk with him."

She pushed off the railing. "Go ahead. Take him for a beer."

He placed his lips against her ear and took a deep breath, letting the scent of her floral shampoo fill his head. "How about dinner at my place. You and me. No Niles," he whispered.

She grew still. "And what would Niles do?"

"As my dad says, he's a grown-ass man. He'll figure it out."

"Caleb! There are no restaurants or food delivery services here. He has to eat."

"Let's ask his social director, Amanda, to entertain him."

Her brows drew in worry.

"While I entertain you." He grinned when she shuddered. "I can be very entertaining."

CHAPTER TWENTY-SEVEN

Caleb sat on one of the two deck chairs he'd placed at the end of the dock, overlooking the harbor. Next to him, Niles scrolled on his phone. "Oh, look at this one. She's hot, yeah? Tinder's the best."

Caleb glanced at the blonde on Niles's screen and shrugged. He popped the top on his beer and held it up in salute. "To Lillian."

Niles rolled his eyes, then held his beer bottle aloft. "To Lillian." He took a swallow. "I thought we were going to go to a bar. You know. Meet some women."

Maybe he'd overpromised. This guy was a real piece of work. Caleb tried to sound casual. "So you could do what? Bring someone back to Lillian's cottage so you could bang a headboard in the room next door to hers?"

His face crumpled, like he hadn't thought of that. "Yeah, I guess not." Caleb suspected Niles didn't think of Lillian's needs much, if ever.

"Do you know why she's filming here?" Caleb asked.

Niles seemed fascinated by Bill Burke's lobster boat as he pulled in. "I figure she just wanted to torture me."

"No. It's not about you at all. It's not about her, either."

Fortunately, Bill decided to go visit with Amanda instead of dealing with his catch, or Caleb would probably have lost Niles's attention completely.

"She's filming here for people she doesn't even know—and some she does."

Niles looked puzzled.

Caleb took a swallow of beer. "She's doing it to save this town from extinction. She's trying to save a whole town, Niles. That's a big goal. What are your goals?"

"My goals?"

He nodded.

"I don't know."

"What kind of things would you like to do?"

He shrugged.

Heat prickled up the back of Caleb's neck. Good God. The guy had no direction in his life at all. He took a deep breath, summoning patience. "Okay. I'll phrase it in an easier way. What do you not like?"

"I don't like being bossed around all the time."

Caleb nodded. "That's a good one. What else do you not like?"

"I don't like being treated like I'm still a college kid on frat row."

"I don't blame you. What else?"

He was really on a roll now. He puffed out his chest. "I don't like it when Lillian and Erin treat me like I'm stupid. I'm not stupid."

He nodded. "You strike me as very smart."

"I am."

Good—he was perceived as a buddy now. Someone on the same side. "I can tell you how to stop those things you don't like."

Niles took a long pull of beer. "Here comes the lecture. Did she set you up to this?"

"Nope. In fact, she'd be pissed if she knew about this conversation, probably. This is not a lecture. Advice. That woman is trying to run a business that affects lots of people who make a living from that business, including you. On top of being responsible for all those people's livelihoods, she's now taken on the task of saving an entire town. In order to do that, she needs your help. What are you doing to help?"

Niles's mouth opened and closed like he was a fish.

"I'll tell you what you're doing. You are letting her do everything for you. She does your research. She plans your schedule. She worries and frets and prods and pokes like she's your mother. She's not your mother. You're a grown man with a brain of your own. You don't want to be treated like a kid? Then grow up. You don't want to be treated like a frat bro? Stop being irresponsible."

Jaw set, Niles started to stand, but Caleb pulled him back down in his chair, hard.

"That woman spends her time covering for the fact you don't know a thing about what you're supposed to be an expert in." He gestured to the cottage across the harbor. "You asked her to come save you from a group of middle-aged women who were asking you questions Niles Sharpe would know."

"But I *don't* know that stuff."

"You could. You *should.* You could do what she does. When we were shopping, she asked every person she met questions so she could pick up new, useful things. How do you think she learned about blueberries? She did online research and talked to people who grew them, just like you could."

Niles looked at the boards under his feet, like a scolded child who knew he was wrong. It was the first time Caleb thought maybe he was getting through to the guy.

"My father said something to me that really made a difference in my life, Niles, so I'll share it with you. People will forgive ignorance; they won't forgive laziness."

Niles met Caleb's eyes directly for the first time since they'd met.

"It's okay to not know everything. Nobody knows everything," Caleb said.

"I don't know anything."

"That's okay. That's the biggest step: admitting you need improvement. Those women in Lillian's cottage today adore you. They'll be fans no matter what. Be charming. Admit you're wrong when you are. Ask questions when you don't know answers. Use your phone for research, not trolling Tinder." He patted Niles on the shoulder. "And start treating Lillian like your coworker, not your mommy."

He looked up to see Amanda and Lillian strolling toward them. Lillian was in a clingy top that made his mouth go dry. Amanda was in some pantsuit that looked like something out of a bad disco movie.

"So, the woman with the curly short hair…" Niles whispered.

"Amanda."

"She's pretty," he said.

"She's taking you to dinner at the Starfish Diner. No work until tomorrow."

"Really? No how-to lessons from Lillian?"

"Nope." But with Niles out of the way, Caleb was anticipating his own how-to lesson from Lillian.

CHAPTER TWENTY-EIGHT

"I should have brought earplugs," Lillian muttered to herself, drowned out by shrill, excited voices in the crowded diner. Roger and Seamus were at their usual booth, looking completely out of place in the room full of women. Across the booth from her, Niles checked his look in the back of a spoon.

Amanda was at the door, collecting money and directing traffic. Sally was in the kitchen with Cassidy, Luke, and Bethany, slinging plates of food faster than she'd thought possible.

And Caleb—her body heated when their eyes met— Caleb was taking plates of food out of the diner service window and placing them on tables in front of eager Sharpies.

She shifted in the booth when she remembered their candlelight dinner he'd prepared last night—frozen pizza this time—and the blueberries with whipped cream he may have gotten creative with. Yeah. Definitely creative.

She crossed her legs and watched Amanda saunter with authority to the front of the room. She was made for this, and honestly, Noms with Niles wasn't a bad idea. The Sharpies could get the gawking out of their systems before the team arrived to film.

"Can I have your attention?" Amanda hollered. "Hello!" Once the room was moderately quiet, she cleared her throat, reveling in the limelight. She was dressed in a business suit, which seemed totally wrong for her, except it was paired with a ruffled yellow tux shirt and matching earrings in the shape of moons. "I'm proud to tell you that we have doubled last year's Quilts at Christmas fundraising total." There was light applause. "Breakfast is making the rounds. Because of the excellent turnout, Sally has limited the menu—like, really limited it, and everyone is receiving the same thing for the sake of ease. If you don't like it"—she shrugged—"too bad."

A couple of people laughed.

Across from Lillian, Niles looked intense as he scrolled on his phone. He'd been quiet all morning, and she wondered if it was because he was still tired from travel or if it was something Caleb had said to him last night. On his houseboat, the infuriating man wouldn't say a word about his conversation with Niles, but she had to admit, she liked his tactic for distracting her from the subject. Amanda had already dropped Niles off when she arrived at the cottage. She didn't see him, but she could hear him muttering and moving around at all hours of the night. He must not have slept much.

"So, as you know, Lillian Mahoney has been in town for a while." Amanda indicated for her to stand up, but she waved instead. "And her company is going to begin filming here tomorrow featuring our town, Blink, for some episodes of *Living Sharpe*." There were squeals from a few members of the crowd who evidently hadn't heard this news yet. Amanda held up her hand for silence, exposing loads of bangles. Her nails were bright yellow to match her shirt and earrings. "This morning's event was not only to raise money for supplies to make quilts for the women's shelter. It was to introduce you to someone many of you will recognize from TV and follow online: lifestyle guru and cooking expert, Niles Sharpe."

Niles paled. He took a deep breath, then stood, waving awkwardly. What was wrong with him? There were more people here than in front of her house yesterday, but no more than forty including the people helping out. He'd handled crowds much larger than this one.

At the counter, Caleb watched him, face expressionless, while everyone around them cheered.

"Come on up here, Niles," Amanda said, indicating the spot at the front of the room next to her. Niles set his phone down and made his way toward her. He'd laid his phone faceup, and Lillian leaned forward to see what woman had caught his eye this time. They were usually blond and tall. This one was…

Lillian gasped and grabbed his phone.

"We are so excited to have you here in Blink, Mr. Sharpe," Amanda said.

Lillian shook her head in disbelief. Blueberries. He was reading up on blueberry cultivation and harvesting.

"Niles Sharpe, from Living Sharpe, everyone," Amanda said, followed by applause.

He was reading up on blueberries, not boobs.

"I know your appearance this morning was last-minute, Mr. Sharpe, so you haven't had time to prepare. I was hoping you'd be willing to answer questions for your fans," Amanda said.

Lillian sat bolt upright in her seat. One article on blueberries couldn't prepare him for a Q&A. She should have pulled Amanda aside and briefed her. Had some questions ready in advance for vetting so she could pick ones he could be coached to answer successfully. She needed to stop this. She slid to the edge of her booth seat, but before she could stand, a firm hand cupped her shoulder.

"Relax," Caleb said, nudging her until she made enough room next to her. "He's not a little boy. It's okay to let him fail."

"He fails, my company fails," she said through gritted teeth.

"He might surprise you."

Well, it's not like she could stop it now. Amanda was already taking questions, and Niles seemed okay with it. At least he wasn't giving her that deer-in-the-headlights terrified look when he was afraid of not knowing something.

"Hi, Niles," a woman with gray hair said in a breathy voice. Then she giggled, which caused others to titter. "I wanted to know what your daily routine is like."

Lillian huffed out a relieved breath. He could talk about himself all day.

"Well, I'm not very good at getting up on time," he said with a winning smile. "But I plan to get better about that." He leaned against the counter, which gave him that nonchalant look that appealed so much to their viewers. "Then I go to the conference room, where the Living Sharpe team meets, and we work on whatever is on the schedule that day. Then dinner, some TV, and back to sleep." He shifted his weight to his other leg. "My life isn't that much different than yours," he said in a complete departure from his usual routine, where he spun elaborate tales about his glamorous lifestyle.

Every muscle in Lillian's body was wound tight. Something was up.

Amanda called on someone else—Fran this time. "How do you keep your hair so tidy?"

He smiled and ran a hand over his perfect hair. "Now, I can't give away all my secrets, can I?" His audience, as expected, giggled.

So far, so good, Lillian thought. Maybe they'd keep it superficial, and he wouldn't get tripped up and give himself away.

"Hi, Mr. Sharpe," a woman Lillian recognized from Amanda's party said. "I'm a huge fan."

Niles flashed his movie-star grin, designed to dazzle. And it did.

The woman blushed, then said, "So, I tried out your recipe for foolproof roasted chicken, and it came out really dry. I followed the recipe exactly, but it was tough, and we could barely eat it. What would you suggest? How much salt do you use when you make it, because I'm thinking it might be wrong on the recipe printed in your magazine."

Oh, crap. Oh, crap. Oh, crap, Lillian chanted in her head, waiting for Niles to give her a panicked look and plea for help before shutting down. He didn't even look her way.

"I'm so sorry it didn't turn out. There are so many things that can go wrong in the kitchen. Trust me, I know. I think I've made every mistake possible." He charmed them all with his smile, then looked right at her and winked.

Lillian's jaw dropped open—like open-in-a-cartoon open.

"I can't possibly tell you what went wrong, but if you email me with specifics, I can run it by our culinary team, and they might be able to help you out. I'm the face of Living Sharpe, but I'm only as good as the people working behind the scenes to bring you great content."

Something was wrong with Niles. "Niles is broken," she whispered. Caleb had to be behind this. She leaned closer. "Did you break Niles?" she hissed.

"Nope," Caleb answered, leaning back in the booth with a smug look on his face.

Amanda called on Charlotte. "Yesterday, we showed you a quilt we were working on, and since you did an entire segment on quilting year before last, I wanted to know if you had any advice for us. And what kind of stitches you would recommend for the border."

Lillian found herself holding her breath. Niles didn't know quilting from knitting, much less have the expertise to give advice on either.

Niles spread his arms wide in that I'm-accessible-and-open pose they'd practiced. "I was so honored that you shared your work with me."

Charlotte practically swooned at his attention.

"But I'll be honest with you. I am not an expert on quilting, despite that segment. My team had researched the topic, and I presented it, which is the case with many topics we cover on *Living Sharpe*."

When Lillian scanned the room, she saw some skepticism and disappointment. She'd feared this for a long time, and now it had happened. The curtain had been pulled back on the great and powerful Oz. Not completely pulled off—just enough to give a little peek. Oh, well. It had been good while it lasted. Maybe word would spread slowly this time because it wasn't about a relationship.

"I have a favor to ask," Niles said. "Instead of asking me lifestyle advice, which I give all the time through Living Sharpe, why don't you share your tips with me? We're always looking for new techniques around the home and in the kitchen. And if I like your tip, we may end up using it and crediting you in the magazine or online."

Gone were the disappointed or skeptical faces, replaced with excitement. "I have the best oatmeal raisin cookies!" someone shouted.

"I can get lipstick off of anything!" another person said.

Amanda held up her hands. "I'll pass out papers. Put your advice, name, and email address on them, and Mr. Sharpe will read them and reply to you."

More like someone on the Living Sharpe team would reply because Niles probably didn't know how to open his inbox, much less reply, but who cared? The group seemed happy as Amanda tore pages from one of Sally's order pads and passed them out.

Stunned, Lillian relaxed and took in the room full of happy, excited women. Niles had turned what could have been a disaster around. Instead of being disappointed in his lack of knowledge, they'd been sucked further into the fandom because they'd been invited to be part of the team and help.

Her eyes drifted over the sea of Sharpies to Roger's

booth. He was staring right at her with a grin on his face. She smiled back.

"Thank you to everyone here for contributing to the quilt fund," Niles said. "Amanda tells me it's a big deal and worthwhile. I'm glad I could be a part of it, and I'm looking forward to my time here in Blink. Thanks for having me."

As applause filled the room, Lillian leaned close to Caleb. "Who is this person, and what did you do with Niles?"

A self-satisfied smile crossed Caleb's face, and she wanted to kiss it off.

"He was researching blueberries, Caleb. Blueberries, not pickup lines or dating hot spots."

Caleb shrugged. "He just needed a little help figuring out who he was and what he wanted." He met her eyes, and her throat closed at the profound sadness she saw there. "Happens to all of us."

She watched Caleb stride to the kitchen to help Sally clear away some dishes from the service window. Around her, people were laughing and talking over coffee and plates of food while Niles made the rounds of the room with a glowing Amanda.

Maybe Caleb was right and Niles had finally figured out who he was and what he wanted. And she hoped that, unlike her, he could make the two work in harmony together. The big city-based business owner couldn't reconcile who she was with the small-town life she craved or the man she needed like she needed air to breathe.

Tired. She found herself terribly tired all of a sudden. After gathering her planner and bag, she slipped out and drove to the cottage. Feeling sorry for herself was an indulgence she ordinarily didn't allow. She had too much to accomplish to take time to be introspective, but dammit, this sucked.

She was leaving.

She didn't want to leave.

There was a strong urge to throw herself on the bed and wail, kicking her arms and legs, but she overrode it and went to the fridge, pulled out one of the test pies, and took it to the sofa with a fork. Nothing sugar wouldn't fix. And time. Lots and lots and lots of time.

CHAPTER TWENTY-NINE

Caleb leaned against the railing of the *Bethany Anne* with Willy and Scout at his feet.

"And, cut," the small brunette woman in a black shirt with "crew" on the back said. Niles put the lobster into the bucket at his feet and shook Bill Burke's hand as the camera crew went about taking down and moving their equipment away from the lobster boat.

The days had flown by since Lillian's people had arrived. Every hour was filled with activity from sunup to sundown as they worked through the schedule she'd laid out. She'd asked him to do something about restoring vintage woodwork, but he declined. That wouldn't bring people to Blink. He was a one-man shop, and these days he was feeling all that one-ness to his toes. He and Lillian had been spending the nights together at his place, but even surrounded by all these people — *especially* surrounded by all these people — he'd never felt more alone.

"Thanks for the segment," Niles said to Bill. "I had no idea how intense being a lobsterman is, and you're third generation. Wow. Big respect, man." Bill flashed a wide, snaggle-toothed grin.

Niles might not have a great grasp of the material he presented yet, but with time he would, and he had something that couldn't be learned through research — a natural ability to interact with people on a personal level.

Yeah, the guy had a pretty face and voice, but Caleb felt certain that his people skills held a lot of weight in his high ratings.

The sun had dipped low enough to touch the tree line. Soon, the Living Sharpe folks would get on their bus and head to their hotel in Machias and he would have Lillian to himself.

Right now, she was talking to a camerawoman, pointing to a clipboard. If this week had made anything clear to him, it was that Lillian was great at what she did. People followed her and loved her, and she had a great way of getting her ideas across. Her success was deserved.

His main takeaway: She didn't belong here.

And that truth hurt with a deep radiating pain, like he had bruises on the inside of his ribs.

But he had her right now, and he'd have her alone tonight, and that would have to do. He knew it going into this. She was always going to leave.

"Isn't this cool, Dad?" Bethany was skipping toward him with Luke trailing behind—no surprise there.

"Very cool," he answered.

"So when are you going to go see her in New York? Can I go with you?"

That thought had never even crossed his mind. As much as Lillian didn't belong here, he really didn't belong there, and long-distance dating was out with no possible endgame. It was best to rip it off like a Band-Aid. Saturday was it. "I'm not, baby."

"You can't just let her go. She's…" Tears filled Bethany's eyes. "She's perfect."

He couldn't agree more. "She's not mine to keep. You

can't make people stay, Bethy, no matter how much you want them to. She has a life somewhere else that she loves and deserves."

"Then go with her. Move to New York. I'll be fine. I have two bedrooms in two different houses, and I'm off to college soon anyway. I can fly to see you on the weekends, and we can see Broadway shows. Lillian says her estate is not that far from Manhattan. Think of it, Dad. It'd be great."

He took her by the shoulders. "Bethy… Baby, I can't. *She* can't. It won't happen." Not once had Lillian mentioned him following her, and he knew why. Upending his life for a person, even someone as wonderful as Lillian, was a terrible idea. If he moved to New York to be with her and they broke up, he'd be left with nothing but a place he didn't like. "This is home. My parents are here. Fern and James are here. My *life* is here." He kissed her forehead. "My heart is here."

Well, except for the part Lillian would take with her when she left.

• • •

Lillian knew something was up before she even reached Caleb and Bethany by the worried looks Luke gave her as she approached.

Caleb kissed his daughter's forehead, and even from this distance, she could tell Bethany had been crying.

Maybe she should turn around.

She stopped, and Bethany looked at her, then turned and ran down the dock, Luke following behind.

Caleb stood perfectly still. "She doesn't want you to leave."

A knife twisted in her chest. Neither did she, but she had to. He knew this. She didn't have to say it again. It was the mantra that ran through her head all day. She held up the grocery bag full of meal-prep items Erin had brought her.

"How about I cook tonight? Coq au vin, asparagus, baguette?" She wiggled the bag.

"You'll never beat my peanut butter and jelly," he said, putting his arm around her shoulders. She loved it when he touched her casually. It felt natural.

"Don't worry about Bethy," he said. "She'll be fine."

It wasn't Bethany she was worried about. Two more days. Two more nights. And then, she'd leave Blink. And Caleb. And Roger and Cassidy and Amanda and… She took a deep breath and, with a smile, stepped over onto the deck of the houseboat to make dinner and then make love like her heart wasn't breaking into tiny pieces.

CHAPTER THIRTY

Caleb was seated next to his dad at the Starfish Diner counter. The place was packed. It was the last day of filming in Blink. Tomorrow, the Living Sharpe crew would cover the pie contest in Machias and then film a piece at Buddy's burger place about Wendy's clam chowder. And then…well, then they'd leave.

Roger and his crew had been displaced from their usual booth so that a woman holding a camera with a lens as big around as her arm could take photos of Sally's biscuits. They'd moved them around and used different types of lights on them and even sprayed them with something from a can to make them shiny.

"Lot of to-do about a plate of biscuits, if you ask me," Seamus said in a loud voice from the booth closest to Caleb and his dad.

"Nobody asked you," Roger said. "Lillian knows what she's about."

"Where is she?" Seamus craned his neck to scan the diner.

Good question, Caleb thought. She was usually among the first to arrive for this kind of thing. The film crew was trickling in, and Sally was pouring coffee left and right. When the Living Sharpe folks left, it was going to be really quiet around here.

The bells clanged, and Caleb found himself holding his breath, hoping to see Lillian. He exhaled as Niles, looking his usual, stylish self, strode in. After greeting some of the people closest to the door, he made a straight line for Caleb.

"Hey. This is our last shoot in Blink, so it's my last day here. I'm off to the hotel tonight so I'm closer to the pie contest shoot in the morning." He held out his hand. "Want to thank you again."

"You're welcome."

He looked left and right, and then his face lit up. "I'll see you later." With a smile, Caleb watched him join Amanda at the far end of the counter, standing close. Really close.

"I'm so nervous," Sally said, running her hands down her apron as she paced behind the counter. "Do I look okay? I've never been on TV before."

"You look fantastic, Sally," Gus said. "Lillian will make sure you're taken care of."

Where was she? Caleb pulled out his phone, but there was nothing new from her. She'd left his houseboat before sunrise to go to the cottage to change and get ready for this shoot, like usual.

"Okay, we're ready, Niles," a woman with wire-rimmed glasses and a clipboard said.

Just like every other time Caleb had watched the Living Sharpe team, they worked together respectfully and efficiently. Niles knew his lines and, for the most part, hit his marks, earning him lots of praise, which made Caleb suspect this level of performance was new for him. Sally was clearly nervous, but it added to the sweetness of the story about a diner in a tiny town with a reputation for the best biscuits in the state. Caleb doubted the reputation was warranted, but anything that drew interest in Blink was gospel as far as he was concerned. Between Lillian and Roger's efforts, he had a feeling that his dying town might get a second chance after all.

From the corner of his eye, a flash of red caught his attention. The sight of the little red car pulling into the lot threw his heart into overdrive. He loved Lillian, plain and simple, if just seeing her could make him react like this.

She wasn't in her boots, jeans, and plaid shirt like yesterday. She looked like someone else. Like her New York self from those first few days.

From the stool he'd been on that very first day, he watched her walk into the diner on high heels, wearing that same tight skirt with the stripes on it and a matching jacket with a shiny white blouse. Her hair was pulled back, and she wore flawlessly applied makeup. This was a beautiful woman whose every facet reflected success. She looked like a fancy statue. Yeah, a diamond watch in a toolbox. She was making a statement, and his heart heard it loud and clear as it squeezed painfully. She was leaving.

"And, cut," a woman next to one of the cameras called, and everyone applauded. Sally flushed bright red and gave little bows to her friends and neighbors.

Lillian spoke with members of her team, then walked over to him. Her face was expressionless, and his body grew cold.

"I don't do goodbyes well," she said, unable to hold his eye contact. "Gus, you made me feel welcomed from the start. Thank you."

"I thought you were staying until tomorrow. Amanda is holding a party on her deck tonight," Caleb said.

She closed her eyes. "I can't." She opened her eyes and finally looked at him. "The team will film the pie contest tomorrow and go do the segment with Wendy at Buddy's about the clam chowder." She blinked rapidly and looked away. "I'm heading out now."

You knew this was coming, he told his swimming head. She'd made it clear she was leaving every day from the day she got here. Over and over and over. But still, now that the time was here, it didn't seem real.

Caleb forced himself to remain calm and still. "Okay."

She swallowed. "Okay, then."

He stood and moved toward her—to what? To hug her?

She put out a hand and stopped him. "Please don't. I can't. I have to go."

"You have to go," he repeated.

And then, she nodded and left.

Just like that.

CHAPTER THIRTY-ONE

"Here's tomorrow's schedule, Ms. Mahoney," Lillian's new assistant said, laying it on her desk. She didn't think she needed an assistant and had made that clear. Erin had hired her anyway.

"Thanks, Sam," she replied, not looking away from the window. A strong gust of wind kicked up the leaves on the lawn, sending them swirling around the tree trunks and Living Sharpe employees' cars parked in the drive.

Today, they were working on a segment for the magazine about creative uses for vinegar, so there wasn't much for her to do since she'd approved the material already.

Niles shifted in his wingchair in the corner of the study and flipped another page in the book he was reading. "So, did you know that Julia Child was six foot two? That's my height."

Niles had been so different since Maine. He researched constantly. In the three months since they'd been back—well, eighty-four days, six hours, and twenty-eight minutes, but who was counting—he had become a fact machine, learning all about a subject before presenting it.

"Julia Child also had never cooked until she met her husband. She grew up with cooks." He closed the book. "You should hire a cook. All I've seen you eat recently is potato chips and junk food."

"I love preparing meals," she said. "I don't want a cook." She just hadn't been in the mood recently. "Shouldn't you be in the studio, dousing yourself with vinegar or something?"

He stood. "I liked you better when you were bossy and intense and telling me what to do all the time. Mopey, sarcastic Lillian is boring." Book under his arm, he strolled from her study.

Maybe Niles wasn't the only one who'd changed.

She sighed and ran her fingers over the edge of her desk. Her sister had been acting differently, too. Totally distracted. Erin spent a lot of her off time in her office. Maybe she was working a side job. Or maybe she was just avoiding mopey, sarcastic Lillian.

She turned back to the window, wondering if the turned leaves were falling in Blink like they were here. Maybe it was snowing already. She heard Roger's voice in her head. *You'll need to trade this car for something more suited for the snow up here.* He was so certain she would stay.

The first of three episodes featuring the town would run next week. Cassidy and Erin had been in contact a couple of times recently about cottage maintenance, and Cassidy said there had been increased activity since Blink had won the pie contest.

As always, her mind did that association thing where every thought circled back to Caleb. Pie contest leads to blueberry pie, which naturally evolves into thoughts about blueberries and whipped cream, which lands her mind in Caleb's creative arms.

Stop it.

A knock came on the doorframe. "I'm sorry to interrupt you, Ms. Mahoney, but the other Ms. Mahoney asked if you'd come take a look at something out in the studio."

"Thanks, Sam. Could you please call me Lillian? The two Ms. Mahoneys makes it confusing."

The young woman smiled. "Yes. Thank you so much, *Lillian.*" Practically bouncing, she hustled away.

Lillian missed those days. Days when little things made her almost giddy. She sighed. It hadn't been that long. Only—she looked at her watch—eighty-four days, six hours, and forty-two minutes ago, now. Though those last hours hadn't offered any giddy moments, only heart-crushing hurt. It *still* hurt, dammit.

She pulled on her jacket to make the short walk to the converted horse barn behind the main house that acted as the *Living Sharpe Magazine* studio. The huge room buzzed with energy and sound. A table was set in the center and ringed with lights displaying artfully placed items. A bottle of vinegar, a bright cobalt spray bottle, and a box of baking soda were at the front, surrounded by a semicircle of items notoriously suitable for a vinegar cleaning, like a coffeemaker, teakettle, blender, and fruits and vegetables. All were tied together with a blue theme woven into the cloth underneath and accents on many of the items. And yep, there were blueberries.

Lillian's jaw clamped tight as she willed her brain to stop.

"Thanks for coming over," Erin said. "I know that we had designed the section on vinegar with a picture featuring a wide range of uses to be covered in the first photo, but I'm thinking the food in the same photo as the appliances is off-putting now that we see it in person. Like food on the cleaning-supply aisle in a grocery store. What do you think?"

"I'm good either way," she said with uncharacteristic ambivalence. She didn't care. Not about the photo shoot. Not about much of anything, really, since she'd finished and sent off the master book for the Blink pie festival plans to Amanda and Cassidy. She'd heard from them occasionally at first but not recently. Bethany had tapered off, too, for some reason. When she didn't reply to Caleb that first week, he gave up, which was best. Maybe. That old adage, out of sight, out of mind? It was a load of crap.

She picked up a blueberry from the table and rolled it in her fingers. A sound like the ocean against the rocks filled her head, and she was transported back to the beach at night.

Stay, Caleb's voice whispered in her mind. *I want you to stay.*

The edges of the berry blurred, and she blinked rapidly. She dropped it back in its bowl and backed away from the table like it was covered in poisonous snakes.

"Sorry, I need to get away from this vinegar," she said, wiping her eyes.

Her sister looped an arm over her shoulder. "You okay, Lils?"

No, she wasn't okay. She might never be okay. She glanced around the room full people. All of these hardworking, talented people depended on her to keep this business running and successful. They'd been with her for years. She didn't have a choice. "Yeah, I'm fine," she said. "Vinegar just gets to me, I guess, like onions."

The room relaxed a bit, with a few people going back to whatever they were doing before she'd melted down. She was fine now. She'd power through this rough patch she was going through and get back on the ball. Her vision cleared, and she took a deep breath, pulling out from under Erin's arm. "I think we're fine combining elements in the introductory photo as long as we can divide them out for the subsections, with one for appliances and household cleaning, then the other for foods. Does that work?"

"Works for me," she said, then leaned close. "You sure you're okay? Why don't you take the rest of the day off?"

"Nah, I'm good. Really." Lillian shoved her hands into her jacket pockets and froze—as did her heart, the room, and the world, when her fingers wrapped around a smooth, hard object.

She opened her hand and stared at the blue sea glass in her palm. It was shrouded in a white haze from surface abrasion, except for the perfect, round spot where her tear had just fallen. That part was the deep, rich cobalt of the ocean off Blink's cliffs. The color of Caleb's eyes.

Stay, his voice echoed in her head.

Go, her heart screamed with a painful hammering behind her ribs. *Go back.*

Breaths coming in pants, she scanned the room of concerned faces. Faces who relied on her.

Don't wait until you're old to finally live, Roger's voice said in her head.

She couldn't do this anymore. She didn't belong here. She belonged in Blink. Blink was home.

And like a wave pulling back from the rocky shore, her panic washed away, replaced with certainty and determination. She had to take care of some things on the way out of town, but she didn't need to take the time to pack. She could send for her things later. She would leave now. Right now.

"I have to go," she said, closing her fist around the sea glass. "I'll call you from the road."

Erin looked more amused than worried as Lillian all but ran to the exit. Without looking back, she muttered an apology to whoever she'd smacked with the door when she shoved it open and sprinted across the lawn, leaves scattering behind her like the life she was leaving behind.

CHAPTER THIRTY-TWO

Lillian hadn't made the drive in one shot this time. She'd savored it, stopping to take in the views and, yes, get gas at every town whether she needed it or not. She'd stayed at a lovely B&B in Kennebunkport, which had given her a ton of ideas for the cottage—and maybe Mr. McGuffy's main house, if his offer to let her in there was still good.

The snow last night had left everything covered in white, like a winter wonderland. As she passed Emmett's gas station outside of Blink, she noticed the boards had been taken off the windows and it appeared someone had begun to repair some of the rotten wood on the front. As she drove over the hill, she smiled as she passed the road sign, "Blink, Maine, population 204."

Not long after, the familiar hand-painted sign for the Starfish Diner came into view. It looked like it had been repainted or maybe just cleaned. Surprised, she pulled into a parking lot that was half full instead of its usual two or three cars.

Her heart squeezed as she parked next to an old, beat-up pickup with the round Wright Boat Works logo on the door. It was Gus's truck. Caleb's was a little newer but just as dirty. She scanned the parking lot but didn't see his truck.

No wobbling into the diner on a broken heel this time. She strode in, not even slipping on the frozen rocky surface thanks to the deep tread of her boots. "Hi, Sally," she said, slipping out of her coat and hanging it on the rack inside the door.

Sally squealed and hugged her so tightly, she thought she might break a rib. "You're back! I'm so happy you're here. Coffee?"

"No, thanks. I'm just dropping in to say hi on my way to the cottage," Lillian said, slipping on a stool next to Gus while Sally scurried off when a customer hailed her.

"Lillian, love," he said, putting an arm around her shoulders. "You decide you couldn't live without us?" he asked with a squeeze.

"Something like that." She scanned the diner. Roger was at his usual table with Seamus. She didn't recognize anyone else there, though. "Who are all these people?"

Gus shrugged. "From the best I can figure, someone from the Blink Church told someone at the Machias Presbyterian Church about Sally's biscuits."

Sally swooped in to refill Gus's coffee, and she took over. "Word got out that Living Sharpe filmed a segment on my biscuits, and people from around here wanted to see what the fuss was." She gestured to the half-full diner. "And now, there's a fuss. It'll get even more crowded when church lets out in half an hour."

Lillian's body hummed with warmth and happiness. It had worked. Her plan had brought people to Blink, and it was only going to get better. *Everything* was going to get better. "Wait until the segment airs next week," she said. "You'll have a line out the door."

Sally beamed. "I already have Luke and Bethy lined up to help me out."

Luke and Bethany were obviously still hanging out

together. Lillian couldn't have stopped her grin if she had wanted to. "Well, I'll see you two around."

Her heart was so full at seeing these people again — at being in this town — but she needed to find one person in particular. Caleb. Her heart lurched at the thought of him.

Sally clasped her hands over her chest, and Gus grinned as she stopped by Roger's booth on her way out.

"Hi, Roger," she said. "You keeping that house in order?"

He laughed and took her hand between his. "I am. Are you finally getting yours in order?"

Her hammering pulse got louder. "I think so."

Seamus gave her a smile and flipped the page of his newspaper as if she'd never left.

"Come see me when you're sure," he said. "Lots going on."

"I will." But first, she had to find Caleb. "I'll drop in later."

Her heart was so light when she pulled into the harbor, she was pretty sure it would float away like a balloon in the crisp, blue sky. She pulled around the right side next to Caleb's truck outside the Wright Boat Works shop. Scout and Willy bounded from the houseboat and greeted her with kisses and wags so dramatic, they were wagging their entire hind ends. "I'm happy to see you guys, too," she said. And she'd be even happier to see their owner. The door to the shop was locked with a "closed" sign on it. It was Sunday, after all.

Amanda's store looked closed as well. Her disappointment at not finding Caleb yet vanished when she noticed the buildings down from her were clearly under renovation. One had a scaffold covering the facade, and both no longer had plywood on the windows. Her body seemed to glow from the inside like the bright winter sun above as she stared at the harbor. She'd helped make this happen. She loved this town, and maybe it could grow and thrive because of her and the other citizens' efforts.

With a grin, she stepped aboard the *Bethany Anne*. "Hello?" she called, Scout and Willy running circles around her legs. Empty. Empty and different.

The things that had been on the kitchen counter—utensil cup, salt and pepper, dish soap—were all gone. The counter was bare, and the furniture in the living area, what Caleb called the saloon, had been pushed against the wall and tied together with straps like her resistance bands from yoga.

A weird, sinking feeling made it hard to put one foot in front of the other as she shuffled to Bethany's room. It was empty of everything except her bed, which was stripped down to the mattress. Even her drawings and easel had been removed.

She wasn't sure she could stand it if the bedroom across the hall was like this. All the way here, she'd pictured that room, with the beautiful wooden ceiling and furniture Caleb had made by hand.

The tension in her shoulders eased as she gently pushed the door open. Both dogs gleefully bounded past her and leaped onto the messy bed. The sheets were rumpled and twisted—like hers had been back in New York from her insomnia. It appeared he had secured the items in the houseboat for travel but he was still sleeping in this room. She took a deep breath in through her nose, reveling in the scent of Caleb—a mix of laundry detergent, mint, and ocean breeze.

Where was he? She peered out the window at Miller Mercantile, which had a new coat of paint. Amanda kept her nose in everyone's business. Surely she'd know.

Only, Amanda wasn't there. Maybe she was at church or something.

After some more pats and kisses and a promise to return soon with treats, she found herself on the road to the cottage. As she made the last turn at the top of the hill, she pulled over and simply stared. The hillside above the cottage was littered with colorful little cabins. The trendy prefab tiny houses like the ones advertised in *Living Sharpe Magazine.*

Maybe Roger had done it as an homage to his dad or something.

"Very cool," she whispered under her breath as she pulled back onto the road. What wasn't cool, though, is that the door to the cottage was locked and her key didn't work. Shivering, she tucked her bare hands into her pockets and pulled out the gloves she'd taken off to work the key. Flexing her fingers into the soft cashmere, she stared in through the front window. The furniture was the same, but there were moving boxes everywhere. Sealed and labeled with the address but no name she could see.

Holy crap. Erin had sold the cottage.

"Well, it's hers to sell," Lillian said, stomping back down the porch steps. It wasn't like she owed Lillian any explanation for the disposition of her own property. She tried to smooth her discomfort by imagining it was a family with kids to help make Blink grow. She could always build her own house—or maybe Roger would let her buy one of the cabins on the hillside.

When she glanced at Roger's house, she noticed the Handyman Hank truck parked in front of the big white Victorian. Maybe Cassidy would know what was going on.

Cassidy was ripping up rotten floorboards in the entry when Lillian found her.

"Lillian!" she cried, bouncing to her feet, knocking a stack of boards over. "You're here!"

Cassidy sounded pleased but not surprised. Just like Gus and Roger. Maybe they'd known all along what Lillian had only recently discovered: She belonged here.

After hugs, she asked, "Any idea why the locks were changed on the cottage?"

Cassidy looked away and started restacking the planks she'd knocked over. "Someone new is moving in."

From her jerky movements and total focus on floorboards, Lillian didn't have to be a psychic or even terribly observant to know that the topic made Cassidy uncomfortable.

The cottage changing hands wasn't a huge deal. Change was good. Change for Blink had been the goal all along, and it looked like that goal was being met. Time for a subject change.

"So, Roger's finally letting you work on this house." For the first time since entering, she looked around. "Wow. What a house," Lillian breathed. Under the dust and outdated mid-century furniture lay a grand old lady of a structure.

Cassidy grinned. "I know, right? Original woodwork and fireplace surrounds." She gestured to an enormous staircase. "It's mostly intact, but Caleb is going to replicate and replace broken parts. Feel free to look around."

"Not now." She was too anxious to clear the air. "Do you happen to know where Caleb is?"

"No." She didn't meet Lillian's eyes. She was hiding something.

"Any idea when he'll be back?"

Cassidy didn't strike her as someone who could lie easily, and that turned out to be true. She was very uncomfortable when she said, "I don't know."

"It looks like he's prepared the houseboat to relocate."

She stared at her paint-splattered running shoes. "I don't know what his plans are. He left three days ago and said he'd be back soon."

Three days. Well, at least she didn't need to beat herself up for taking her time getting here. He'd already left Blink before she would have gotten here, even if she'd done the drive in a day like before.

There was nothing to do but wait. And she knew where she'd do it. "I'm driving to Machias to buy some groceries. Need anything?"

"No, thanks," Cassidy said, then her sunny smile returned. "I'm glad you're here."

"So am I."

Before Lillian had made it off the porch, she saw Cassidy pick up her phone and furiously type on her screen. Something was going on around here involving

Caleb, and she suspected everyone knew about it.

She clenched and unclenched her fists in frustration as she strode to her car. She'd find out what it was, eventually. Until then, it was time for some power shopping and then some stress baking. Caleb may not be in the houseboat, but his very fine kitchen was.

CHAPTER THIRTY-THREE

"Ohhhhh," Amanda said, fending off the pups as she stepped inside Caleb's houseboat. "This place smells like heaven."

It should. Lillian had been cooking on and off for two days. Caleb had secured the furniture and moved items from the counter, but the cupboards were basically the same as they had been before she left. They'd had latches to keep them closed already, and he'd only moved around breakable items from what she could tell. She'd bought a new set of mixing bowls and some pots. His were too basic for her needs right now. Needs that had only intensified since she'd arrived. Two nights wrapped up in sheets that smelled like him had been simultaneous bliss and torture.

Lillian narrowed her eyes at Amanda. "No 'Welcome back' or 'Hey! What are you doing here'?"

"Oh, no. I always knew you'd come back," she said, peeking under the towel covering bread dough.

"Don't touch anything," Lillian said, slapping her hand. "It's proofing." No damage done, though. Despite the snow and frost coating the windows, the cabin was toasty from all the baking.

"How long are you staying?" Amanda asked, pulling a dining chair closer to the counter, where Lillian was rolling out sugar cookies. "Because if you keep making things like this"—she held up a fudge square she'd

plucked from a container on the corner of the counter—
"I might have to hold you hostage."

"It depends," Lillian said.

"On what?" Amanda took another bite and made an
mmmmm sound.

"It depends on whether I am locked up for murdering
the town gossip for not telling me what's going on around
here." She set the rolling pin on the counter and ran a
flour-covered hand over her shirt. A red one she found in
Caleb's drawer with "*The Happy Hooker*" emblazoned
across the back. A fishing boat, she assumed.

"I don't know what you mean," she said. "Wow, you've
cooked enough food for the whole town."

No topic change was going to blow her off track.
Something was going on, and Amanda, of all people,
would know what it was. "Where is everyone?"

Amanda looked confused. "Everyone is here. Bethany
is with Shemom and Shedad this week, if that's who you
mean. I just got back from a small business owner's
conference in Bangor."

"Where is Caleb?"

She let out a long breath and adjusted her fuchsia
scarf. "I don't know exactly where he is. He left a few
days ago to arrange for another place for his houseboat.
His plan was to move farther down the coast."

He was leaving Blink after he said he couldn't leave
here? For a moment, her blood pounded in her ears as
she allowed her anger to swell, but it deflated just as
quickly. She'd never asked him to come to New York with
her. She'd never even hinted at it. He'd hate it there. And
when he'd worked up the guts to ask her to stay in Blink,

she'd said no, despite her clear love for the place. She was the one who left.

She straightened her shoulders, then turned and picked up the rolling pin. Still, it hurt.

She rolled forward, then back. Then smiled. There was only one solution. It was her turn to ask *him* to stay.

• • •

Lillian pulled the hood of her coat tighter around her face. The wind coming off the water was bitter, like her mood had become.

Everyone around here was avoiding her and had been for days. They were nice enough but found something else to do when she appeared. She'd decided it wasn't about her but rather about something they were hiding or covering up. Roger hadn't answered when she dropped by his place a half hour ago, despite telling her to come see him that first day. She knew he was inside. *Wheel of Fortune* was blasting from the TV, and his car was in the drive.

Even Amanda said she was too busy to chat — Amanda was *never* too busy to chat, and when Lillian had dropped in on Cassidy at Roger's main house, she suddenly needed to use power tools. Loud ones.

She carefully followed the path down to the rocky beach where she'd first met Bethany. It had snowed this morning, and it looked like someone had taken a shaker of confectioners' sugar to the rocks, frosting them lightly on top. Beautiful.

She sat on the flat rock and watched the gulls until

her backside went numb from cold. Usually, the sound of the waves cleared her head, which was way too full. She was in limbo, waiting to start her life, which seemed ridiculous. She stood and turned into the wind. Why was she waiting? She was staying in Blink whether he sailed off into the sunset or not. She had a lot to do. It was time to arrange to have a house built and have that awful conversation with Erin about how to handle Living Sharpe. To be honest, she was surprised Erin wasn't blowing up her phone.

She took several steps toward the ocean, then folded her arms over her chest. All her life, she'd studied and researched ways to make her life organized and orderly. She'd observed human behavior and adjusted her approach to maximize the potential of those around her. To make her business more profitable and her employees content. Right now, though, she couldn't tell up from down. Nobody was acting as she expected.

"It's impossible," she shouted at the waves. Totally impossible to figure people out.

"A very wise person once told me—" a voice began behind her, and she almost screamed.

She spun to find Bethany grinning at her. She was wearing a cranberry coat with black trim that made her blue eyes seem lighter. Eyes so much like her father's.

"A very wise person once told me that nothing was impossible," she said. "But, I'll admit," she added, "finding you was almost impossible. Everywhere I went, I was told you had just been there." She grinned. "You make really good fudge, by the way. And chocolate chip cookies."

From the bottom of the trail, Luke whistled and

waved his arms, and Bethany waved back.

She took Lillian's hand. "That wise person who told me nothing was impossible also told me there was always a compromise," Bethany said, leading her past the flat rock to the trail. "You, wise person who makes excellent baked goods, are about to witness perhaps the most impressive compromise in the history of Blink, Maine — maybe even the whole Downeast region."

Breath puffing out little clouds in the cold air, Lillian followed, not feeling chilled at all anymore. Maybe she liked not knowing how people would act after all.

As they neared the harbor, Bethany picked up the pace. "Did you see that they are fixing up the two old stores? Mr. McGuffy has sold every lot on the harbor, and Hedad says there should be four new buildings breaking ground in the spring."

Still tugging Lillian, she broke into a run when they hit the wooden walkway at the harbor. Fortunately, someone had sanded it, or Lillian suspected she would have ended up on her backside, boots or no boots. They passed Amanda's place and ran past the houseboat and into the parking lot, where, thank goodness, Bethany stopped next to Luke.

Gasping for breath, Lillian leaned over, hands on her knees. "I'm too old for this," she said.

"Whoa, is that your car?" Bethany asked, gesturing to her new Land Rover.

"Yeah, that's Brutus."

"Ooo. Can I drive it?" she asked.

"When I die from heart failure from running for the first time in twenty years, I'll leave it to you in my will."

A car pulled into the parking lot, then another. More poured in, and people she recognized from her new hometown got out and lined up along the parking-lot entrance like they were about to witness a parade.

"Want to tell me what's going on?" Lillian asked when little Tommy Lassiter waved at her and jumped up and down from across the parking lot where his family huddled together next to Roger and Sally.

"Yes, but I can't," Bethany said. "They'd run me out of town."

"You just ran me into the ground. Fair is fair."

Applause broke out, and Fran and Charlotte squealed and jumped up and down with excitement like they had when Niles had come to town months ago.

If this was about Niles Sharpe coming to visit, Lillian was pretty sure her head would explode.

Sure enough, the Living Sharpe bus turned into the parking lot.

Seriously? What the heck were they doing here?

Gus came up on her other side and patted her shoulder as the doors folded open and Niles bounded down the steps of the bus, waving at the thrilled Sharpies with a volume of "The Joy of Cooking" under his arm.

No way would Erin send Niles here for her to look after. No. Stinking. Way.

"Be patient," Gus said, holding her in place. "No scuttling off like a crab. You've got a harder shell than that."

After a brief pause, Erin came down the steps, followed by a dozen or so of her team members and people she assumed were their families. There were even some dogs, to Scout and Willy's delight.

Bethany waved, and Erin strode over, pulling her coat tight. She stopped directly in front of Lillian with that serious, big-sister look on her face. "You didn't think you were going to leave me holding the bag like that, did you? Just skip town in a huff."

"I do not huff," Lillian said.

"You most certainly do," Erin said, wagging a finger.

"You huff!" Niles called from several feet away, where he was signing an autograph.

"You stay out of this," both Erin and Lillian said at once before returning to their stare-off, fighting smiles.

"If you had not huffed out in such a hurry, you would have noticed who you slammed in the face with the studio door."

Erin gestured to the bus, and Caleb stepped out with two black eyes. Well, not really black — more like a putrid shade of olive green.

Lillian's hand flew to her throat as she tried to catch her breath. He'd been in New York when she left. Amanda said he was looking for a port south of here...

As he neared, it was like people became vapor. They stepped off and back and moved away to give them privacy.

She gently touched under his eye. "I did this to you? I'm so sorry."

He shrugged. "I've had worse. Bethany gave me a real shiner when I was teaching her to fly-fish." He touched the bridge of his nose, which was also discolored. "It's a lot better now than a few days ago."

For a moment, they simply stared at each other, white

puffs of breath mingling between them. He was here. For now, anyway.

"Why were you in New York? Why didn't you let me know you were coming?" She gestured to the bus, where her team was boarding again. "What were you doing on the Living Sharpe bus?"

He held up a finger.

"If you put that over my lips, I swear I'll scream," she said.

He leaned very close and whispered, "You can scream later."

Okay, so right there, in front of the whole town, she almost burst into flames, or melted, or both. From the corner of her eye, she could see Erin returning.

Finger still up, he said, "I was in New York to secure a place for my houseboat. There's a lot of business up there, and it would have been a sound move career-wise...and to see you, of course." He raised a second finger. "I didn't tell you first because I was worried you wouldn't agree to see me." He added a third finger. "And I was on the bus because Erin felt bad I'd been smacked in the face and offered me a ride back here." He smiled. "Besides, I have it on the best authority that Blink, Maine, is the new headquarters for Living Sharpe and the beautiful Lillian Mahoney."

"Wait a minute. Hold on." Lillian's thoughts tumbled around her head in a jumbled mess. "I've eaten way too much sugar the last few days, so someone's going to have to break this down slowly for me. Pretend I'm Niles from the old days and spell it out, please. Maybe with pantomime or illustrations for clarity."

Erin laughed. "When you were here, you sounded different. Better. So I did some asking and got a pretty good picture of what was happening."

"Cassidy," Lillian said.

"She adores you. Then, the team came, and they started acting weird, too. They returned, talking about this place and even mentioned wishing they lived here. I did a poll of our employees. After analyzing cost of living for them and overhead for us in New York, versus Blink, Maine, I determined moving here was a sound business decision."

The buzzy feeling traveling up her legs and into her spine wasn't from the cold. "Everyone is moving here?"

"Well, not everyone. Some have extended family in New York and don't want to move. I'm trying to get some online job descriptions together for them if they want to stay with the company. Almost everyone from the crew who shot here is on that bus, along with some who had stayed with me. Others will join once they tie up loose ends at home — sell their houses and apartments or whatever. Short version. Living Sharpe, LLC is moving to Blink, Maine!"

Now all the avoidance made sense. The whole town was in on it.

"So, you've been planning this for months." The secrecy. The phone calls. Long hours in her office with the door shut.

"I have."

She rounded on Caleb. "And you were in on it?"

He held his hands up. "No. I didn't have a clue until Erin picked me up off the floor after you brained me with the door."

"To be honest with you, it's a big change," Erin said. "I was having some doubts until Caleb showed up. Then I knew for sure I'd made the right decision."

"And you didn't see fit to run it by me?"

"Not even a little bit." Erin grinned. "I'm your big sister and know what's best for you. It's why you pay me the big bucks."

"I might have to murder you," Lillian said.

"You'll have to do it later. I need to get everyone moved into their cabins."

Now those made sense, too. "Those cute ones on the hill?"

She nodded. "Got a great group rental discount, and Roger McGuffy was a dream to work with. Once we get into a routine and used to the area, our people can build their own homes. Roger says there's a discount on lumber at some mill nearby and he has lots of land he wants to see developed."

The bus horn honked, and people cheered. "Wait a minute," Lillian said, grabbing her sister's arm to keep her from walking off. "Where are you staying?"

"In the cottage, of course. I had my stuff shipped weeks ago. You're welcome to stay in the guest bedroom, unless you have someplace better to stay." She gave her sister and Caleb pointed looks, then strode toward the bus past the cheering crowd, including the Lassiter children, who were holding a sign written in crayon that said, "Welcome to Blink."

"Party on the patio!" Amanda shouted, waving her neighbors over to where several people were setting up tables on the deck in front of her place. "Food courtesy of

Lillian Mahoney."

She couldn't help but grin. "Did you raid the refrigerator?" Lillian called to her, hands cupped over her mouth.

"You betcha. And the counters, pantry, and bread box, too."

Caleb took Lillian's hand and placed it over his chest, where she could feel his heart beating a constant, steady rhythm. Constant and steady like the waves against the rocks. Like this town.

"Let's go home," he said, leading her toward the houseboat.

Home. This was truly home. Blink was home. Caleb was home.

She sighed and leaned her head on his shoulder as they walked. "We're going to have to make an appearance at that party, you know," she said.

He pulled her to him and kissed her like she'd imagined him doing since she'd left. Closing her eyes, she relaxed into his tall body, reveling in his heat. She jerked back when a few people still hanging out in the parking lot cheered. Yeah. She'd eaten way too much sugar. That had to be it.

"We'll make an appearance at the party *later*," he whispered in her ear.

The electric thrill in her spine devolved into dull ache as they boarded the houseboat with its chairs and tables secured to the wall, ready to sail. He'd said a move was sound for him career-wise. As they entered the cabin, she ran all the practiced lines through her head that she'd worked up to convince him to stay with her in Blink instead of moving away—the persuasive arguments that were designed to appeal to his logic and common sense—but instead all she could come up with was, "I love you, Caleb Wright."

He froze, and for a moment, her heart stopped and stuttered as she stared at his broad back. His shoulders rose and fell with a breath before he turned to face her. "I asked you to stay, Lillian, and you said you couldn't." Before she could panic, he caressed her cheek. "But you did stay. You stayed right here." He thumped his chest with his fist. "And I want you here forever." He opened the door to the bedroom and pulled her inside and against him. "I want you to be happy. And I'll do whatever it takes to be with you, even if it means leaving Blink."

She shook her head and wrapped her arms around him. "I don't want to leave. I love Blink."

"And I love *you*, Lillian Mahoney," he said, lowering his mouth to hers.

They made it to the party two hours later.

EPILOGUE

Lillian pushed her sunglasses up on her nose and leaned back in the lounge chair on the back deck of the *Bethany Anne*. She raised her wineglass in salute as the last of the pie contest attendees loaded up in their cars in the newly paved harbor parking lot.

In the chair next to her, Caleb groaned and rubbed his belly. "Remind me of this moment the next time I'm asked to judge a pie contest."

Since Blink was now home to Living Sharpe, the pie committees from the area churches felt it was unfair for Blink to enter after their win last year, which had merit, considering the company had a brand-new studio test kitchen and culinary experts on staff. Even if nobody associated with Living Sharpe was involved with the town's entry, there would always be speculation that they were. Instead, Blink would now host the contest every year, and *Living Sharpe Magazine* would publish the recipe and some photos and information about the winning entry.

"You'll be asked to judge again soon because Sally's already lining up the panel for next year," she said.

He groaned again.

She swung her legs over the side of the lounge chair and pushed to her feet, smoothing the front of the sleeveless magenta dress she'd purchased specifically for today's event. "I don't think it was judging the pie contest that got you. It was probably the lobster rolls, clam chowder, and funnel cakes." They'd had almost two dozen vendors rent tents this year, with twice that already committed for next year. "Oh, and the ice cream cone with extra sprinkles. Don't forget that."

"Stop. I surrender," he said. "I will never eat again."

She tugged on his hand. "No surrender. Never surrender. Rally your forces; it's time to go help Amanda with cleanup."

He sat up at her tugging but stayed in the lounger. "We helped with setup. It nearly killed me."

She dropped his hand and put her fists on her hips. "Only because you tried to fly the new entry banner like a kite."

"Because Niles let go of his end."

"It looks great, though." The large printed banner that said "Hideaway Harbor" was strung between two poles at the entrance. At one of the first town planning meetings, held where the new city hall would be built, it was decided that "Blink Harbor" didn't have enough commercial appeal, so a team of local residents brainstormed names and Living Sharpe designers created the logo. "Welcome to Blink, Maine, home of Hideaway Harbor," she said.

Caleb grinned. "And Hideaway Harbor Boat Tours."

She looked to her right, where Billy Burke was polishing the railing of his tour boat. "It was really great of you to work that old boat up for him. It looks fantastic."

"He needed to stop lobster fishing with that arthritis, and he certainly knows the area." He stood with yet another groan. Scout and Willy, who had been under his chair, jumped to their feet. "Besides, it was a great excuse for him to get his son back to Blink. Billy captains, and his son narrates the tour. Beats troubleshooting online orders at a phone bank or whatever he was doing in Bangor."

Caleb took her hand, and they wandered down the walkway toward Amanda's deck, which was still covered in round rental tables draped in yellow and pink tablecloths that matched the patio umbrellas, just as Lillian had planned. As she took in all the new construction around the harbor and up the surrounding hillsides, it was hard to believe that only a year ago, she had walked away from this place, never intending to return.

He squeezed her hand. "So that lot we were wondering about that was framed out for a foundation pour—the one next to where Blink City Hall is going up?"

"Yeah? Did you find out what it was going to be?"

He grinned and led her up the steps to the deck. "A family clinic for a Dr. Tristan McGuffy out of Portland."

She stopped on the second-to-top step. "No!"

He dropped her hand and picked up a couple of cups and napkins from one of the tables, then pitched them into a trash can in the corner of the deck. "I judged the pie contest sitting next to Roger. He's pretty excited about it. He said it took some real persuasion and a year of free rent, but he convinced Tristan to come home."

Behind her sunglasses, Lillian blinked back tears and folded a tablecloth. A couple of other people were working on the tables on the other side, including one she recognized as her social media director, Ellen. "Roger must be so happy."

"Yeah. He seems to be. And he's happy about David Jr.'s progress at the mill."

Seamus rolled a low cart to the middle of the deck. "Chairs here, please."

Lillian folded the chairs they'd rented from the party-supply company while Caleb placed them on the rack.

"They have over thirty full-time employees at the mill already," Caleb said, straightening the stacked chairs. "Several of them had worked there before Roger pulled the plug on it over a decade ago." He grabbed four more chairs. "And you know why he closed that mill?"

Lillian stopped folding chairs. "I have no idea. He said it was because of petty foolishness, but he was in a rare mood when he said that."

Caleb leaned on the cart handle. "He wasn't far off. He closed it because Tristan said he wasn't coming back after undergrad to run it. He'd decided to go to medical school instead. His mother was thrilled. Roger wasn't and closed the mill to let him know he'd burned a bridge and words had consequences."

Wow. Petty was right. No wonder Roger had felt so bad about the Lassiter family. She resumed folding chairs and leaning them against the table. "I think Roger's the one who learned the biggest lesson about consequences and burned bridges from that."

"He has. And he's totally turned it around. And it's because of you." He placed his hands over hers on the chair she'd just folded, and his touch made her body buzz, like it always did. "You helped him change his life."

"Fair's fair," she said, blinking rapidly, glad once again for the dark sunglasses. "He helped change mine."

He brought her hand to his lips and kissed her fingers, then nibbled on one.

She laughed. "I thought you weren't hungry."

"I changed my mind."

"Hey, guys," Bethany said as she climbed the steps to Amanda's deck with Luke close behind. "I wanted to give you a heads-up."

Heads-up was generally teen code for something bad happened or was about to. Lillian's hands tensed on the edge of the table. Luke studied his shoes. Yep. Code cracked.

Caleb folded his arms across his ribs in his best stern-dad pose. He knew the code, too.

"So, Luke and I are going camping tonight—maybe tonight and tomorrow."

A muscle in Caleb's jaw twitched while Luke memorized the shoes on his shuffling feet. Lillian knew this was a tough one. Caleb respected and adored Luke. No way was she getting involved in this, so she studied Luke's shoes, too. Nice, steel-toed construction boots like Caleb wore when he worked.

Bethany laughed. "Oh, lighten up, you old-fashioned old people. I'm just kidding. We're going to take my jeep and have a picnic on the beach. We'll be back by ten."

Caleb let out a long, slow breath as he watched his laughing daughter bounce down the steps, arm in arm with Luke.

At a picnic table in the far corner of the deck, Niles, with his arm around Amanda, regaled Erin, Cassidy, Sally,

Alice, and Gus with the history of cinnamon. On the walkway in front of Wright Boat Works, Scout and Willy hassled the resident seagulls. Over the treetops, the sun was sinking, painting the harbor amber and crimson. And next to her, Caleb grinned. "Let's go home and do some old-fashioned, old-people things."

ACKNOWLEDGMENTS

A huge thank-you to Liz Pelletier, Heather Howland, and the entire team at Entangled Publishing.

Hugs to my husband, Laine, and to my kids and friends who put up with me on a daily basis. I love you all.

And most of all, thank you to my readers—you make it possible for me to do what I love the most.

Three sisters + a small town where everyone knows everyone else's business... what could possibly go wrong?

the
SWEETHEART DEAL

MIRANDA LIASSON

Pastry chef Tessa Montgomery knows what everyone in the teeny town of Blossom Glen says about her. *Spinster. Ice Queen. Such a shame.* It's enough to make a woman bake her troubles away, dreaming of Parisian delicacies while she makes bread at her mother's struggling boulangerie. That is until Tessa's mortal enemy—deliciously handsome (if arrogant) chef Leo Castorini, who owns the restaurant next door—proposes a business plan...to get married.

Leo knows that the Castorinis and the Montgomerys hate each other, but a marriage might just force these stubborn families to work together and blend their businesses for success. The deal is simple: Tessa and Leo marry, live together for six months, and then go their separate ways. Easy peasy.

It's a sweetheart deal where everyone gets what they want— until feelings between the faux newlyweds start seriously complicating the mix. Have they discovered the perfect recipe for success...or is disaster on the way?

Secret crushes, stolen kisses, and a scandalous confession set the course of this clever new rom-com.

the best kept secret

USA TODAY BESTSELLING AUTHOR
TAWNA FENSKE

Nurse Nyla Franklin knows three things to be true. Taking care of others brings more joy than a basket full of kittens. A triple-fudge sundae can cure just about anything. And no good ever comes from keeping a secret... So when her best friend spills his biggest one ever, Nyla knows she's not just holding a secret. She's holding a ticking time bomb.

Mr. Always Does the Right Thing Leo Sayre knows three things to be true. Piloting smokejumpers over burning forests is the best job in the world. His best friend Nyla is the smartest, funniest, and okay, sexiest woman ever. And pain meds are apparently his truth serum. Now his post-surgery confession has everything flipped upside down and turned inside out... including his relationship with Nyla.

Secrets have a way of piling up, and it's just a matter of time before someone lights a match. Because while the truth can set you free, it can also burn completely out of control...

AMARA

an imprint of Entangled Publishing, LLC